The Hidden Past of Pippa McGovern

Dodd Diaries
Secret Agent Romantic Comedy

HOLLY KERR

The Dodd Diaries

Spy Romantic Comedy series

The Secret Life of Charlotte Dodd
The Missing Files of Charlotte Dodd
The Best Worst First Date Ever
The Hidden Past of Pippa McGovern
The Last Stand of Charlotte Dodd
The Second Love of Charlotte Dodd (exclusive content for
newsletter subscribers)

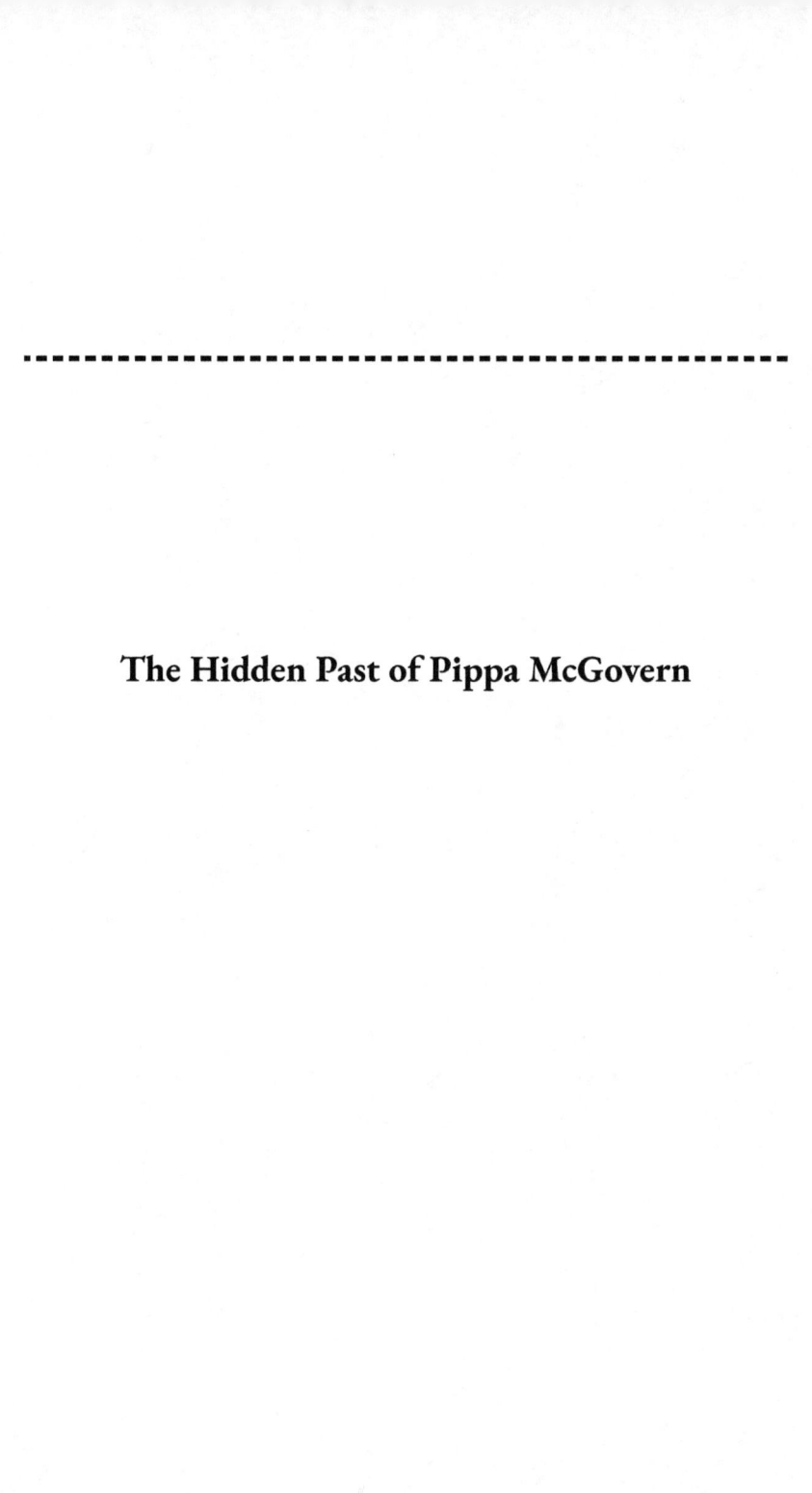

The Hidden Past of Pippa McGovern

Prologue

THE ELASTIC PULLS MY red curls back from my face so tightly that it gives me a headache only a double whiskey will help. Braids, hairpins, some plant and faux pearls have created a Princess Leia-worthy hairstyle.

I poke my head with irritation. They used so much hairspray that I'd not like to stand near an open flame.

And the makeup.

I tilt my head to the right. Who knew such gorgeous cheekbones could be created out of such cheeks? My eyebrows have been waxed and plucked, the ordeal going on so long, I almost murdered Alessia. My lipstick is a colour not found in nature and makes my lips look like some sort of Kylie Jenner miracle puff up.

I've endured torture by of Iraqi agents and getting prepped for my wedding is worse.

But I have to admit, I do look pretty *focking* amazing.

The door to the washroom opens. They've given me the accessible bathroom to use as a private bridal suite. I don't even turn, not wanting to give him the satisfaction of my surprise.

"Hello, Colin."

"Pippa."

I'm still not used to him without the fake frames he's been wearing for the last year. His blue eyes look brighter without the glass lenses. "You do look lovely."

The London accent inspires a hollow ache of what might be homesickness in my chest but I have no time for it.

"What're you doing here?"

Colin Darcy leans against the door. "How could I possibly stay away? I assumed my invitation must have gotten lost in the mail."

I smile, adjusting the sparkly tiara caught in my red curls. "I meant here. In the loo. *Private* bridal lavatory means *privacy*."

"I do apologize, but I wanted to give you my best. Congratulations, my darling girl." Colin steps forward, dropping a kiss on my upturned cheek. "All the best, Pippa."

"Thank you. But Colin, how could you possibly think it's a good idea for you to be here? Your old girlfriend is here. I'm sure the new boyfriend won't be pleased to see you."

"I've no intention of letting either of them know I'm here." He touches his hair, now a dark brown rather than the reddish colour I'm used to seeing him with. "You're not the only one who is good at disguises."

I scrunch up my nose at the colour. "I wouldn't have gone as dark. You know, her daughter Lucy is adorable. But then, I doubt you've met her, have you?" My gaze flickers to Colin's reflection in the mirror and I notice his jaw clenching, a sure tell that my jab hit the target.

"No, I've not had the pleasure."

"No? Just stalking her?"

Colin gives me a tight smile. "I may have checked up on her occasionally but I wouldn't call it stalking. Now, that's something *you* know about."

"It's not stalking when you're ordered to do it. Have you heard that my new boss wants your head?"

Colin's smile doesn't reach his eyes. He may be closer to me than most people, but there's still an unspoken layer of competition between the two of us.

At least there is for me. But then again, I'm competitive with just about everyone.

"I fear you're exaggerating," Colin says, his voice as polite as always. "Ham's made it perfectly clear that he would love to discuss the situation with me, not remove my head from my shoulders."

"Then why don't you talk to him? No, don't answer that." I hold up my hand. I'm wearing *gloves* for God's sake. "I don't want to get in the middle of it."

"But you are in the middle of it," he reminds me. "You just married into the Agency. MI-6 knows full well your alliance has changed. Not to mention the Irish Intelligence Party."

"Nothing's changed," I hiss. "This changes absolutely nothing." The Irish lilt is always stronger when I'm annoyed.

"I don't believe that," Colin says in a mild tone.

"I'm not asking you to." I do my best to compose myself. The two constant observations people have made about me are the quickness of my reflexes and how my mood can change just as fast. "You should go."

"It might be best if I do." Colin makes a half-turn before he pauses.

"Tenley's lovely, you know," I offer. "Much easier to get along with than Charlotte." This time I don't hide my grimace. "I think Charlotte must be the kind of woman who doesn't play well with other women."

Colin gives a ghost of a chuckle. "You know me too well."

"I do," I reply, ignoring the embarrassment betrayed in the quirk of his brief smile. "She's doing fine. Tailor-made for this life."

"Is she really?"

"Would I lie to you?"

"I don't suppose it would be the first time."

I laugh, a little too heartily for the dress and feel like I'm about to pop the dozens of buttons that march down my back. "Whatever will you do without me, Colin?"

"If I honestly believed this is the last I'll see of you, I'd be very happy. But something tells me this isn't it for us." He stares at me questioningly.

He can stare like that all day; it's not like I'm about to tell him anything.

"Go dance with your husband," Colin finally relents. "And Pippa? Try to behave."

I wink, the fake eyelashes swiftly brushing my cheek. "Well, what's the fun in that?"

But I take his advice. After waiting the appropriate amount of time for Colin to sneak back into the kitchens, or wherever he came from, I head back out to the dining room where less than fifteen minutes ago, a bunch of strangers watched me get married.

I slip up to my husband, admiring the way he fills out his tuxedo. His blond hair gleams in the light. I agreed to the big frou frou event for his sake. I would have been happy eloping somewhere with a beach.

I'll do anything for this man.

I've done so much for him.

He looks down at me as I twine my arm with his. Even with the toe-crushing heels, he still towers over me. "Hello, Mrs. Dodd."

My heart melts like a plate of butter left on the stove as Declan Dodd smiles down at me.

One

Six days ago...

THE SMELL OF THE chicken satay is making my stomach rumble so loud that the man next to me glances around.

"That's me," I tell him with a grin. "I'm about ready to eat the twelve apostles, handing these out. Better take some before I make a run for it."

He shakes his head over my offer.

"More for me," I say cheerily and move away.

The accent's not quite right. I've got a Buffalo whine in my voice rather than sounding Canadian born and bred.

But at least it masks the Irish. During missions, it's best not to call attention to yourself. Sounding like a big red version of Saoirse Ronan lets everyone know I'm here.

The hair's always the most noticeable, along with the chest. I hold the tray higher to hide the girls. There's not a man within a fifty-feet radius that wouldn't be begging for a glimpse of these puppies, which is why my girls are basically strapped down with not one, but two heavy duty sports bras.

And my riot of curls—my best feature, in my opinion—has been pulled back in a no-nonsense bun. The red is easy to mask with an easy wash-out hair dye. Tonight, I've gone for a black-cherry colour which makes me look even paler than usual. A heavy application of makeup erases any evidence of pink in my cheeks and the smattering of freckles along my nose along with muting my features.

The glasses help too. I learned that a long time ago from a friend of mine. Studies show that people wearing glasses are believed to be more intelligent as well as trustworthy. And glasses help mask other features; a man could have a big, honking nose the size of Mount Rushmore and if he wore a pair of glasses, no one would even notice.

I'd go so far as to say my best friend would have trouble recognizing me. If I had a BFF, that is. I've always been more of a lone wolf type of gal. It's easier that way.

The waiter attire let me wander around, practically invisible since there are plenty of high-rollers at this party, and studies show the one per cent normally takes little or no notice of the help. I've already recognized three CEOs, two professional athletes, a politician, and the Toronto-born, world-famous rapper, Drake. Or at least someone who looks an awful lot like him.

It's not like I can wander up to him and ask. But I would if I wasn't in this getup.

There are also a bunch of women at the party, all tarted up. I like a little skin showing myself, but I'd freeze my arse off in that dress. I smile at one poured into a gold lamé dress as she takes one of the satays. I'd bet my last quid that she's a lady of the night.

Tonight's party is at the home of Robert Revello, the latest tech genius to come out of Silicon Valley. He recently married a Canadian woman and moved to the Land of the North, setting up residence in a mansion on Toronto's fancy-pants Post Road.

Revello must be as smart as *fock*, like that Facebook guy. He came up with a new search engine, bigger and better than Yahoo or Bing, and rivaling Google. Tonight's party was billed as a "celebration of his achievement."

A waste of money, if you ask me. Go have a pint with your mates and give a good who hoo. Sounds like more fun to me than some fancy schmanzy shindig.

A couple other *ladies* catch my eye as I circle the room with a platter of coconut shrimp, which are tasty, but not as good as the satays.

One of the girls is a redhead, but it's doubtful that the colour is natural, the other wearing a pink wig. The colours clash as they bend their heads together. There's a big height different—Red is almost as tall as me, but Pink Wig is tiny with a body like a teenage boy.

The women may be dressed for the part, but if I had one more last quid, I'd bet those aren't getting the hourly wage for being here. Something about them doesn't fit. Maybe I'm wrong, but I doubt it. Anyone getting paid to be here would be taking full advantage of the champagne flowing as fast as the St. Lawrence River. I've seen Pink Wig dump no less than three full glasses into the potted bamboo tree behind her.

If she keeps it up, the bamboo isn't going to make it.

And neither of them is going to be making any extra money if they don't stop whispering to themselves.

Do prostitutes make a flat fee at parties like this or are they paid when they hook up with someone? Do they get tips? I've known my fair share of working girls, and I've never asked them.

Something to wonder about.

I continue my serving circle and keep my eyes peeled for anything worth reporting, and also for the opportunity to get upstairs.

The party's being held in the front foyer of the house, with a black marble floor and towering columns that reach at least twenty feet to the ceiling. Security guards in black suits stand at the top of the sweeping set of stairs with folded arms and frowns, making sure no one takes a self-guided tour of the house.

I gnaw on my lip as I hand out tiny meatballs skewered on tasselled toothpicks. For someone with a boatload of money, this guy should be able to find a caterer with a little more originality.

How am I supposed to get upstairs?

Out of the corner of my eye, I see a flash of colour up above on the second floor. What the...? But a shriek fills the air and my attention is diverted to the other side of the room.

"Oh, my gawd!" Pink Wig is standing in front of the centrepiece of the lobby, pointing her finger at it with an expression of amazement. "What is *that*?"

The *that* in question is a block of solid glass with what appeared to be a tiny canoe in the middle of it. I noticed it myself but let it go, knowing that rich folks often had strange taste in art.

Robert Revello pushes his way through the crowd to Pink Wig. "I'm so glad you asked," he cries with delight. "I've been waiting for someone to."

"I'm so happy that I made you happy," Pink Wig enthuses, without an ounce of sexual innuendo. This strengthens my argument that she's no more a working girl than I am. "What is this and how did you get it inside that block?"

"*That* is a replica of the very same canoe I sank the afternoon I met my wife." And Robert Revello proceeded to tell Pink Wig and the surrounding hangers-on the story of how he met his wife.

Bingo. Thanks, Pinkie.

The security guards move halfway down the stairs, listening to Revello. I've got to give the guy credit—he tells a good story, especially when he tells it in a most inappropriate fashion. He better hope his precious wife doesn't hear the things he's saying about her.

I let the security guards listen with the others as I hurry with my tray to the kitchen. "Toilet," I mumble to the guy in the chef's hat as I drop my tray on the counter for a refill and head to the hallway leading to the second set of stairs.

It's going to be tight, but I've always been handy at getting in and out of tight spots.

Racing up the stairs, I stop at the corner before the balcony looking over the foyer. To get to the room I need means I have to pass right in front of the balcony, looking over the foyer, right across from the men in black. My only hope is they are still halfway down the stairs listening to the story.

I can't even check to see if anyone is watching me. Holding my breath, I push off the wall and quickly walk across the balcony, head down, and trying to look like I'm in dire need of a washroom.

Crap cover story, but better than nothing.

The laughter from the bottom of the stairs tells me that attention is still diverted so I hightail it down the hall, like I'm doing the Irish walk out of the pub, hurrying to get home. No one downstairs can see me now.

Third... fourth door... how many rooms does this place have?

My lock picks are in my mass of hair, disguised as hair pins. Such is the power of hair spray that only a tiny curl escapes when I pull them out.

Slide it in, wiggle the wire and listen for the click.

I'm in. Easy peasy. With a grin, I ease open the door, then turn to close it gently. *Click.* It locks after me. Time to have a gander at what that Mr. Revello thinks is so special.

Two

I TURN AROUND.

"Feck off! Whaddya doin' there?"

The tall redheaded girl stands behind the desk, the laptop open before her, exactly in the position I need to be in. Her eyes are as wide with shock as mine.

"You're not supposed to be in here," I say, thinking fast and falling back on the waitress story. And I grab hold of my accent. Surprises can make me slip up.

"Neither are you." She bends over the laptop, fingers dancing across the keys before tapping one with authority. I knew something was off about her.

What gives her the right to bungle my job?

"What's the matter, party not to your liking?" Sliding my lock picks back into my hair, I step closer to the desk. She continues typing without glancing up at me.

I never like to be ignored.

"I always need a bit of quiet time during a party." Her hand brushes along her temple. "Gives me a headache."

"I hear you. What's that you're doing?" I take another step.

"Checking Facebook," she says blithely as she pulls out what appears to be a USB stick from the computer. "Forgot my phone."

"Facebook's always important," I agree. "Anything new on Tay and Travis?"

"Didn't see anything." She closes the laptop with a smile. "Time to get back to the party."

"I don't think so." I cross my arms. "I think you should hand over that there USB you just stuck in your skirt."

I see her fist tighten, her expression blank.

"We about to hop on, then?" I grin, cracking my knuckles. It always shocks me how loud the sound is. "I'm always good for a tussle."

"You shouldn't crack your knuckles," she chides. "You'll get arthritis in your joints."

"*Ta*, but my joints are just fine."

I hate to admit I'm distracted by the quick exchange and not ready for her move. Instead of dodging around the desk, which would have been *my* move, the girl jumps on the desk, then flies off, straight at me.

Her fist grazes my cheek before barrelling into my shoulder. "You *hussy!*" I hiss as I reel back from the hit and straighten my glasses.

She ignores me again as she legs it for the door. I grab her arm before she gets there. "I don't think so." Swinging her around, I send her crashing into the wall.

She bounces off it like a drunk after too many pints. With barely a shake of her head, she's right back at me.

I don't know who this girl is, but she knows a thing or two about fighting.

There's at least a twenty-second exchange of punches without either of us landing the money shot. Finally, I go low, with a cheap crotch shot.

What can I say? I fight dirty.

She leans away at the last second so it hits her thigh, hard enough to give her a nasty charley horse, but it doesn't even slow her down.

She retaliates with two uppercuts that knock the breath out of me, and follows it up with a backhand that sends me reeling. This time the glasses fall off.

Then she's out the door into the hall.

I snatch them up and shove them back on my face. They may be fake glasses, but they weren't cheap and I'm not leaving them behind. "I said, I don't think so!" I cry, right behind her. "Not on my watch."

I catch her by the shoulder, but she slips out of my grasp, and opens the next door, this one unlocked. I get my shoulder against it in time before she can shut it in my face.

"Sorry, no time to chat," she says breathlessly.

"I think we're beyond that." She's strong and puts all of her weight behind the door to close it. But I'm taller and have to admit, quite a bit heavier, so I win. I give the door one last good shove and she staggers backwards. I stride into the room. She picked a bedroom to hide in; never a good idea for a fight.

This is a nice one with shiny silver wallpaper and a black satin spread on the bed. Too fancy for me, but nice. And really big.

"Now, who the *fock* do you think you are?"

She clicks her tongue at me. "Language," she says in a voice that is surprisingly reminiscent of my mother's, god rest her soul.

"Eff off, is that better?"

She smiles thinly, already in fight stance with fists held shoulder high.

Instead of a punch, I give her a hard shove and the end of the bed catches her against the backs of her legs. She falls onto the bed, short skirt sliding even higher up on her thighs. Striding over, I grab hold of her ankles, notice she's wearing ugly, practical shoes, and flip them up, sending her tumbling off the side of the bed.

I grab her by the hair, only to have the red wig come off in my hands. "I think maybe you need to do something with your hair before you go back to the party," I tell her, glancing between the wig and her short dark hair.

She takes advantage of the pause to wriggle away from me. "I don't think I'll be going back."

"I have to, if I want to get paid."

The lamp on the nightstand tips over, she manages to throw me onto the bed and then jumps up there with me.

"This is kind of fun," I laugh, still in full attack mode.

"I don't think it's supposed to be," she says as she plows her fist into the side of my head. A ringing noise bursts through my ears.

The door bursts open, startling us. The girl with the pink hair stands there. "Tenley, we gotta go."

"Good idea," my opponent says, hopping off the bed. I give her a shove mid jump, which sends her tumbling into Pink Wig.

"You're not going anywhere with that info," I tell her, jumping off the bed. "*Tenley*."

What kind of a stupid name is that?

"Who the hell is this?" Pink Wig scowls as she sets Tenley on her feet and gives her a push towards the window. "Get out of here."

She faces me and blows the hair off of her forehead as Tenley pulls open the curtains. The cool air rushes in as she slides open the window.

An alarm shrieks.

"Damn Perry," Pink Wig mutters.

"That's why it's better to work alone," I say. I dodge Pink Wig and head for Tenley, who already has a leg out the window. Roughly, I pull her back in, throwing her onto the floor.

I need that USB stick and I'm not leaving here without it.

I straddle Tenley, who is trying to wriggle out of my grasp. "You had to hide it somewhere," I mutter, groping at her waist and hips.

Before I can find any hidden pockets, I'm tackled from behind, causing me to lose my balance and giving Tenley a chance to get out from under me.

My glasses fall off again. I'm surprised the things have made it this far.

"You should always ask before you start to grope," Pink Wig says from the floor beside me. "It's polite."

"I'm not polite," I tell her, and punch her in the face.

"Stop!" booms a loud voice.

Pink Wig and I turn to the door in unison. Three security guards block the doorway with their shoulders.

"What do you think you're doing in here?" He looks more interested than angry to find the two of us tussling on the floor.

"Does he really expect us to answer?" Pink Wig groans.

"Maybe. We're having our own party," I say to the guard. "And you're interrupting."

"And that's rude," Pink Wig adds. She blows the hair off her forehead.

I've already figured out that's her tell, and I'm ready when she moves.

She somersaults her way to the nearest guard, bounces to her feet, and with an impressive leg sweep, knocks not one, but two guards off their feet. They fall to the floor in a heap of arms and legs. I hear the thud as Pink Wig smacks their heads together.

At the same time, I take out the third guard with a quick jab to the throat and a sharp kick to the crotch. "That'll show them."

"You seem to like to hit there," Tenley observes. She's back to her original position of halfway out the window.

"Does the trick."

Without another word, Tenley throws her leg over the railing and slides over the edge. We're on the second floor and she just disappears. I'm still goggling at her vanishing act when Pink Wig gives me a sharp jab to the face and takes her own leave out the window.

"No focking way," I mutter. A quick glance over the side shows the thin rope ladder dangling down to the ground. "Aren't you the little Girl Scout?"

My planned exit was to be through a bedroom by the back stairs, where I could swing over to the garage roof and jump down from there. But this will do nicely.

I slide down the sides of the ladder, throwing in a kick at Pink Wig before jumping the last few feet.

The Tenley girl is already hightailing it across the lawn. I'm ready to give chase, but a shout from the balcony makes me reconsider. The three security guards have been joined by friends.

I grin at Pink Wig, who is clearly as torn by the fight-or-flight instinct as I am. A shot rings out overhead, deciding it for me.

"Till next time, then," I tell her, taking off at a sprint in the opposite direction, right to where my bike, a Kawasaki special, is parked by the side of the house.

A second alarm wails as I throw a leg over and gun the engine. I have just enough time to get the helmet on before security begins streaming out of the doors.

"I still expect to be paid!" I call as I roar away.

I overtake the Pink Wig's getaway car as it races down Post Road—a black catering truck with a *Good Eats* decal.

I give a jaunty wave as I catch up, glancing over at the last moment.

A blond god stares back at me. It's only a moment, but I can tell he has eyes the colour of the Mediterranean and a toothpaste-white smile. He gives me a salute and I almost lose control of my bike.

Where in holy hell did he come from?

Three

THE ADRENALINE RUSH FROM the fight has all but worn off by the time I unlock the door to my hotel room. Not only that, but I haven't been able to get the image of the driver out of my mind.

Who is he? Was he with the dynamic duo from the party? He had to be. A dark van racing away from the scene of the crime is like asking if bears shit in the woods—it's obvious some agency sent their people in to retrieve the list.

But which one?

I set my helmet down on the table and glance around the room with a sigh. It's a kip, but not the worst place I've stayed in. It's far from the best. My boss, Eugene Mochrie, is as tight as a duck's arse and begrudges me every time I hand in my invoice showing a hotel for more than twenty quid a night.

He'd probably prefer me to still be sleeping rough on the street, just so he wouldn't have to put out for the lodging when I'm away on a mission.

"Sleeping rough shows you have character," he boomed when I once asked for an upgrade from the sleazy motel he'd booked me into.

"No, it shows I'm collecting bed bugs to bring you back as a souvenir," I had retorted.

I begin the slow process of pulling out the pins holding up my hair. Every time I yanked one out, a curl corkscrewed out. I have Julia Roberts hair, circa 1990s—long, red and a mass of curls.

I think back to Pink Wig. Maybe I should use a wig. Braids, chignons and the odd hat have done the trick hiding the hair so far, but maybe it's time for something new.

Not a pink one, though. I have Irish skin—creamy white and dotted with freckles, and pink does not flatter such paleness. Plus, it looked kind of cheap.

Just as slowly, I unbutton the no-nonsense white top I had to buy to serve at the party. It had been brand new, but there's no way I can return it now. There's a long rip down the seam and another under my arm.

Is that blood or sauce from the shrimp?

Blood, I decide after a quick look. I have a nasty gash over my eyebrow and dried blood around my nose.

I'm suddenly completely knackered. Even the bed looks inviting, or it will be when I wriggle out of the sports bras. There's no way anyone can sleep with these things cutting off the circulation.

As I change into a battered jumper, I go over the events of the party. Who were those girls? I hadn't heard that there was any other interest in the info I had been sent to retrieve. Were they freelance? There was no excuse for me not to have gotten the information off that laptop before they did.

Like me, they had been after Revello's list.

My mission—that I chose to accept—was to come to Toronto, get access to Revello's hard drive, and download the list of beta testers he used for the new search engine.

I'm sure the search engine will be kick-ass whenever he gets it up and running, if he ever does. But in the meantime, I'm guessing the important thing for Mr. Robert Revello is all that private information he'd gleaned from the beta testers.

See, our whizzkid came up with a funny little glitch in his search engine that allows a third party to gain access to the personal information of those using. Like Facebook running ads based on what you're searching for on Google, but worse. This little glitch can weasel its way into a computer and check out important things like favourite shows on Netflix, frequented porn sites, and, oh yes—banking information.

And a lot of other fun stuff.

The malware will do a lot of damage when it's released to the public, but that's not my problem. Revello took a year to test his baby on a select group of friends and investors, most of which make up some of the world's movers and shakers; celebrities, politicians, and those with lots to hide. This list of beta testers, as well as access to their computers, phones and basic life, is worth a bloody fortune.

Revello is in town to set up a sweet deal to sell it.

I was at the party to steal it before he could do that.

Before I do anything else, like sleep or eat or run and hide, it's time to contact Eugene and tell him about the night's events.

Belfast is five hours ahead, which makes it—I wince. It'll be the middle of the night over there, but I suspect Eugene will be awake and waiting for me to report in.

And as I connect to him via Zoom, I see that he is, sitting at his desk in his office that smells of cigars and whiskey, wearing the worn cardigan that makes him look more like a grandfather than one of the most feared and respected men in Northern Ireland.

"Pippa," he booms, favouring me with a warm smile. "How goes it?"

Of course he's happy with me; he thinks my night was a success.

"Not good. Made a bit of a right bags out of it," I admit heavily, the Irish in my voice coming out loud and clear now that I don't have to hide it. "I had to leg it out of there."

The smile vanishes. "Report."

"There was another interested party involved." I give him a brief recap of what happened, without coming right out and saying I almost got my ass kicked.

I didn't—the fight between me and Pink Wig ended before a clear winner could be called, but seeing as how I lost the info, I was obviously the big loser.

Eugene's expression of displeasure deepens the more I explain. And I don't bother giving excuses. It had all come down to timing. Blondie and her friend saw an opportunity before I did, and took it.

"Who d'ya think they are?" I finally ask.

"Has to be NIIA, but I didn't think they had the bollocks for a job like this, given the mess they're in. Hamilton Short is losing agents quicker than he can train them."

"I heard the name Tenley. I don't know if that's a first or last."

Eugene frowned. "Don't recognize it. Was one of them a blond?"

"Maybe. She had a on a pink wig. Scrappy little thing."

That was high praise indeed from me.

"Probably Charlotte Dodd." He makes one of his noises deep in his throat; I never know if it means he's pleased or disgusted or had just scheduled a mission for me in Siberia.

The name sounds vaguely familiar. "Who's she when she's home?"

"Top agent and heir apparent of NIIA. If there'll be anything left for her to inherit after Short gets finished with it," Eugene says with a rude laugh.

I've heard mention of the NIIA. The intelligence community isn't tight, but based on gathering intelligence, we know who the other players are. I've actually heard of Hamilton Short, the young and brilliant head of the Canadian spy association, mainly because Eugene's son Lysander has a hate on him, bordering on murderous.

"Dodd," I muse.

"You met her grandfather. He was here for dinner once, before you started with us. Seamus Dodd. Wily old cat."

It's the *wily old cat* reference that brings a set of memories crashing down on me, as intense as the time I was thrown through a wall.

"I don't remember him," I lie, keeping my face as smooth as a mask as the images of a tall, grey-haired soldier type flit through my mind.

"Not much to remember. He's dead now."

Unfortunately, I do remember exactly how he died.

"What d'ya want me to do?" I ask, a leaden feeling starting in the pit of my stomach. I don't need to ask what he wants—I know.

"Get me the list. And while you're at it, see what you can find out about NIIA. See if you can find a way in, do some damage."

"I'm not sure they're going to be welcoming me with open arms if I steal the list back from them."

"You're a smart lass. I'm sure you'll figure something out."

Eugene Mochrie wasn't just my boss; he was more of a father figure than my *oul fella* ever was. Eugene had found me when I was fifteen and living on the streets of Belfast. I had made a decent attempt to pick his pocket, enough to impress Eugene with my skill and speed, so instead of belting me around the ears, he took me home and fed me.

Since that day, I've been a card-carrying member of the Irish Intelligence Party, a less violent but more radical offshoot of the IRA. Eugene made me the youngest agent working for the IIP.

And then he joined a group called Mielson, who are looking to combine the worldwide intelligence communities into one powerhouse faction. Instead of each country being in charge of their own secrets, Mielson wants them all under their control, able to use and sell for their own advantage. Picture agents for the CIA, M1-6, NIIA, IIP all working together, without any loyalty to any country and with a much better paycheck.

I should know, because they pay me. Eugene is now second-in-command of Mielson.

And looking to run the whole thing. When I left Dublin, he was pretty close to taking over. Getting the information from Revello might just give him the leg up to do it.

Eugene makes it sound like having all the spies working together is the cat's arse, but I'm not so sure. Obviously, there's more he's not telling me, but that's above my pay grade. And the more I find out worries me. If Mielson gains control of the CIA, M1-6 and NIIA, not to mention the other intelligence communities, then who would control them?

The more I think about it, the more I wonder if that makes *me* one of the bad guys.

Four

ONCE EUGENE GIVES ME his instructions, he ends the call without much of a goodbye. Typical Eugene.

Leaning back in the chair, I rest my feet on the table beside me and study the ceiling. Maybe there's a plan up there among the water stains and spiderwebs. This is the first mission I've ever failed at. I needed that information and I didn't get it.

Should I go back? I could get back in without a fuss.

No, Eugene's right. By now, Revello's place will be locked up tighter than Spanx on a four-hundred-pound-woman. I've lost my chance. He'll be out of town as soon as his private jet is ready to go. Probably already is. I can track him, but it will take time, time Eugene doesn't want to give me.

No, the best way to get it is from NIIA.

My feet hit the floor with a thump as I turn back to the laptop. I do what every ten-year-old has been trained to do when they want to find out something; I Google Charlotte Dodd.

There's not much there. She is a spy, after all.

But I have my ways to find out things. I pick up my phone and about two seconds after I send the text, my phone buzzes with a response.

"Colin!" I don't have to pretend to sound pleased to hear from him. "I think you're the only person I know who refuses to text."

"Pippa. Actually, I prefer face-to-face but this will have to do. By the way, usually you lead with a quick, *how're things*, when you drop a line to a person you haven't seen in a few months." His British accent sounds sharper when he's irritated.

"Pish. You still in Canada?"

"Why?"

"Because I want you to help me break into the CN Tower. Why d'ya think? I need some info? Please. Pretty please. With some poutine on top, since that's all these folks eat. Nasty curds and gravy."

"I agree, poutine's a bit overrated. What do you need?"

I've known Colin forever, even before he went to work for MI-6. We met in London when we were kids and I lived there with my mother. He was the only one I kept in touch with when I moved to Belfast. There was a time when I had wanted to be more than just friends, but that's long past us. Colin's a mate, and one of my only friends outside the family.

Why is an agent of Britain still friendly with a lowly Irish lass with ties to Irish intelligence? A few years ago, Colin got recruited by Mielson, so we work together. Sort of.

"Have you had any run-ins with agents from NIIA?" I ask Colin, popping my finger in my mouth. Some of the sauce from the chicken satays survived my hand washing, tucked deep into the nail bed.

"Why do you want to know?"

I heave a martyred sigh. "Not for anything dodgy. I need this for *me*, nobody else."

Colin may have been recruited by Mielson, but he still works for M1-6. And as close as we are, I'm not entirely sure where his loyalties lie. I suspect wily Colin is playing both sides.

But I'm not about to call him out on it, especially not if he helps me.

"How 'bout the basics," I suggest. "That Hamilton Short is the pretty-boy head of things. And there's this Charlotte Dodd? Small, wee thing, a bit annoying."

"I've actually never had the pleasure of meeting her," Colin admits, and I smile. "But from all accounts, she's a bit of a dynamo."

"Uh huh," I prompt.

"She's with Ham Short. Her four brothers work for NIIA with her. It's like a regular royal family of Canadian spies."

"Names?"

"Perry, Caleb, Declan—he drives. Seamus. You might have heard of the senior Seamus. He started NIIA back in the 1970s."

I ignore the information on the senior and focus on two words—*he drives*. What is the chance of the hot guy driving the getaway van being Charlotte Dodd's brother?

Pretty good chance, if you consider my luck.

"Uh huh. Where do they hang out?"

"Are you asking me where the NIIA is located?" Colin's voice turns icy. It's times like these that I suspect he likes M1-6 more than Mielson.

"Of course not. I want to know where this royal family *hangs out*—pubs, gyms, dog parks, things like that."

"Why?"

"Because I want their autographs, why d'ya think? There's no hit on them, so again, nothing dodgy about me asking."

"I didn't think you'd turned paid gun."

"Nope, just paid thief," I say cheerfully. "Anything else interestin'?"

"Not really, no," Colin says slowly.

"Mmm, ta." I can tell Colin has lots more he's not sharing, so I decide to wait him out. "So what's with you? Who is she?"

"Who's who?"

"Whoever it is that's keeping you here in the Six? I hear that's what they call Toronto. I don't get why," I muse.

"It has to do with the amalgamation of the city," Colin explains.

"Always was a smarty pants. But who is she?"

Colin chuckles. "Have you ever thought of doing proper intelligence work?"

"You're proper enough for the both of us. Now, be a love and tell Pippa all about your lass."

"Nothing to tell," he admits. "It didn't work out. I thought I'd check in with her before I head home."

"Did *you* put her in danger?"

"*I* didn't."

"Because she works for NIIA." It was a shot in the dark, but I don't miss Colin's sharp inhale. Bingo. "She does, doesn't she? Please tell me it's not this Dodd chickie."

"No, it's not Charlotte Dodd. And that's all I'm telling you."

"G'wan wi' you." I fake a loud yawn. "Well, I'm off to beddie. Thanks for the info, Colin. Got time for a pint before we head back across the pond?"

"That would be lovely," he says in his proper English way before ending the call.

Maybe I should go to bed. It's late, and all the bowing and scraping with trays of food at Revello's was bloody exhausting, much more than the scrap I got into upstairs. But first, I need to check out this Dodd family.

Google doesn't tell me much, so I log on to my second favourite way of tracking someone.

Facebook.

Maybe I'm old school, because I much prefer Facebook over Instagram or Twitter.

I hit the mother lode when I type in Declan Dodd.

"Bingo again," I mutter, leaning closer to the screen for a better look. I was right. "What a ride." Declan Dodd, looking sexy with his blond hair and blue eyes, was indeed driving that van tonight.

I scroll through his feed, looking at pictures. His setting is private, but it doesn't take a genius to break through the security.

Or maybe it does, and I'm just that good.

The whole Dodd family is so bloody good-looking. And fit. Nicely fit. I pause on a picture of Declan with his shirt off. He's very pretty.

And what's this? The next picture shows Declan with someone, obviously one of the brothers. The brother has his arm around a girl who looks suspiciously like Tenley from tonight.

"Well, look at that," I mutter.

It doesn't take me long to find out Seamus is the brother, and he changed his status to IN A RELATIONSHIP not too long ago. A few more clicks leads me to her name.

"Tenley Scott," I read. "Soup du Jour. Looks like I found a place for breckie tomorrow."

I read everything I can find about Tenley and the Dodds. There's nothing to be found about Charlotte, which tells me she's agent through and through. Or that she has no life, whereas Tenley still does.

When my eyes begin to cross with exhaustion, I finally close things down and get ready for bed. Of course, when I'm all tucked in with lights out and booby-trapped door, my phone buzzes again.

"It better not be you, Colin," I grumble, reaching for it in the dark.

Lysander.

I accept the FaceTime call and run a hand through my hair before I paste a smile on my face. "Hey."

"Da told me what happened."

There are no pleasantries or greetings between us, just a serious expression on Lysander's handsome face. And he is handsome and charming—at times. Smart and well-read and well-off... Lysander Mochrie has a lot going for him.

"I've got it covered." This time I try to hide the yawn with my hand.

"Do you, Pippa? It's not like you to let an easy mission slip past you. Are you all right?"

I know Lysander isn't asking about my physical well-being, or even about my mental state. He wants to know what the hell is wrong with me that I didn't get a hold of the USB stick.

Lysander is the second son to Eugene. And like the second sons of old, he has a huge chip on his shoulder when it comes to not inheriting the family business. The heir apparent to Eugene is Niall; Eugene has earmarked him to take over Mielson as well as the family's own interests. Lysander had been sent to France to oversee a dirty little operation that was supposed to end with Mielson gaining control of the Directorate General Intelligence by the end of the year.

At least, that was the plan. I don't think it's going well for Lysander.

But I know enough not to ask about it.

Eugene's always said he wants to bring me into the family in a more permanent way. "You're my daughter in everything except name," he told me more than once. "We'll see what we can do to make it official."

This means Lysander's been set up to marry me.

Even though the union of Pippa and Lysander has been unofficially planned for years, I still haven't got my head around it. But I'm not about to tell Eugene this, especially since possible husbands aren't exactly crawling out of the woodwork looking for me.

Not that I'm looking for a husband. It's not something people in my line of work aspire to.

"Just a slip-up," I assure him. "It's covered."

"How? What's your plan?"

This time I don't bother to hide my yawn. "Lysander, it's the middle of the night here, and I'm knackered. Trust me on this, will you, and let me get some sleep."

"Are you alone?"

"Yes, Lysander, of course I'm alone." Along with intensity, Lysander shares his father's jealous streak. It's not one of his better qualities. I pan the phone so he can see there's no one else in the room with me.

"I miss you," he says dutifully.

"I miss you too." The words are automatic, even when the sentiment isn't always sincere. I do love Lysander, in my own way. It's complicated.

"I'll let you get your rest. Keep me updated, please."

"'Course I will."

Why does Lysander want to be updated? I report directly to Eugene, and if he's not available, to Niall. When I have to report to anyone, that is. I've been doing this so long that Eugene lets me run my own ops. I work better alone.

Except for this time.

It's not like me to botch a mission.

I don't like it.

Five

I SLEEP THROUGH MY alarm the next morning and I don't
make it to the cafe for the early breakfast I had planned. But
I still make it before lunch.

It turns out the little cafe Tenley runs is a quick stroll from my
fleabag hotel. It's a brisk, chilly walk; it's like the weather finally
decided that it was time to be autumn, but it works for me. I'm not
going in undercover, but I don't want to call attention to myself,
so once again, the hair needs to be covered. I've plaited it, and
while most spies use the traditional baseball cap, I always come off
looking incredibly dorky, so I pull out my black knitted toque.

It's a Canadian thing; I've noticed lots of people wearing one,
even in the summer.

The bell on the door jingles merrily as I swing into the cafe.
Despite the bright morning sun, a gust of chilly air follows me
inside.

I breathe deep, savouring the smells of freshly baked muffins and
the rich aroma of coffee. Being Irish with a side of English, I can't
stand the stuff, but even I have to admit it smells darn good.

"Morning," chirps the girl behind the cash. "What can I get for you today?"

I notice Tenley arranging muffins in the display at the other end of the counter. "Are they fresh baked?" I point to the tray of muffins, and Tenley looks up. "They smell lovely."

I let the accent fly free. Even on the off-chance Tenley thinks I look familiar, anything coming out of my mouth will sound completely different.

But I still hold my breath until Tenley gives me a friendly smile, without a trace of recognition.

Pulled it off again.

"Still warm," she says. "Just got them out of the oven. Apple oatmeal."

"One of those, please, but the cheddar scones look yummy too..." If this is the same Tenley who tried to kick my butt last night, what is she doing here, all bright and perky? And did she bake all this? My last attempt at baking got me burnt biscuits, and a broken smoke detector.

My mouth waters. Last night's stolen satays were a long time ago.

"Everything's good." The girl behind the cash, whose name tag reads Brianna, smiles eagerly at me. "First time here?"

I nod, trying to look like I'm having difficulty deciding, while in fact I'm watching Tenley. Friendly, obviously in good shape... nothing about her screams spy.

That's the point, isn't it? No one seeing me could tell what I'd been up to last night either, especially since I hid the bruises with a thick layer of make-up.

"Well, how about a coffee while you're making up your mind?"

"Tea, please. Earl Grey, with two sugars and a shot of vanilla, please. And in a mug? I'll hang out here for a bit."

Brianna turns to make my tea, and I notice Tenley staring at me. "That's an interesting way to take your tea."

"Is it? Cheaper than a London Fog latte, but the same taste. I'm too skint to fork out for the frothy milk."

She nods slowly. I don't like the way she's looking at me and fight the urge to run. There's no way she recognizes me from last night. The hair is back to red and no glasses. Plus, I'm wearing my baggiest pants and a thick jumper with a hood. While I may be a big girl in the tits and hips department, this getup makes me look huge all over.

I stand my ground and smile cheerfully at her. "I think I want the muffin."

After paying Brianna, I take my tea and muffin and head to a corner table, one that gives a good sight line to the door as well as the counter. Pulling my book out of my bag, I settle in to observe.

The cafe is long and narrow with about a dozen little tables in two neat rows, with a few stools at the long counter. It's bright and cheerful, despite the sparse décor. Almost impersonal, I decide. Nothing about this place tells me anything about the owner.

I guess that's the point.

The door to the kitchen is directly opposite me, so I can watch without seeming to stalk, but lets Tenley observe me as well. Not that I'm giving her anything interesting to see—just eating my muffin and reading my book.

About a half hour into my stake out, Tenley approaches my table. "Can I get you a refill?"

"Lovely." I hold up my mug with a smile. "Earl Grey with—"

"I remember."

I watch her prepare my tea, chat to Brianna. I hope for Tenley's sake this place picks up. When she returns, she has a cheddar scone on a plate.

"On the house," she says, setting the plate on the table. "Since it's your first time here."

"Ta."

Tenley stands by my table, and I glance up expectantly. "I knew someone who used to take his tea like that," she says.

Bloody hell. Colin! I'm the one who introduced it to him.

Tenley can't be the girl he's hanging around for. What would be the chance of that?

It's a pretty good chance, now that I think about it.

"Must be common," I say with a laugh. "I can't be the only one trying to save a few quid."

She frowns and I fight the urge to wince. "He was English too."

I give my head a firm shake. "Well, now, I'm Irish. A whole country apart."

"Sorry. I love the accent but I can't tell them apart. Do you live around here?"

"Not too far." I take a sip of tea to signal the conversation is over, and end up burning my tongue. Tenley doesn't leave, but watches me with narrowed eyes.

Just as she opens her mouth, supposedly to continue the interrogation, the bell on the door signals. Tenley's face softens into a smile as she looks to the door.

Seamus Dodd. I recognize him from my Facebook stalking of last night. He's a few inches taller than I am, with a barrel-like chest and arms rivaling Dwayne Johnston.

Maybe not that big, but big enough.

But Seamus doesn't hold my attention long. I'm too busy watching the man who jostles into the cafe after him. I'd recognize the blond hair and blinding white smile even if I hadn't been pouring over his pictures last night. It's the driver of the van, Declan Dodd.

"Excuse me," Tenley says automatically to me. Seamus greets her with a hug and a quick snog. I tuck my chin into my neck and try to disappear behind my book.

If Tenley hadn't, there's no way Declan is going to recognize me from last night. Plus, I had my helmet on, and he only saw me for a brief moment as I flashed by. But the memory of his cheeky grin, his two-fingered wave stayed on my mind.

He waved like he *knew* me. Or at least like he wanted to know me.

At the counter, Declan leans on his elbows and says something to Brianna, the girl behind the counter, who giggles and tosses her hair. He looks a randy sod, a player if I ever saw one, and I've seen my fair share. So why do I want him to turn around and smile at me?

Stop being thick. I give my head a shake as Declan laughs at something Brianna says. There's no way he'd notice me in this getup, anyway.

Gulping down my tea, I stuff the scone in the pocket of my jumper and get up from the table, purposefully leaving my book. Tenley is distracted by the thousand-watt smiles of both Dodd brothers and I slip out without her noticing.

It's a good first contact.

I spend the rest of the afternoon wandering in and out of the stores around Tenley's cafe. For a moment I'm tempted to follow Seamus and Declan when they leave, but stay put, smelling every single sample in The Body Shop as I watch out the front window of the store as they cross the street against the light.

I watch as Declan throws his head back as he laughs at something Seamus says, and I smile in response. Both men are attractive, but there's something about Declan. He looks happy and carefree, unadorned by worries.

It would be easy to do a quick meet with him. He has no idea who I am and—

Why would I do that? Tenley is my target. Declan is nothing but a pretty face. And more importantly, what could that pretty face do for me?

"Can I help you with anything?"

I turn away from the window towards the sales clerk who has approached me. It's the second time, which means I've been in here too long.

"No, thanks, I'm just on my way." I give her a cheeky grin and slide past her towards the door.

As soon as I'm outside, I immediately look across the street to the last place where I'd seen Declan and Seamus before they disappeared into the crowd. There's no sight of his leather coat nor bright blond head.

"Look at you in that get up."

Colin Darcy looks completely different without the glasses, which proves my point. He's dyed his hair a dark brown. Shame—I much preferred the reddish brown.

"I could say the same about you." I feign indifference, even though Colin has done well to sneak up on me. "So you're stalking now?"

Colin nods towards Tenley's cafe across the street. "Pot calling the kettle black, Pippa." Another smile. "Got time for that pint?"

Colin leads the way to a nearby pub. It's a little more upscale than what I'm used to, based on the number of micro breweries on tap. I make a mental note to let Colin get the tab.

"Why are you watching her?" I demand as we take our drinks over to the table beside the front window.

"Me first. Why are you here?"

I ignore his question. "Are you here for MI-6 or Mielson?" No sense beating around the bush. There's no way I'm telling Colin anything before we've straightened out who he's working for today.

"My loyalty has never been in question."

"Yes, but to who?"

Colin only smiles. "Do you like her?"

"Tenley? I haven't even met her. Not really. But she doesn't really seem the type—you know, to be an agent." I take a mouthful of my Guinness. "How'd that happen?"

Is it my imagination, or does Colin appear a wee bit guilty? "Well, that might be my fault."

I give him a *come on* gesture with my hands. "Continue." It's always fun to get stuff out of Colin, especially supper. I pull the menu close to me and flip through.

"We were on a date, actually. Long story short—and it is a bit of a long story—Tenley, *erm*, got a bit mixed up in some unfinished business. An associate of mine—former associate now—took the liberty of downloading someone's memories into her head."

I burst out laughing. "Get out of the garden! That's as mad as a box of frogs!"

"Unfortunately, it's true."

"True? That's a crap date."

"Actually, there were a few surprisingly good points."

"What's all this about the memory stuff?" I demand before Colin starts to reminisce about his date.

"Apparently, Charlotte Dodd had her memories pulled out to go undercover. Unfortunately, the file with the memories was stolen by Benjy Lionel— "

"Ah, Benjy." I sigh. "So that's what he's been up to this week."

"And downloaded into Tenley's mind."

I whistle under my breath. "Does Tenley think she's Charlotte? No, she can't because Tenley owns the cafe and how does Charlotte... I'm confused."

"No, Tenley still has her own memories, but has Charlotte's as well. Now Tenley knows about missions and moves and top secret information from the National Information and Intelligence Agency. The Agency is Canada's version of MI-6."

"How come I didn't hear about this?"

"It's not something you want broadcast."

"Did Tenley turn like insta-spy then?"

"Yes, exactly. NIIA recruited her right away." Colin frowns. "I'm not sure how she's doing with that." He glances at me expectantly.

"'Fraid I can't help you. Only got me tea. But..." I trail off, thinking of last night. "She seems okay. Like, okay in the head."

"I'm glad."

"But does Tenley still have Charlotte's memories stuck in her head? Or her own back?"

"No idea."

I file away that tidbit; the little I know about Charlotte is that she's a fierce competitor. I can take her, but help is always nice, and I've been known to play dirty.

Colin and I chat, both of us surreptitiously checking the street for any sight of Tenley. I'm not sure what their history is, but Colin seems hung up on her. Too bad for him; as fond as I am of Colin, Seamus Dodd is pretty cute. Not as much as his brother, but enough.

It's a nice way to spend the rest of the afternoon; chatting with Colin, trying not to think of Declan. Colin even pays for my burger.

My hard work is rewarded when I notice a man and a young girl knock on the door of the cafe a little after four. Tenley had already changed the sign hanging on the door to closed, but let them in.

A few minutes later, the man leaves, followed by Tenley, now holding the hand of the little girl.

Ah. Does Tenley babysit on the side, or does she have a kid? From the matching hair colour, I'm going to go with Tenley has a kid.

Six

- -

A FTER SAYING GOODBYE TO Colin, I head back to the hotel
to spend most of the night researching Tenley Scott. I've
picked up some handy hacker skills in my years working for Eugene
and put them to good use. A few hours after I start, I have the be-
ginnings of a dossier, including the name and age of her daughter,
as well what school she goes to.

Not that I would ever use that information, but it's handy to
have.

I've never had the maternal instinct, but it's not that I don't
respect those who do. It's not their fault I had a mother who only
saw me as a meal ticket.

Not that I've ever been able to figure out a way she could make
money off me through gymnastics.

I was competing by the time I was five, travelling across Britain
and Europe for competitions. Lapping up the attention I got from
my prowess on the uneven bars and showing off my floor routines.
Mum pushed and pushed and finally got her reward when I made
the British gymnastics team when I was eleven. Mum had one

goal—I was going to be the first British gymnast to win Olympic gold.

I was good, but not that good.

Especially when my own body betrayed me. Puberty hit, and within six months, I grew eight inches and gained a chest that got in the way of everything. Mum tried everything she could to stop me from growing—she put me on the pill, cut out protein in my diet, everything she could think of to make my body obey her commands. I wasn't having any of it. Years of watching everything I put in my mouth, sore muscles and never making friends were enough. I put my size nine foot down and said no more.

Of course that didn't work. I get my stubbornness from my mum.

Looking back, I always wonder if I should have given in. It would have made her last months a bit more peaceful.

After she died, I was packed up to live with my uncle in Belfast.

I lasted less than a year with him. My gymnastics skills helped make me a darn good pickpocket, which was how Eugene Mochrie found me.

But that was a long time ago. I have more important things to do rather than get teary over the past.

I focus back on the laptop, coming across a sweet little picture of Tenley in her high school yearbook.

It's easy to find information on Tenley Scott. She's all over the place – education, a little piece telling about the opening of her cafe, marriage and divorce from a guy named Simon Stein. Birth certificate for Lucy, age nine.

She must have gotten knocked up pretty young.

I find her on social media, although not much in the last few months. Mostly pictures of the cafe, with Lucy. No profiles on the dating sites.

In comparison, I find next to nothing on Charlotte Dodd, other than a fuzzy picture of a little blond thing with braids at a track meet in 2003.

So she's fast. Good to know.

All this tells me that Tenley is indeed the newest recruit for the Canadian National Information and Intelligence Agency.

Eugene checks in with me around midnight. "Any news?" he asks in his no-nonsense way.

"I don't have the list, but I know how to get it," I tell him.

The next morning, I show up at *Soup du Jour* around eleven o'clock. It's chaotic, but not nearly as bad as I expected.

Tenley's behind the cash, smiling, but I notice the stress furrow marring her forehead. About half the tables are full and every one of them has dirty dishes or balled up napkins strewn about the surface. I immediately switch into waitress mode, piling up dishes with a mound of soiled napkins to take to the counter.

"Where can I put this for you?" I ask Tenley after she finishes with her customer.

She blinks her brown eyes. "You don't have to do that."

"I do. It's in exchange for the on-the-house scone yesterday." I grin when the recognition flashes across her face. I've dressed in more flattering attire, but the hair is still braided and hidden under the toque.

"Oh! You were here yesterday. The Earl Grey with a shot of vanilla. You forgot your book."

"That's what brought me back." I glance around. "You're a bit busier today."

"Brianna called in sick at the last minute." For a moment Tenley let the harried expression cross her face.

"That sucks. Let me help. I'm an awesome waitress."

"I can't let you do that."

"Why not? Hand me a cloth and I'll do the tables. You'll be getting your lunch rush soon." When she pauses, I know I have her. "Don't bother arguing, just hand it over."

With a grateful sigh, Tenley passes me a damp cloth. "Your tea is on the house today, and I'll throw in the frothy milk this time."

I wink at her. "Deal."

For the next four hours, I work my ass off for Tenley. After I tidy up the tables, she gives me a quick lesson on the cash before heading to the kitchen to ready for the lunch crowd. I find out there's a cook in the kitchen, a beast of a man covered with tattoos, with a Jamaican accent as strong as the whites of his teeth. I also discover most of the crowd are regulars, quite a few who ask about Brianna. I like to think I've made a few friends, since the tip cup on the counter jingles with change quite often.

Finally, it's over. The cafe is empty save for an older gentleman nursing his coffee and a young mother with a sleeping baby in the stroller.

"I don't know how to thank you!" Tenley enthuses. "I couldn't have handled that on my own today."

"Glad I could help."

Tenley pushes the tip cup in front of me. "Take this. Usually they share, but Leo insists it's all yours today. He's grateful for you stepping up like that."

"Seriously, it was nothing. I didn't have anything to do today. I'm between jobs."

"Are you looking?" Tenley demands, just like I knew she would.

As we iron out the details of me starting to work for her tomorrow, I deal with two other customers, pouring them coffee with a smile on my face like I'm really looking for a job. I can't believe how easy it is.

A few hours later, Tenley tells me to leave after the last customer, says she's okay to finish up for the day. I protest just enough to sound sincere, when in reality, my feet are killing me and I'm ready to call it quits.

Especially when I get a text from Eugene.

> *New package to pick up this pm.*

To translate, the text means Eugene has a mission for me tonight.

"Are you sure you'll be okay on your own?" I ask Tenley, shoving my phone in my pocket without answering it. Eugene always sends details via the encrypted email address.

"I'll be fine," Tenley says. "I'm closing early today."

"Got a hot date?" I tease, and I'm justified when her cheeks flush a faint pink. "You do!"

"No, not a date," she says reluctantly. "Just... a thing."

"A thing with a boy? A man, I guess. Or woman," I correct hastily.

Tenley laughs with embarrassment. "There's a man," she admits.

"I hope your *thing* has to do with him."

She cocks her head. "I'm actually not sure. But I think I'm seeing him tonight."

I frown. I'm surprised to find I've already developed a soft spot for Tenley. "You think? You don't know?"

"It's complicated."

"Nothing complicated about it. Tell him to shit or get off the pot. Dangling you about's not good for either of you." Both of us look at the door when the bell jangles.

"Seamus!"

It takes a supreme amount of control to keep my jaw from dropping when Seamus Dodd and his brother Declan walk in to the cafe.

Seamus takes no notice of me. His eyes are for Tenley, and Tenley only. And from the way her face lights up, she feels the same.

Colin had no chance.

Any concern for Colin vanishes as Declan turns his blue eyes to me. "Well, now. You're new."

"This is Pippa," Tenley introduces me, after disentangling herself from Seamus' embrace. "She saved my life today."

That catches Seamus' attention.

"Brianna called in sick," Tenley explains quickly. "Pippa stepped up to help."

"Do you know each other?" Seamus demands.

"I like her scones." I flash a winning smile at him. "Happy to help."

"That's very nice of you." Up close, Declan's looks are even more heart-stopping. Nose that's a shade off perfect, probably because it's been broken, a faint dimple nestled into his right cheek and at least two days' worth of stubble.

I like how he's looking at me, interested but not being offensive about it. It's a fine line to balance these days.

"I'm a very nice person," I say with a cheeky smile of my own.

"You look like a very nice person."

"And you can tell this how?"

"No one with hair that colour could be anything but nice."

I tug at a curl that escaped from my braid. "Maybe it's not my natural colour."

"Eyebrows that match, milky white skin and that smattering of freckles—I'd bet money you're a natural redhead. And that accent."

"Considering I worked hard for that tip money, I won't take that bet."

"Is that all Tenley is paying you?" Declan exclaims. Tenley and Seamus had vanished while Declan and I had been talking and I hadn't even noticed.

That never happens. I'm one of the most observant people I know.

"We're working out the details," I reassure him.

"Does that mean you'll be back?"

My heart does a gold-medal-worthy backflip at the hopeful tone in his voice. "At least for tomorrow. I'm not about to wear out my welcome."

"Can't see that happening." His gaze holds mine for a second longer than necessary, and I can't stop the smile that spreads across my face.

Of course that's when my phone signals a text. Instinctively, I pull it out.

> *Emailing you details. Confirmation within the hour*

"Boyfriend?" Declan asks sadly.

"What? No," I say, wiping the frown off my face. Eugene isn't usually so demanding. "No boyfriend here," I wave my phone at him. "Or anywhere."

Lysander would understand. This is *Declan Dodd*, pretty boy driver for the NIIA. It might not be the same as cozying up to Hamilton Short, but I'm sure I can make it worth my while.

Is that a twinge of guilt? Guilt for Lysander – I'm sure he's enjoying himself immensely in France and not giving our "relationship" a second thought.

It's not even a relationship. It's more of an understanding. Like an arranged marriage, but I'm free to socialize before the event without the threat of being stoned to death.

No, it's not the thought of Lysander that produces the twinge.

"Is that so?" Declan asks hopefully.

"That is so." I'm sure my smile of satisfaction matches Declan's.

"So, Pippa," Seamus interrupts us. When did he come back? "You from around here? Are you familiar with *Soup* and that's why you pitched in?"

"I'm new in town," I say, switching my attention to Seamus and the wariness in his voice. "Like I said, I was here yesterday, and came back today. Tenley was going crazy, I'm a good waitress. Call it my Good Samaritan act of the week."

"Where're you from?" he persists.

"A little place in County Cork." Which is about as far from Belfast as you can get.

"What's with the third degree, bro?" Declan says mildly. "You're like mother bear possessive. Tenley's a big girl."

Seamus frowns, but before he can respond, Declan continues. "Besides, I have my own questions for Pippa."

"You do?"

That smile makes Declan absolutely irresistible. "Are you busy tonight?"

Seven

I'VE BEEN RUNNING MY own ops for a few years now. Eugene agrees that I work better on my own, but Lysander's never been convinced. I think it's easier to move when it's just me to worry about. I hate someone telling me what to do, and cost-wise, my ops are a lot cheaper without the added expense of a handler.

Since I have plans to meet Declan for a drink after I'm done, it works well that I'm solo tonight.

Of course I don't tell him what I'm doing before our date.

Is it even a date? Meeting for drinks—that can be classified into the date category, can't it?

When Declan suggested seven o'clock, I countered with eight thirty, praying this would give me enough time to steal whatever info Eugene needs.

I add Declan to my contacts just in case and head back to the hotel to prep for the mission.

I even have time for a quick nap.

There's a swirl of anticipation in my stomach as the elevator stops at the eleventh floor, and it has nothing to do with me sneaking into the housekeeping room at the Four Seasons and borrowing a uniform as well as a master key. After I give the grey dress a tug to prevent the gaping between the buttons, I push the laundry cart into the hallway.

Room 1121. I can guess what room it is since it's the only one with two men standing guard outside the door. Eugene didn't give me many details about who is staying here, but either he's pretty important, or he's pretty afraid.

He's not going to be worried about little old me, though.

I smile at the bodyguards, but to give them credit, neither one of them changes their expression. I'm quick to notice the earpieces and the bulge under the suit jacket—a dead giveaway that they're packing. Taking two pillows from my cart, I widen my smile. "I need in the room, please, boys. Someone needs some extra fluffy pillows."

Tall, dark, and threatening number one holds out his hands. "I'll take them in."

"N-uh." Hugging the pillows, I give my head a flirtatious shake. "It's my job and I wouldn't want to bother you, since you seem so busy."

That produces a crack of a smile from number two.

"It'll just take a sec—I won't be a bother."

"I think he's in the shower," number one grunts.

"Perfect. I'll turn down his bed while I'm at it, so it's all ready for you boys to tuck him in." The teasing wink seals the deal, especially with the triple layer of mascara. I'll have to run out of here to be on time for my date with Declan and I don't want to have to worry about not having enough time to get ready properly.

With a swipe of the key card, number one opens the door for me. I hold my breath after the door closes behind me. I didn't expect him to stay in the suite with me, but you never know.

"Hello?" It's not the penthouse suite, but it's close enough. I wish Eugene would splurge for me to stay in a place like this once in a while.

I hear the noise of the shower, and go to work.

The briefcase is right where it should be, on the table in the bedroom. Throwing the pillows on the bed, I pull on my gloves. Breaking into things was among my first lessons when I started with Eugene. He always said being a former street thief gave me an edge.

Maybe he was right. It takes me sixteen seconds to get past the lock on the briefcase.

"No pictures, give me the actual papers," Eugene had instructed. It's quick work to find the file he wants and no time at all to tuck it into the elastic belt I wear under the uniform. Now to fix the bed and get out of here.

But before I do that, I head for the room safe.

I always find they are the easiest things to break into. Taking a little vial of powder from my pocket, I blow it onto the keypad and *voila*. Fingerprints appear on four of the keys.

It takes me two tries to get the code, but the door finally swings open.

This is where he hides the good stuff. Stacks of bills, a gun and—what's this? I pull out the blue velvet bag and stick my fingers in.

"Pretty," I murmur as I pull out a few diamonds. Who is this guy?

A minute later, I close the door of the safe, after helping myself to about five thousand in cash and a handful of sparkling, uncut diamonds. I have no idea how much the jewels are worth, but they'll feather my nest egg nicely.

I don't see the need to let Eugene know about the extras I acquire. As much as he professes to care about me, I'm not family, and that means I'm expendable. I always look out for myself because nobody else is going to do it.

Another minute to turn down the bed, tuck a chocolate onto the pillow and I'm finished. The diamonds are tucked into a finger of one of the gloves, which are then shoved into my bra. The money goes into the belt with the papers.

The shower is still running.

"Have a good night, boys," I tell the guards as I let myself out of the room. I give my hips an extra sway to direct the attention there, rather than on the papers strapped to my back, and push my cart to the elevator.

It pings its arrival just as I get to the door. Keeping my head down like the good maid I'm trying to be, I wait for it to empty.

Two women get out.

A quick peek tells me one is short, with violent pink hair.

I smile as the door closes. I guess Charlotte Dodd got her wig back.

Eight

- -

I'M SEVEN MINUTES LATE for my date, which is good for me, not even considering I had been across the city in a hotel room only forty-five minutes ago.

"Sorry I'm late," I say, trying not to pant from my run as I slide into the booth across from Declan.

"You're worth the wait," he teases.

"You're right," I tell him, laying on the sass. His dimple is *adorable*. And he's wearing this blue sweater that exactly matches his eyes, with a V-neck that gives a glimpse of a wee bit of chest hair.

I drag my gaze back up to those blue eyes. Even his lashes are impressive.

Thank god the waiter appears because I'm gawking at him like eejit. This is brutal. I've dated lots of men, *countless* men, and never once has anyone got me drooling like Declan has.

I'm dumbstruck to realize that I'm *nervous*.

I'm never nervous.

"So what'll it be tonight?" Declan asks.

I swear I never heard the waiter ask what I wanted to drink.

"Um—" I glance around. It's a nice place, even more upscale than the pub that Colin pulled me into yesterday. A pint of the black stuff would go down nicely, but this is supposed to be a date, so I'd better start playing the part. "Red wine, please. And if you were a wine list where—?"

The waiter points at the wine list on the table before me.

"You'd be right in front of me."

Quickly, I chose the pinot noir and Declan orders a beer. As the waiter disappears, Declan stretches out his hands across the table so that they're inches from mine.

I resist the urge to grab one. I should be okay as long as we don't touch. I'm really not sure what's going on here. I drink in his face like fine champagne. His lips look soft...

I snatch at a thought that nudges its way through the cotton candy murk at the front of my brain. "How long has your brother being going out with Tenley?"

Declan frowns. "I don't think I said he was my brother."

That oversight deserves a swift kick. "Of course he is, you look identical," I bluff, since they really don't.

Pay attention, Pippa.

"I've always thought I look more like my sister," he muses. "Or she looks like me, because she's the baby."

"A sister and a brother—any others?" Stick with the simple questions, just like any date.

This is a date. Nothing more.

And as Declan and I get to know each other, talking and teasing and smiling so much my cheeks ache, I forget all about Eugene and IIP and any thoughts of missions. I forget about Lysander and Revello's list, and finding out more about NIIA.

All I want to do is find out more about Declan.

It's a heady sensation—being able to forget about my past and put my present aside—to pretend I'm just a normal girl, sitting across from a regular boy, hoping he likes me. But I'm still nervous, sitting on the edge of my seat, like I'm a keener in school ready to raise my hand at the drop of a hat.

As we talk—and there's no shortage of subjects—I play with my cutlery, my wineglass, the edge of the table and finally, my hair until the alcohol hits my system. It's like a flashing red light—calm down!

Declan tells me about his three brothers and Charlotte, although he never mentions their names. I find out he lost both his parents, and is very close to his grandmother. I tell him the brief, albeit fabricated version of my life—only child, parents still happily married. We moved around a lot, and Bob and Margo are currently residing in County Cork, accepting that their daughter is a bit of a free spirit.

I'm very convincing in my story because I would really like it to be the truth.

One glass of wine leads to another. Declan orders us a plate of sweet potato fries to share and I eat most of them since I haven't eaten anything since that morning. Declan orders a second plate.

"I like a girl who isn't afraid to eat," he says as I liberally dunk the fry into the aioli.

"That's me. So what d'you do, Declan, when you're not meeting strange ladies at cafes?"

"This is a bar," he points out.

"But we met at a cafe." I give the image of me speeding past Declan on my bike the other night a firm face palm to move it aside.

"I wouldn't call you a strange lady."

"But I was a stranger. And I am a lady. Sort of." I give him a wink.

"Not the lady-like type?"

"Nope."

Declan leans forward. "Good," he whispers, and my stomach does another one of those backflips I used to be so good at.

"So what d'you do?" I persist. "Or you just some rumbly bloke?"

"What is a rumbly bloke?" he asks with a laugh.

"A dodgy sort. I don't think that's you. Are you some man of mystery?"

Declan nods. "That's tempting. I could be a man of mystery."

"Not tempting to me. I like the open book bloke—no secrets."

A twinge of something I can't read flashes across his face and I smile to myself. Considering the line of work I'm in, I really don't mind secrets, as long as the person keeping them feels guilty about it.

"I'm kind of like you, in between jobs," Declan admits, toying with his half-empty glass. "I drive. I used to work the NASCAR circuit."

"A race car driver?" I don't have to fake my excitement about that. I'm an adrenaline junkie, have always had a thing for extreme sports. Speed is one of my favourite vices.

"For a time. I worked the pits. Now..." he shrugs. "I do some driving with a service, work as a mechanic now and then. A little bit of this, little bit of that."

"Never gets boring."

"Never does."

Another glass of wine, and then I switch to water. I'm hesitant to order it, not wanting Declan to think I'm ready to call it a night.

I'm not. I may be knackered, but there's no place I'd rather be, not even my lumpy hotel bed. Even with the aching feet.

I like him. I like him a lot.

We talk and talk, and somehow, I'm telling him that I've never met a man I've felt so comfortable with so quickly.

"I feel the same way." Declan pours the remaining water from the pitcher into my glass. "Normally, the girls I meet..." he smiles ruefully and taps his head. "Nice girls, but not enough up here to keep me interested for almost six hours."

"*Six hours!*" I grab for Declan's wrist, pulling it toward me. "It's almost two o'clock in the morning! How's that?"

Declan shrugs. "Is it bad that I don't want it to end?"

I sink back into my seat and smile shyly. "Neither do I. It's been a craic."

"Is that a good thing?"

"Aye, tis," I say, stressing the accent.

I really don't want the night to end. It's been so perfect that saying good night to Declan would break the spell. And I don't want to go back to his place, as enjoyable as that might be. For once, I don't want to go home with a guy I really like.

I never like the guys I go home with as much as I like Declan.

To move forward would mean this blanket of intimacy and comfort will change. It might change into something better, but right now, I don't want to take that chance.

"Do you want to go for a walk or something?" Declan asks. "It's a nice night and I think they're getting ready to close up."

"I'd love that. But first," I point to the back of the bar. "All that water..." I trail off with a lopsided smile. He must think my bladder is the size of a peanut. I've already excused myself three times.

"I'll be right here when you get back."

"Okay," I whisper. As I head away from the table, I can feel the weight of his gaze watching me. For once I don't work it. There's no swinging of the hips, no cocky stride.

There's just me, hurrying to the washroom so I can get back to him.

As I wash my hands, I stare at my reflection. No makeup would be able to mask the purple shadows under my eyes, but nothing can dim the sparkle. I don't think I've ever looked this happy.

I've certainly never felt it.

I scrunch up my face with excitement. "Eek!" I whisper scream. "This is *so* good."

Then, of course, my phone decides to ruin my elation.

Or rather, Lysander does.

Nine

I T'S JUST A TEXT, and it's the middle of the night, so I'm justified in not answering it. Even if I did, I wouldn't have any clue how to respond.

> *Will be in Toronto within 48 hrs. Call when you wake up*

"Dammit," I mutter, pressing the screen against my forehead as if I could will away Lysander's message.

I'll tell him it's part of the mission. That's all it is. I'm just trying to get intel on NIIA.

There's that twinge of guilt in the pit of my stomach. I much prefer the elation.

Wiping any concern off of my face, I take a deep breath and head back to Declan.

He stands up as soon as he sees me. This time, I can't miss the way he watches me walk back to the table. "You're so graceful," he says. "Were you a dancer?"

"Gymnastics," I admit, before I stop myself. While many say that a good lie is based on the truth, I prefer my stories completely made up. Pippa with the happily married parents wasn't a gymnast. She played soccer and Bob was the coach.

Declan nods. "I paid the bill. I think they're excited we're leaving." A quick glance tells me that other than a man seated at the bar, we're the only customers left. "I think he's the cook," Declan whispers, seeing my attention on him.

"I don't remember the last time I closed a place down," I confess as we leave.

"You mean this isn't your first time?"

"First time with you." I give the image of Lysander a mighty shove out of the way as I smile up at Declan.

"I admit, I have no idea what to do this late," Declan confesses. The chill night air hits me like a slap in the face. "We could go to my place, but..."

"Let's walk," I suggest. "I've never done that. It's like I'm breaking some rule."

"Do you like breaking rules?"

"Don't you?"

Declan gives me a sideways glance but doesn't answer. "There's no rule about walking late that I know of, unless you're falling-down drunk."

"I'm no half-langered, so there's no chance of me acting the muppet."

"I have no idea what that means," Declan confesses.

"I'm just takin' the piss out of you," I say with a laugh. "I don't usually sound that Irish. Besides, you're the one with the accent."

"That's what they all say." Suddenly he takes my hand. "Is this okay?"

I nod, any joking passed aside as he rubs his thumb along mine.

I don't remember the last time someone held my hand. But then it hits me—Henry used to hold my hand any chance he got. He used to—

I am not going to think about Henry right now.

Toronto is a bustling city, with non-stop noise and activity. It's not on the same level as New York, or even Tokyo, but it's pretty busy. Seeing it without people milling about, without the line of cars flashing by, is a brand-new experience.

Declan drops a coin in the basket in front of the sleeping home-less man as we walk by. A group of men laugh uproariously on the other side of the street.

"They're acting the muppet because they're langered," I point out to Declan. "Drunker than skunks, from the sounds of it."

"Thanks for the translation."

Two or three cars drive by, but that's the end of it. The street is blissfully quiet.

"I think it'd be busier if we were downtown," Declan says, sounding apologetic. "There are more bars and clubs and—"

"I like this."

We walk for at least an hour, still talking, only stopping when Declan decides I'm cold.

I lost feeling in my toes a while ago, but I didn't want to mention it.

He takes me to a Pho place that's open all night. The steaming bowl of noodles and broth warms me enough to continue walk-ing.

We end up at what Declan tells me is Queens' Quay, the very bottom of the city, seated on a bench overlooking the water.

"It's beautiful," I say, like Declan arranged the boats in the harbour just for me.

"I think the sun's going to be up soon." With a smooth movement, he tucks his arm around me. I lean into his warmth.

"I don't want it to end," I whisper.

"What are you doing tomorrow? Today, I mean."

"I'm working for Tenley," I say with a laugh. "Pretty soon, actually. She asked if I could be there for seven."

"That's late for Tenley. Usually she's there at the crack of dawn. Are you going to be okay? I feel bad that I kept you up all night."

"It's not all night yet. And I'll be fine. I'll head back to my place to shower and change before I go in."

"Now?"

"No?" I tilt my face up. Declan's gaze takes in all of me.

Is he going in for the snog?

But he doesn't. He stares, like he's memorizing my features, and hugs me closer. "I have to give you breakfast."

"You just gave me dinner not too long ago."

"Still." He stands up and extends his hand. "You need breakfast. It's the least I can do after making you stay up all night."

"You didn't make me." As much as I like walking with him, my feet rebel, and my pace noticeably slows. I may be in good shape, but I'm not used to non-stop walking. But as hard as he tries, Declan is unable to find any restaurant that is open twenty-four hours.

"Here," he says finally, stopping in front of a grocery store. "This is open."

"And they do have food." As much as I want to, I can't deny the rebellious grumblings of my stomach.

Shopping at five thirty in the morning is another new experience. And it's fun.

Declan collects a cart and, without warning, sweeps me off my feet and deposits me into the bottom level with my legs dangling over the edge.

"I don't really fit in here," I protest, laughing.

"I've walked your feet off and you'll have to stand on them for hours. You need to rest."

He does have a point.

There are more employees in the store at this time than customers, and we say hello to every one of them. Only one looks vaguely disapproving at me riding in the cart, but when we get to the bakery department at the back of the store, two of the cashiers join us with their own cart and we have an impromptu race among the hamburger buns.

We win, of course.

"You didn't bring your car tonight, did you?" I ask as we turn into the cereal aisle.

"That would be pretty funny, wouldn't it? No, I walked over to the bar. I live pretty close to it."

How do I tell him where I'm staying? Luckily, the hotel isn't that close to Tenley's cafe, so I should be able to get there without Declan seeing the dingy dump that I'm calling home.

Lysander is coming in two days. The thought returns relentlessly to my mind, no matter how much I want to forget it.

"What cereal do you like?" Declan asks. He stands in front of the cart, staring at the colourful boxes.

I tear my thoughts away from my dilemma with difficulty.

Maybe it's not a dilemma. Maybe this is a one-night thing. Maybe Declan will be different in the light of day.

"The sugary kind," I reply.

"Of course you do." There's that smile again. I'm never going to be tired of it.

How can I be having all these feels? Like, how amazing it would be to go shopping with Declan on a weekly basis, what it would be like to spend the night with him curled up on a couch watching movies, cooking his favourite meal.

I can't even cook.

I don't know what his favourite movie is.

Does he have enough income for weekly shopping for two?

"What's your favourite movie?" I ask.

Declan gives me a look like I should know the answer to that. I'm amazed that I can already read his expressions so easily. "The *Empire Strikes Back*."

"Of course. Such a guy answer."

"What about you? *The Notebook*?" he teases.

"Do I look like a *Notebook* type of girl?"

"You look like my kind of girl."

Then as I sit in the shopping cart, the edges digging into the backs of my legs, Declan leans down and kisses me. His lips are as soft as they seem.

I'm done.

Ten

D ESPITE BEING COMPLETELY KNACKERED, I somehow float through the day with a silly smile on my face.

Brianna has returned to work after her bout with stomach flu, looking pale but determined. "It came on so quick," she keeps repeating with an incredulous shake of her head.

I feel a twinge of guilt. In my arsenal, is a little wonder drug that brings on flu-like symptoms; only a bit is needed but I might have smeared a little too much on the five-dollar bill I gave Brianna when I paid for my tea yesterday.

As tired as I am, I work extra hard to make it up to her, insisting that Brianna take frequent breaks and making her a cup of tea.

I like the cafe, and I find myself liking Tenley more and more as the day goes on.

She's smart as a whip and her serious demeanour hides a wicked sense of humour. I'm not sure what her role with the NIIA is, but being the owner of *Soup du Jour* is the perfect cover. She comes across as a hard-working, dedicated single mom who loves her daughter more than anything. If this was a different life, maybe we could be friends.

If I didn't know better, I wouldn't believe that Tenley had anything to do with a secret spy agency.

There's been no recognition from her, so I relax a bit. Tenley has no idea that it was me she had quite the tussle with the other night, or that we were minutes away from having another one last night at the hotel. I've no doubt she would have been as pissed as a wet hen had she caught me there.

The sparkly diamonds are tucked away in a secret pocket in my knapsack. I'll wait until I'm back in Belfast to cash them in. I have someone in the old neighbourhood who helps me out with things like that.

"What did you and Declan do last night?" Tenley asks halfway through the morning as she arranges muffins in the glass case. She's an awesome baker. I've already sampled two muffins and an oatmeal cookie. Working here is not going to be good for my figure.

I finish with the latte I'm making and hand it to the waiting customer with a smile. For the first time that morning, no one is waiting in line.

For the first time in my life, I wish I had someone to confide in.

Tenley would be the perfect person to talk about last night with.

I don't have a lot of friends, and even if I did, I wouldn't have a lot of good gossip to share with them. Things like how a new guy makes you feel, sharing the excitement of an intense infatuation, details about the first snog.

Despite the overwhelming urge to confide in her, I stop myself. "Not much," I say casually. "Had a few drinks, went for a walk."

I don't tell her about the hours in the bar, the walk through the city, the snog in the shopping cart, the second one when he puts me in the cab that takes me back to the hotel, the third one when he crawled in after me.

The cab driver had sat and waited with the meter ticking as Declan kissed me on and on.

I don't tell her any of it, as much as I want to.

"He's a good guy. Granted, I don't know him very well, but I don't think he makes too much effort for a girl. I don't think he's met the right one yet," she finishes diplomatically.

"He's a player, isn't he?" I groan.

"*Yes*," Brianna says, displaying more than a touch of the green-eyed monster in her tone. "That's the last you'll see of him."

I don't feel guilty for making her sick any longer.

"Like I said, I don't know him very well." Tenley frowns at Brianna.

"How long have you been with Seamus?" I ask.

"Not long at all," Tenley admits.

"How did you meet him?"

The bell jangles and saves Tenley from answering. She greets the customer with a smile, chatting about the weather and effectively side steps my question. I plan on asking again, but after the man in the business suit leaves with his triple chocolate mocha with extra whipped, she pulls the conversation back to Declan.

"Are you going out with him tonight?"

"Not sure," I say, wishing I had made some sort of plans with him. We left it that he would text me later today. I still haven't heard from him, and I'm tired of checking my phone.

When my shift is over at one thirty, I head back to the hotel with a bag of day-old scones. BLTs were the sandwich of the day and I really need to shower off the faint smell of bacon. I should check in with Eugene or Lysander or both, but the lumpy bed calls to me like the honey-toned voices of the sirens that beckon sailors and I can't resist.

I wake up with a start seven hours later. My shoes are still on and my head is back in Ireland, wandering the green hills with Henry.

It's a dream I often have, usually when I'm happy; the two of us, walking hand in hand on the Howth Cliff Path, outside Dublin, feeling the wind in my hair and the salt on my tongue.

Henry kissing me as the wind threatens to push us over into the gorse.

This time, even though I can still feel the way my hand fits into Henry's, his face has somehow morphed into Declan's, so I'm not sure who I was dreaming about.

Henry died seven years ago and I still haven't found a man to replace him. Nor do I want to. But what is my dream trying to tell me?

I yawn and roll over to grab my phone from the nightstand. It's telling me it's just a dream.

My eyes feel like I've rubbed sand in them as I scan the texts I've missed.

Most are from Eugene and Lysander, with instructions and questions and wanting confirmation about last night. I had time to photocopy the papers I took from the hotel and Fed Ex the originals to Eugene before I met Declan last night, but I must have forgotten to tell him they were on the way.

The questions get more pointed. Lysander used shouty letters in his last two texts, so I know he's royally annoyed.

"Jeeze, can't I take a nap without having to check in?" I grumble. They should have the papers by now, so I hold off on responding.

There are four messages from Declan.

Despite the urgent need for a bathroom, I take a moment to read them, the smile on my face helping to wake me up.

> *I had a really great time last night. How do I say that in Irish?*

"Bhí am iontach," I murmur in Gaelic, rolling over onto my back.

> *Sorry I kept you out so late. Hope it wasn't too painful being in the café. At least there was coffee!*

He doesn't know I don't like coffee. That feels like something I should have told him. How did I not tell him that?

> *I was a complete zombie today and as much as I'd like to see you, I need to be responsible and considerate and let you catch up on your sleep. Being responsible and considerate sucks!*

"Got that right," I mutter. I can't stop smiling after I read the fourth message.

> *I know I said no for seeing you tonight, but can I renege? How is it possible that I miss you already? I don't miss anyone? Who are you?*

> *Your dream come true.*

He responds immediately.

> *I think you might be. Tomorrow night?*

> *It's a date. But I might impose a curfew.*

> *That might be a good idea.*

Before I respond, my phone signals an incoming FaceTime call. It has to be Lysander. I sigh as I smooth away the giddiness and the bedhead.

There's really no way to prepare myself as Lysander's face fills the screen. He's so very good-looking, like Jude Law, David Beckham and Tom Hardy rolled into one—but in a good way, not one of those creepy, *what would your baby look like* morphs.

There's nothing creepy about the way Lysander looks. He's just a devastatingly handsome Irish man. For once, I don't appreciate it.

"Pippa, love."

Lysander means it as a term of affection, but it always comes across as a sort of command.

"Hey, Lysander. How's Paris?" I ask, my voice still groggy from sleep.

"Beautiful this time of the year, or at least that's what they tell me. I haven't had much time to see the sights."

"Aw, no? That's too bad."

"Not really. Where've you been?"

I turn the phone so Lysander can see the bed, with the tangle of sheets I've just crawled out of. He will also be able to see there's only one head imprint on the pillow.

"Asleep. I got a job. Working's overrated, don't you think?"

Lysander wastes no time shifting into work mode. "What's going on? You've been MIA for almost twenty-four hours. That's not like you."

I cover my yawn with a hand. "I'm helping out at a cafe. The owner sidelines as an agent with NIIA, so I've got my in."

"How is that supposed to help you get that list?"

"Because NIIA has it? Remember?"

Suddenly an idea pops into my head, one that's both brilliant and not so great.

"Look, Pippa, Da says you've got things under control, but I'm going to pop over to check, see if you need help."

"I don't. Need help." I also don't need a babysitter, but I don't say that to Lysander. I've worked hard to get where I am in Eugene's organization, and I don't want one little slip up to get in the way. "It would be lovely if you want to come for a visit, but everything's under control. I have a plan and it will be brilliant."

"No distractions?"

"When have I ever let myself be distracted?"

"Let's hear your plan, then."

I tell him about meeting Tenley, working at the cafe. About meeting Seamus, and after a moment's hesitation, about meeting Declan.

I keep my voice flat and businesslike. For this to work, I really can't have any distractions.

A text pops up on my screen.

Curfews are overrated.

"Do they trust you?" Lysander asks, bringing me back to the problem at hand.

"I think so. Yes," I say, the admission sinking like a stone in the pit of my stomach. Declan trusts me. So does Tenley.

But so does Eugene, and he's been my family for a long time. "I know how to infiltrate the head office of NIIA."

"It can't be done," Lysander flatly retorts. "Get a better plan."

"I'm going to get invited inside. The info is in there, so all I need is to get in and I'll be able to find it."

Lysander looks skeptical, but has enough respect for my thieving abilities not to say anything. "Da expects that information," he says, his voice sounding loud in his intensity.

"I know."

"I don't think you do, Pippa. He already has a buyer lined up, one who won't be happy if you don't finish the deal."

"I can finish! Who's the buyer?" I ask like it's an afterthought.

"You wouldn't know her."

Her? "Try me."

"Jacqueline Robineau. We don't know much about her. She's good at hiding off the grid."

"You can't hide from me. I'll have a poke around, see what I can find out."

Again, Lysander knows my hacking skills and doesn't respond, but the tightness around his lips suggests he's not pleased with me. I make a mental note to go to him with any intel first before Eugene.

Lysander's a bit of a baby that way—he always needs to be first with things.

"Robineau's organization is up and coming. We have evidence that she was behind the Tokyo Plan."

I whistle under my breath. The Tokyo Plan took place eight months ago but is already legendary in the scope of the complexity. A group broke into the Yoyogi Building in Tokyo and got away with info on the shareholders, as well as the subscribers of NTT Docomo, Japan's biggest telecommunications company. Authorities still don't have any idea how they got in and out of the building. There was literally no evidence left, no fingerprints, no trail, no exit route. It was like they got in and then just disappeared. Whoever this Robineau is, she's good.

But so am I.

"So she's the new big gun. Fair enough. I'll deliver the goods, Ly; you can tell your Da that."

"When?"

"Seventy-two hours," I say without thinking, and then proceed to kick myself.

"Are you sure?"

I hate hearing the doubt in Lysander's voice and it fuels my spirit of competition. "Of course I'm sure. Eugene wants that list and I'll get it for him."

"He has a lot of faith in you."

"And I won't let him down."

For the rest of the night, I compile as much information on the mysterious Mme. Robineau and the Tokyo Plan, while frantically trying to come up with a way to get inside NIIA head office.

I have to admit I get a bit distracted from both of my tasks by the flurry of texts flying back and forth between Declan and me, but by the end of the night, I have a plan.

Now to carry it out.

Eleven

- -

TWO NIGHTS LATER, I stand in the chilly air with my coat pulled tight around me, waiting for Declan to pick me up.

This is our third date and the first time I've let him pick me up.

I've told him I live in an apartment building half a block from the hotel. I now have a pass card for the front door, thanks to a little stalking and a quick bit of pick pocketing on the subway. There's no concierge in the lobby, which makes it easy as well. There is an apartment building right beside the hotel, but it had Ronald, in his natty waistcoat and nametag on duty when I scoped it out, so I went for the lower-rent one.

I shiver from excitement, rather than the cool breeze, and can't keep the smile of anticipation off my face.

I like Declan. I like him a lot. I've known him for exactly seventy-six hours and I like him a lot more than I should.

I've even fantasized that my arrangement with Lysander fades away, and Declan and I have a future together.

I have to stop myself before the fantasies go too far.

Other than the fantasies—which aren't exactly PG—I haven't given much serious thought to where this is going. To a bystander, dating might seem innocent—he likes me, I like him—but there are a dangerous amount of secrets under the surface between both of us.

I've only ever told Henry the truth, and that was a mistake.

A blue sports car purrs to a stop beside me. "Heya, sexy!" Declan opens the door from the inside before my hand is even on the handle. His fancy car is almost as pretty as he is, with the colour matching his blue eyes. "Going my way?"

"Hey, pretty boy." As I slide into the oh-so-comfortable leather seat, I keep sliding over until I catch his lips with a kiss. And then another, until the sound of an angry horn pulls us apart.

The car must have some pick up because it flies down the street like someone kicking it in the can.

This must be the Audi R8. He also has a Lexus and a BMW.

I've been doing my research, asking the right questions. The NIIA must pay a lot more than Eugene if Declan can afford a stable of sexy cars like this.

"How was your day?" he asks.

Declan asks me that every day. Not the unimaginative litany of questions about what I did, how I did it and what I did wrong, but a simple question that shows he's interested in the answer. He's interested in *me*; just me, not what I've got or what I can do for him.

No one in my past has been interested in just me. Starting with my mother, everyone close to me had always seen me as a means to something. What could I help them with? What could I do for them? How could they use me?

Henry liked me for me, but he was the only one.

I hide my happy sigh as I buckle my seatbelt.

"You smell incredible," he adds with a grin, his hand already warming my knee.

Declan told me last night that he can't seem to stop himself from touching me. I told him as long as his hands were warm, I didn't mind.

"You're lucky I had time to shower because while the broccoli, beer, and cheddar soup Tenley made *tasted* incredible, it didn't smell quite that good. Did you know that cooked broccoli smells a lot like a dead rat?"

"How would you know what dead rat smells like?" Declan shifts into third, and my knee misses the warmth of his hand.

The car is so small that when I lean closer, my shoulder is almost touching his. "You don't want to know. But I sucked it up and washed the whole ginormous pot because the soup tasted so good, it sold out in less than an hour."

"Tenley's a good cook. She has you washing dishes now?"

"No, I did it to help Leo in the kitchen. I might be crushing on him a wee bit."

"Is this something I should be worrying about? Because I've met Leo and he's a lot bigger than I am."

His hand returns to my knee and I pick it up, kissing his fingers. "You, pretty boy, have exactly *nothing* to worry about."

He's not the only one who isn't able to stop touching.

"I made lots of tips today, so I'll be able to splurge on the jumbo popcorn tonight," I add, wincing as Declan turns up the volume on his impressive sound system. "What exactly are you listening to? It sounds like... is this the *Backstreet Boys*?"

"'NSync, actually."

"Is that the one with Justin Timberlake?"

"Don't you like it? I thought ladies of a certain age loved this stuff."

"A certain age? What's that shite? Maybe I liked it when I was twelve." I glance at Declan, who has a sheepish expression on his handsome face. "Hang on—you're not playing this for *me*—you like those bands full of prepubescent boys with pretty hair, don't you? Oh, my good gosh darn!"

"Please don't hate me," Declan pleads with that grin that has me forgetting anything he's done wrong, as well as anything he has yet to do.

"How can I not? You're a grown man still listening to 90s boy music!"

"It has a certain appeal," he argues. "A good beat. It's happy music."

"*Happy* music?" I echo.

"I play it when I'm happy."

Most of my insides melt as quickly as a pat of butter on Tenley's warm cheddar scones. "I guess you can listen to it, then."

I don't have to see my reflection in the mirror to know that I'm grinning like an idiot. Which only widens as Declan picks up my hand and kisses my fingers.

"How was *your* day?" I ask, savouring the touch as he runs his tongue over my pinkie.

Oh, I've got it bad. So very bad.

"I spent some time in the shop, did some tinkering."

What does that mean? Has he been at NIIA head office? Is that where he spends his days?

This is the problem; my loyalty to Eugene is waging a war with my feelings for Declan. When I'm away from Declan, I'm all Eugene's, ready to do what needs to be done for the company.

But when I'm with Declan, everything else flies out the window, leaving me in a confused muddle.

"I talked to Lottie today," Declan says, his tone fighting for casual, but failing miserably.

"Lottie—that's your sister Charlotte, isn't it?" I've gotten him to open up about his family, so it doesn't seem strange that I know so much about the Dodd brothers and their super-spy sister.

She can't be that good of a spy if I bested her at the hotel.

"She wants to join us tonight."

That catches me flat-footed. "Oh?" My voice is weak, and nerves are making a mess of my stomach, worse than any mission I've been on.

Declan's sister is coming with us tonight.

Charlotte Dodd, from the NIIA, wants to meet me.

This is big. This is huge. This might just work out better than what I've planned.

"Is that okay? She wants to meet you. Tenley must have been talking about you... I guess I have too."

"Does she normally want to meet your girl—" I stop myself before I say the word. I have no idea if Declan thinks of me as his girlfriend, or if I want him to.

"My girlfriends?" Declan finishes as casually as if I asked what he had for breakfast. "Not usually. Well, I guess everyone met Hannah Bromley because I went out with her all through high school, but after that, not really. No one really hangs around long enough for a family meet n' greet."

"A family meet... that's two out of the four of them going tonight..." I'm meeting Charlotte Dodd tonight. This is even better than I expected when I suggested the double date. The Declan fog of happiness lifts, making my plans crystal clear. "Is there anyone else coming? Any other brothers?"

"Well, Ham's coming with Lottie. At least, I think he is. Hamilton Short, her boyfriend. They'll eventually get around to getting married, so he's pretty much family, too."

Hamilton Short, head of NIIA, the organization I'm attempting to infiltrate, is coming on my double date. My triple date.

Fecking hell.

By the time Declan pulls into a space in the underground parking at the mall, I've steeled myself for the meeting.

I'm Pippa McGovern, new to Toronto, employee of the month at Tenley's cafe, nothing more. I should be nervous meeting my boyfriend's all-important sister, but nothing more.

Declan called me his girlfriend!

He takes my hand as we head to the elevator. "Your hand is freezing."

"I'm a bit chilly."

"You're not nervous about meeting Lottie and Ham, are you?"

"And Seamus. Don't forget about him."

"Are you really nervous?" Declan stops, pulls me closer. "I never thought you would be. I don't want you to be upset."

"I'm not. It's just..." Pippa, the new girlfriend. Nothing more. "I know how important your family is to you."

"They are, but so are you."

There's the melted butter again, oozing all over the place.

"Pippa, I know we've only just met, but I've never met anyone like you. I can't stop thinking about you."

"Me neither," I whisper.

He tucks a stray curl behind my ear. "I know it's too soon, but I'm completely crazy about you." He leans down and kisses me, so I don't have to find the reply.

I'm not sure what I'm supposed to say.

"Ahem, ahem." I'm still in the haze of Declan's kiss when I hear a voice, as if from a distance. "I thought you were supposed to do the kissing at the end of the night. At least that's what Tenley tells me."

I pull away to see Seamus and Tenley walk towards us.

"I thought that blue flash was you," Tenley says with a teasing smile.

"She thinks I drive too fast," Declan explains. His arms are still around me, one of his hands dangerously close to my ass.

Is it bad that I want Tenley and Seamus to go away so Declan can keep snogging me? But as I reluctantly step out of Declan's arms, I decide it's better that I meet Charlotte with some backup.

Twelve

THE SHORT ELEVATOR RIDE up to the main floor of the mall takes all of thirty seconds, but Seamus uses twenty-nine of them to pepper me with questions.

"Do you like working at Soup? Where are you from? How long have you been in Toronto? Are you planning on staying for a while? Where are your parents from?"

"Seamus, enough," Declan protests after the parent's question.

Even though my story is rock solid, I don't have to make up the nervous tremor in my voice.

What is this? I've been interrogated by Mossad agents, brought in for questioning by M1-6 on more than one occasion. I've even talked to the CIA, and no one has thrown me as much as Seamus does.

He'd make a darn good interrogator.

I know he doesn't trust me and I can't say I blame him. But I'm good and I know there's no reason he should see through me.

If Seamus doesn't like me, I'm not sure what I can do about it. But why wouldn't he like me? I'm very likable.

The elevator door slides open. "Where's Lottie meeting us?" Seamus asks.

"At the concession stand." Declan stands aside to let the elevator clear and gives me a wink as he squeezes my hand. "Sorry about that," he whispers.

"He doesn't like me."

"No, that's the problem—he does." Declan slows down, allowing Seamus and Tenley to walk ahead of us to the theatres. "Seamus doesn't trust easily, so he thinks there's something wrong with you."

"Oh."

"There's nothing wrong with you," he continues, bringing our clasped hands to his mouth for a kiss. I smile foolishly at the gesture until his expression turns suddenly serious. "Is there?"

I stiffen for a second until I realize he's teasing. "There's a lot wrong with me, but I don't think it's anything for you to worry about. Or your brother."

"That's what I'll tell him," Declan promises, hurrying to catch up.

"Don't tell him that! He'll know we were talking about him!"

"But we are talking about him. We're talking about you, Seamus," he calls, but luckily, they are too far ahead to hear.

I smile all the way up the escalator, enjoying the way Declan stands behind me and slides his hands under my jacket.

My smile fades. I like him too much for this to work.

And then I catch sight of the tiny blond standing in line at the concession stand.

Charlotte Dodd.

Taking a deep breath, I paste the smile back on and allow Declan to lead me over.

The first thing I notice is that Hamilton Short is incredibly good looking. He looks like he just stepped out of some swanky men's store in a pair of tailored pants and a V-neck sweater.

I'll bet my last quid that the sweater is cashmere.

The second thing I notice is that no one hugs.

This is an evening out between siblings and their significant others. And this is a close family. But Charlotte and Tenley don't hug, nor does Declan or Seamus give Ham the half-assed man hug that always makes me laugh when I see Lysander do it.

It's like they've only seen each other a short while ago. Like they work together and see each other too often for a more affectionate greeting.

"So you're Pippa." There is absolutely nothing friendly about Charlotte's tone. And it's not just me, because I catch the surprised expression on Tenley's face.

I turn and meet Charlotte's wary blue eyes. There's no gasp of surprise, not even a flicker of recognition. I knew there wouldn't be, but until you come face-to-face, you can never be sure.

She's really little. I knew she was from our tussle the other night, but seeing her standing before me, I really don't know what all the fuss is about. I could toss her into the popcorn machine with one hand. "Pippa McGovern-Stock. Lovely to meet you."

Charlotte doesn't break her gaze until Ham steps forward to offer me his hand. "Hamilton Short. I'm Charlotte's partner."

Charlotte rolls her eyes, but her expression softens immediately at Ham's voice. "That always makes me sound like your business partner," she scoffs.

"Boyfriend, then," Ham corrects, with a gentle look at Charlotte, who grins as foolishly as I did earlier.

There you go. There's the super-spy's vulnerability—Ham Short. I file that little piece of information away for a later use.

Charlotte turns back to me with a quizzical expression. "You look familiar."

I should hope so since I kicked her ass at Revello's only a few days ago. But it's my confidence in my disguise that keeps the smile on my face. Not exactly a disguise, but without the hair, makeup and boobs in someone's face, I do look completely different. "I don't know why. I think I'd remember you," I tell her.

"She may be small, but she's mighty," Seamus says.

"I meant the hair—it's so blond, so much lighter than the rest of you." I tuck my hand around Declan's neck, toying with his hair.

It may have been a touch possessive, but I think I deserve to show them who's boss here.

"I was the one who got blessed with the hair," Charlotte says with a dramatic swing of her head so her ponytail whips around, hitting Seamus in the shoulder. "Among other things."

Seamus grabs her ponytail and gives it a yank. "I can still take you any day."

"In your dreams."

"They're such an affectionate bunch," Tenley says to me as Charlotte and Seamus begin to roughhouse, causing a few in the lineup to move out of the way.

"I can see that." I also see that neither of them seem to be pulling their punches, but neither of them flinch when the blows land. Ham eventually puts a stop to it as we reach the head of the line.

While we wait in line, Seamus and Charlotte continue teasing each other, bringing Declan in as well, as Tenley and Ham talk quietly. I observe, hoping to learn more about them like any girlfriend would do.

The only other information I discover is that Charlotte has a huge sweet tooth and Ham doesn't drink caffeine. As we finally take our popcorn and drinks and head to the theatre, I feel Charlotte's gaze on me more than once.

I sit between Tenley and Declan, feeling the safest there. Charlotte may not have recognized me, but there's no sense pushing my luck.

Declan holds my hand.

The movie is about a Russian spy, which is somewhat ironic since the six of us could give a more accurate depiction of the life of a secret agent than any movie could. But it's a good flick and holds my interest until my phone vibrates in my pocket.

I excuse myself and head to the washroom. I don't want to explain myself to Declan if he decides to follow me out of the theatre.

As expected, it's a text from Eugene.

He's left three voicemails and tried to FaceTime me. Luckily, I turned the ringer off and the only thing that vibrates was text.

Deadline is 1900 hours.

Quickly calculating, I come up with mid-afternoon tomorrow.

I'm on it

As soon as I hit send, Charlotte enters the washroom.

I should have known one of them would keep me in sight. "Facebook," I say waving my phone. "Can't get enough of it."

"Oh, really? I couldn't find your profile."

Of course, she checked me out on social media. "I'm there," I assure her, which is, of course, a lie.

Charlotte nods and pushes open one of the stalls.

What am I supposed to do now? Wait for her? That would be the polite, double/triple date thing to do, but Charlotte's obvious scrutiny is making me nervous, as much as I hate to admit it.

I wash my hands twice. I'm still at it when Charlotte comes out and catches me staring at myself in the mirror.

"You really do look familiar."

Shaking the excess water off my hands, I head to the automatic dryers. "I must have one of those faces."

"With that hair, no one could forget about you."

Was that grudging admiration in her voice? Was that—dare I say it—the beginning of a compliment?

I scrunch a handful of red curls. "I'm the only one in my family with this hair, too. I must have had a bunch of redheaded ancestors."

Which is true, since half of Ireland has red hair.

"It's cool," Charlotte says.

"Thanks. So's yours. Everyone with curly hair wants straight..." I smile, nailing the perfect-girlfriend-meeting-the-sister voice.

"Right." She finishes drying her hands and we turn to the door in unison. "You like the movie?"

"It's good. There's so much I don't know about the life of spies," I tell her.

"Me too," she agrees.

We're almost at the door of the theatre before she speaks again. "You and Declan..." she trails off.

"He's great."

"He is. He's never set up something like this before."

"He—Declan set this up tonight?"

Charlotte nodded. "It's kind of a big deal for him. He's never—I guess he thinks you're pretty special."

"I think he is, too."

This is going well. This is going well. Take away who we work for, and maybe Charlotte and I can get along.

"Don't do anything to screw it up, then. And if you hurt my brother, I'll kill you." With a toothy grin, Charlotte pulls open the door and leads me into the darkened theatre.

That was more like what I expected.

Thirteen

A s WE FILE OUT of the theatre, I duck into the washroom again.

I had a big drink to go with my popcorn and I've been holding it for the last twenty minutes. Plus, a quick absence will give them a chance to talk about me.

It works like a charm. When I come out of the washroom, the five of them are standing in the lobby, forcing the slow-moving crowd to separate around them like mean girls stepping around the geeks, and allows me to walk up to them unseen, catching snippets of their conversation.

Only they're not talking about me.

"We have no leads," Charlotte says loudly. "Whoever it was, just vanished."

"I haven't heard any chatter." Seamus rubs his hand over his short-cropped hair like he's frustrated. "There's nothing out there."

"Someone has to know something," Tenley says.

Ham holds up a hand. "This isn't the place for this conversation."

Declan ignores Ham's unspoken order and continues. "I'll check with my sources and—" He looks up in time to see me lurking behind Tenley. "Pippa! Ready to go?"

"I didn't want to interrupt." I drop my eyes demurely and hide my smile.

I'd bet my last quid that they're talking about the hotel heist the other day when I snuck in right under Charlotte's nose.

Despite the hurried end of the conversation and the dark matter of the movie, everyone seems more relaxed as we file out of the theatre. At least Charlotte and Seamus are more smiley.

"Time for a drink?" Declan suggests as the escalator carries us down to the floor of the mall. The stores have closed, but there are still people milling about.

Tenley shakes her head at Declan's offer. "I can't, another early morning for me tomorrow."

"Me too," I say apologetically.

"Are you working full time at the cafe now?" Charlotte looks first at me and then Tenley.

"I'm between jobs and Tenley's been nice enough to give me a few shifts."

"She's a great help," Tenley says, a little more vehemently than necessary. So I'm not the only one who feels the hostility from Charlotte.

I watch Charlotte as she walks ahead of me. She really doesn't look like much, all tiny and cute, like a teenage girl before discovering the joy of makeup. Her white-blond hair pulled back into a ponytail makes her look even younger.

I bet her bouncy ponytail has got split ends.

She turns her head and I see the edge of the bruise on her jaw, right below her ear, barely visible under the makeup.

I gave Charlotte that bruise at Revello's party. It's gone from vivid red-purple to greenish-yellow.

I do my best to hide my smile of satisfaction.

Easy chitchat flows about what we liked about the movies and plans for the next day. Even though my mind is elsewhere, I make the right contributions.

Declan holds my hand. I can get used to this.

But I'm not going to be able to get used to lying to him. He's planning on driving me home in his pretty blue sports car and coming up to see "my" apartment.

How am I supposed to get out of that?

A headache, early morning, bag of popcorn not agreeing with me? All lies; big whopper lies because all I really want to do is take Declan somewhere private and have my way with him.

It doesn't even have to be that private.

I have to persuade him to take me to his place instead. It's clearly not ideal because I'm going to have to leave in the middle of the night and he's going to want to drive me home. I'll have to sneak out without him noticing...

"It was nice to meet you, Pippa," Ham says politely.

Reality rushes back; the elevator has stopped on our level in the parking garage. Ham and Charlotte will continue on to the lower level. Tenley is out the door and Seamus is holding the door for me. Declan gives me a questioning look.

"You too, Ham." I smile shyly at Charlotte. "See you again, Charlotte."

Declan has a huge grin on his face as the door slides shut behind me. "That went well."

I blow out my breath. "Yeah. She's nice. So's he."

"Ham's great," Tenley pipes in.

"I'm great too," Seamus reminds her with a grin.

"No one said you weren't," she says with a roll of her eyes at me.

"It was lovely to meet you too, Seamus," I tell him dutifully.

"That's more like it."

All of us are laughing as we walk to where the cars are parked. It surprises me how many cars are still there, scattered around the parking garage.

A white van has parked close by Declan's car.

"Maybe next week we can—" Seamus is saying when the back doors of the van burst open.

Six men and one very tall woman jump out of the back doors of the van and arrange themselves in the diamond formation facing us.

These are professionals—uniformed, armed, professional mercenaries.

My heart sinks.

"What the—?" Seamus mutters, pushing Tenley behind him.

Why are there so many?

A man wearing a hoodie under a jacket hops out of the driver's side with a friendly smile on his face. "Well, if it isn't Tenley Scott. How *are* you, sweetstuff? And Seamus. Nice to see the two of you ended up together."

"What the hell do you want, Benjy?"

Benjy Lionel raises his arms. "Just to talk, old friend, just to chat. I guess we're interrupting your date?"

It had been Benjy that I called after Lysander threatened a visit. "I need a favour."

"Yeah? I like having you owe me favours," he'd replied like the tosser he is.

Benjy Lionel, the former NIIA agent, and friend of Charlotte Dodd, has been working for Mielson, and therefore Eugene Mochrie, since his departure from NIIA. He brought enough information with him to ensure Eugene's goodwill, as well as bringing Minka Grace, the Amazon-like woman known for her size, strength and general badassery.

Since I've been in Toronto, Benjy has proven to be a good contact.

I met with him yesterday to explain what I need. "Make me look good," I instructed. "Let me win, but make me look good. And no Minka."

"Oh, come on!"

"Seriously, Benjy, no way."

"Are you scared of big bad Minka? Don't worry, she scares everyone—that's the fun of her."

"You should go a round with her and see how fun it is for you." I have a few, never to be forgotten, memories of Minka back when I was starting out with Eugene's organization and she was still with NIIA.

"So what's your endgame?" Benjy asked shrewdly.

Lysander once told me Benjy's nothing more than a laid-back boyo, out for a good time. That he's a fun tosser to have around. Lysander was wrong.

Benjy's a lot smarter than his cute face gives him credit for.

He brought Minka.

"Get out of here," Seamus blusters, stepping in front of Tenley. "You're not getting your hands on her again."

"Hey, chill, bro. I just want to check in with her. See how those memories are behaving themselves." Benjy takes a step around the crew towards Tenley.

They stand ready, waiting for orders.

What's the story with this? I wanted a small gang, easy to take out, not a little army.

I take my eyes off the men for a split second and turn to Tenley. "What is this?"

She looks scared, but more determined than I'd ever seen her. "They want me," she says in a quiet voice.

And then things click into place.

According to Colin, Tenley had been kidnapped and Charlotte's memories forcibly downloaded into her head. Was that Benjy? Was he behind it?

And now I've all but delivered Tenley to his hands.

It wasn't supposed to be like this!

"Actually, just your memories," Benjy says. "It's been a while, hasn't it? I hope you've had fun with them, but I don't think you need them. You don't, do you?"

This isn't right. This wasn't supposed to happen. This was for *me*, not for Benjy and some dodgy plan that's too high tech for me to understand.

How do you get memories out of a head?

Benjy folds his arms across his chest. "Okay, boys—and Minka. Grab her and let's boot."

But it's Declan who moves first, and it's Declan who goes down when the butt of a rifle slams into the side of his head.

"Declan!" The guns don't have live ammo, are just for stun, but still. "Don't bloody touch him!" I shout, stalking towards the goon that hit Declan.

Seven against four isn't a fair fight. Eight if you count Benjy, but he's not going to step into this if he doesn't have to. This isn't what I had planned. There's no way I'm going to come out of this looking good, especially if they get their hands on Tenley.

I have to stop them.

I take the first one down easily with a simple kick to the crotch. The second one is ready for me and blocks my punches. After I manage to kick the gun out of his hands, I catch his arm and flip him over my head.

He lands hard on his back with a thud. Grabbing his weapon, I stun him, sending his body into a proxy of spasms. That should keep him down.

Then I shoot the goon that has his hands on Tenley. Declan distracts me when gets to his feet with an incredulous expression on his face and I mis-aim, almost hitting Seamus with the electric current.

"Jesus Christ, Pippa!"

This time, I find my target and another goon falls with a shaky seizure. Another one has Tenley in a choke hold, who is still putting up a fight, but I can tell she won't last long.

I'm extra careful when I take him out.

Then it feels like a full-size lorry hits me as I'm tackled, like I'm playing in the Six Nations championship game. The gun slides under a nearby car. Crawling to my feet, I stay in a crouch and swing my leg around to catch the rugger bugger at his ankles, knocking him off his feet.

Straddling him, I grab him by his vest and haul his shoulders up. "Leave him alone," I hiss. Then I give him two sharp jabs and a mighty right hook and watch his eyes roll back in his head.

Jumping to my feet, I survey the rolling mass of flying fists. Who's next?

Tenley seems to be holding her own, with Seamus and Declan acting as defenders. Benjy is squawking like a duck as he shouts instructions. "Just put her in the goddamn van already!"

Tempting, but before I can target him, a couple of goons catch sight of me.

After a brief tussle, I knock the first one down without much difficulty. The second one has a head as hard as the Blarney Stone and might take a little more effort.

I hop onto the bumper of a parked SUV to get a little more height. Luckily, this one doesn't have an alarm and when I jump down, my fist aims for his leather-clad shoulder. His shoulder is as hard as his head, but there's enough weight behind the punch and it knocks him off balance. This allows me to get in a nasty crotch shot that takes him to his knees.

I'm a dirty fighter.

Sometimes you have to be.

His friend catches me across the cheek with a backhand and before I can retaliate, grabs my shoulders and throws me into another SUV, leaving a Pippa-sized dent in the side. The alarm squeals a protest as I drop to the ground, pulling myself under the car to avoid being kicked and booted.

As he reaches under the car for me, I get him first, catching his thick ankle with both hands to yank him off his feet. Then I roll out the other side, surprising the two goons that have the balls to try to take out Declan.

With a yank of his shoulders, the first one swivels to face me, and I drive my fist into his face, once, twice, only stopping when I hear the satisfying crack of nose cartilage.

"*Focking* wanker," I mutter. No one is allowed to touch my man.

His hands cover his face and I drill him in his stomach before shoving him to the ground.

Another goon wants his turn, towering over me with a determined expression on his ugly face. I dodge the fist, but can't avoid being thrown to the ground.

"Pippa!" Declan shouts. "Are you okay?"

"Just... great..." Tucking in my legs, I lash out, this time hitting the goon in the chest and sending him staggering back, right into the goon Seamus is trading blows with, which allows Seamus to take them both down.

Declan seems okay, but Tenley is two cars away, with two of them on her, and Minka heading that way. Scrambling to my feet,

I hop from car to car—sedans, not SUVs—feeling the roofs buckle under my weight.

The move used to work better when I was younger, and smaller.

I throw myself down on the goon that just got Tenley in another sleeper hold.

His shoulders feel like a solid rock as he dances around in a circle, trying to shake me off. I keep a tight hold until he slams me into the side of an Escalade, which sets off another alarm, adding to the chaos.

I slide to the ground, taking a moment to catch my breath.

"Hello, Pippa." Looking up, way up, I find Minka Grace towering over me.

I scowl because no one is supposed to know me here. "Shut up."

Minka smirks and lifts me up by a handful of my shirt. I'm a big girl, but I'm no match for her.

Physically.

As she dangles me about a foot off the ground, I smack her a few times. She holds me too close to get a good punch, but I'm the perfect distance to grab hold of her ponytail and give it a good yank.

She drops me, and I land in a crouch. While I'm down there, I take the opportunity to throw a few punches into her midsection, and the side of her thigh.

A good charley horse can slow anyone down.

Anyone, except for Minka.

"Declan!" Tenley's scream cuts the air and as I turn, Minka clips me with a right hook that sends me on my ass.

"You leave him alone!" I cry. I don't know what training Declan has had, but it can't be as good as mine. But Minka blocks me and I can't get to him.

So I move her. Jumping to my feet, I attack with a flurry of punches. The Amazon gives as good as she gets and, with her height, seems to have the advantage over me. But she's not trying to fight her way to Declan.

The squeal of tires signals an approach, and I have a fleeting wonder about how long it's going to be before the police arrive.

With a final roundhouse, I kick Minka into the side of a car. Once she's out of the way, I see Charlotte has arrived.

She flies out of the car before it even stops, and I have a moment to appreciate the grace of Charlotte launching herself into the melee. And then I sprint over to Declan, who is on the ground, being systematically kicked by two goons.

I grab a leg and yank it, spinning him around and sending him into the boot of another car before burying my fist into the other goon's stomach.

"Ham, get her out of here!" Seamus shouts over the racket.

"I'm not going anywhere." Tenley cries, fighting her way free. She is impressive with her martial arts moves and dance-like poise in the face of much bigger opponents. Either NIIA has an awesome training program, or Tenley's retained quite a few of Charlotte's fight memories.

But Ham doesn't listen to her. He fights his way to Tenley and grabs her around the waist, carrying her to the car. Then he pulls away with a screech of tires.

Fourteen

O NE OF BENJY'S GOONS makes an attempt to run down the car, but Ham floors it and is out of the garage before Charlotte finishes an impressive no-hands cartwheel with a kick to the head from the guy who's kicking Seamus.

Benjy gives a shout of frustration and then whistles like he's calling a dog. The goons immediately drop back and trot to the van. They're out of the parking garage just as fast as Ham.

What the holy hell was that?

I want to yell at Benjy for botching up my plan, but part of that plan is that I'm not supposed to know who they are. So I can't.

"What was that?" I shout at Seamus.

"How did he know we were here?" Seamus yells at Charlotte.

"How the hell am I supposed to know that?" Charlotte retorts.

Declan is the only one who keeps his cool, mainly because he's still on the ground, trying to catch his breath. I crouch beside him and touch his face with trembling fingers.

I can handle them coming after me, but not him. Benjy will pay for that cock-up.

"Are you okay?" Declan seems more worried about me than the blood trickling down his forehead.

"I'm fine, but *you*." Declan winces as I use his arm to pull him to his feet. "You're hurt."

"I'm good." He's battered and bruised, but still manages to tug me into his arms. I run my hands over his arms, his back looking for injuries. He hisses with pain when I touch his side.

"But you... How...?" Declan pulls away to look down at me. "You're okay."

It's not a question. I am relatively unhurt. A few bumps; I'll have a bruise on my hip where the goon threw me into the SUV, but nothing major. Declan wants to know how that's possible—a regular girl like me taking on a crowd of goons and coming out unscathed.

Charlotte and Seamus join us as I try to slow down my racing heartbeat. Charlotte has the same incredulous expressions as her brothers, which makes it easy to see the family resemblance.

"How did you do that?" Seamus demands. "You were against two and you took them both out."

I shrug. "Classes. I picked up some moves from movies. You, though—that was a great move back there... with the punch, then the kick."

I step away from Declan, wanting the attention off of me, even though it's taking everything I have not to preen and boast. "We should get out of here in case they come back. You need a hospital," I add, looking at Declan with a girlfriend's eye. "You're hurt." I gently pull up his sweater to see a stomach that's already covered with purple and red blotches. "I think your ribs are broken."

"I've had worse," he says, gesturing to Seamus and Charlotte with his chin. "Growing up with them wasn't always fun."

"Let's go to H—" Seamus begins, but Charlotte cuts him off.

"Ham's. That would be best. He owns a security company," she says to me. "He'll know what to do."

"Tenley had been doing some work for him," Seamus adds. "That's probably why those guys seemed to be after her."

"Good, because I can't see Tenley doing anything dodgy," I say, eyes wide and innocent.

I don't miss the sideways glance Charlotte gives her brother as I help Declan limp to his car. Luckily, it hasn't been damaged in the brawl.

The three of them are so busy covering their own secrets that I've gotten away with the worst acting job ever.

"Why don't you leave your car here and we can go with Seamus?" I suggest. By the laboured way Declan is breathing, I really think he has a broken rib.

"I'm fine." He waves away my idea with a grimace, unlocking the door with a push of a button. "I don't leave my car."

"At least let me drive."

"My car, I drive. Get in. I'm fine."

"Bloody hell, you're not!"

Declan ignores me as he gingerly slides behind the wheel. I'm a mass of worry and frustration as I climb into the passenger side. "Bloody damn man!"

"Yes, I am."

"That's not a compliment."

Declan gives me a ghost of a smile. Popping the car in reverse, he backs up at top speed, the car curving in a tight figure eight so that he's idling beside Seamus' equally sporty black car. Then we all take off, tires squealing, in a race to the exit of the parking garage.

Declan wins.

"It's not a pissing contest," I rage, even though my heart gives a thump thinking about what Declan might be capable of when he's at a hundred percent. But not now. He's only being a baby, showing off to his brother. He's hurt and he shouldn't be—

This is my fault.

My anger deflates like an actor getting a bad review and shame washes over me.

It makes my heart hurt to see Declan's bruised and bleeding knuckles on the steering wheel. His face is a mass of red and purple blotches that will undoubtedly become bruises. Even the slight movement of shifting gears makes him wince.

"Just letting you know I'm fine," Declan assures me. He pulls out of the mall exit, driving as slow as a nana. No one would ever guess he was zero to sixty below in the parking garage.

My adrenaline always spikes after a fight, but this time I'm numb. I can't take my eyes off his hands, the hands that had been holding mine so tenderly. The hands that cupped my face when he kissed me...

I swallow the sudden lump in my throat.

I have a job to do. I can't let pity for a pretty boy get in the way.

Eugene is counting on me to get Revello's list. He's got the buyer lined up and is counting on me to produce the thing. I won't let him down.

I'm afraid to.

Eugene may be powerful, but Lysander is the vindictive one. As I've moved up in Eugene's organization from a lowly messenger to one of his most respected agents, I've heard tales of those who let the big man down. And what Lysander did to them.

So I don't have an option here. I put this plan into motion and it better work.

It bloody well better.

I force myself to think ahead about how I'm going to obtain the list. They're taking me to the belly of the beast—NIIA. No one else has ever had this kind of access.

This is good. This is a coup for me. Eugene will finish the deal and Lysander...

My gaze keeps drifting to Declan's hands on the steering wheel. Against my will, I gently stroke his thumb with my finger. "You need to put ice on this."

"It's not my first fight, Pippa."

"I know. I don't know, but you grew up with brothers, so I can guess." I kiss my fingers and touch his cheek. "I'm so sorry this happened to you."

"Don't be. It's not your fault. I don't know what they wanted, but I'm glad they didn't get Tenley. Or hurt you." He takes a hand off the steering wheel and puts it on my knee.

My heart swells with emotion and then shatters.

I hate this *focking* job.

In the time it takes to drive downtown, I've cleared my mind.

My heart is another matter, but I'm ignoring that right now.

I have to end things with me and Declan. It doesn't matter how much I like him, as much as I like spending time with him, snogging him and him making me laugh and...

It doesn't matter because when he finds out I was the one who set up Benjy's attack—and he will find out—he'll never trust me again.

I shouldn't have trusted Benjy. I should have found some other way for me to gain access to the NIIA servers.

Should've, could've, would've. It's done now, and I have to finish it.

If play my cards right, I can get away with it. Get in, get out, get the info to Eugene and goodbye Declan. It works.

If it's such a bloody good plan, then why do I feel like I'm going to burst into tears like some blubbering baby?

Declan parks outside a huge, sprawling office building. The sun has set hours ago, but the lawn surrounding the building is lit with strategically placed lights. It's a lush green, full of early spring flowers and trees with baby leaves slowly unfurling. Beautiful, but an odd place for the head office of a secret spy organization.

As I stare across the lawn, thinking longingly of the green Irish countryside, a raccoon lumbers across the grass. Immediately, lights flash, a siren wails and the area of the lawn is lit up like a firefly.

"What the holy hell!"

I've never seen a raccoon run so fast.

"Ham's security company has had some issues with homeless people," Seamus explains. His car is parked behind Declan's and he's supporting Declan in a half-carry. "They're working out the kinks."

"They're going to have to work out who's picking up the raccoon poop because that thing just shite himself," I tell him. "Pretty grass, though."

Charlotte gazes at me coolly before turning her attention to Declan. "Think you can make it, big brother, or should we get you a stretcher?"

"I'm fine," Declan grunts with an attempt to shake off Seamus' help. Mindful of his male pride, I hover beside him without touching.

I'm afraid to make it worse.

"Ham's waiting for us," she says, leading the way across a path to a side entrance. They appear to have worked out the bugs on the cobblestoned path. Either that or Ham's turned off his rodent warning system.

It's not a great distance but seems to take forever to get to the door because Declan is walking so slowly.

He's really hurt. Seamus' reaction and protectiveness tell me Declan is no field agent like Charlotte and Tenley. I'd bet my last quid getting jumped like this isn't going to be in his job description.

I did this to him.

Unfortunately, that's in *my* job description.

Charlotte has the door open by the time Declan limps along the path. She waits, tapping her foot impatiently, obviously already having a password and whatever else is needed to get into this fortress in the middle of the night. I imagine there's heavy security to go along with the rodent patrol, but I can't see anything out of the ordinary.

I follow them inside, surprised to see a brown and gold marble floor and towering pillars like the Knocknakilla stones in County Cork. It looks like an everyday high-end office building. Good cover. Nobody'd think it was anything but a simple security company.

I notice the sign. Mutual Liberty Insurance.

"Ham's office is on the lower floor." Charlotte leads us to the elevator. I follow, taking in my surroundings, searching for exits, security cameras and other obstacles. My heart rate hops like a bunny.

I need a computer and at least two minutes by myself.

And a way out if they catch me.

Ham and Tenley are there when the elevator door opens to a tasteful reception area, minus the gilt and gaudiness of the lobby above.

Only three floors, so stairs are an exit option.

"Everyone all right?" Ham asks as Tenley flies into Seamus' arms. Ham gazes at Charlotte and I imagine he's analyzing her for any injuries, but he doesn't give her the welcome Tenley gives Seamus. But then, she's not flying into his arms, either. Trouble in paradise? Or is this work mode?

I scan the room, my gaze locking on the desk in the middle of the room. It seems like the usual reception desk, neat and tidy and unmanned at this hour, with a phone and a PC patiently waiting for me.

"I want to look over Declan." Charlotte takes her brother's arm and leads him away from me. "Do you still have that first-aid kit in the back room?" she asks over her shoulder to Ham.

"He should go to the hospital," I say in a worried girlfriend voice, trying not to stare at the computer.

"I've got this." Her voice is cold, having lost all the heat of her earlier anger.

"Are you a doctor?"

Charlotte stiffens at my question. "Are you? I said I've got this. Seamus, give me a hand for a sec."

"I'll just be a minute," Declan says with an apologetic glance over his shoulder. "It's better to let them do what they want with me."

"I bet." In a moment, the three of them vanish through a door and I turn to Ham and Tenley. "What is this place? Is this where you work?" Normal girlfriend questions. "Is Declan going to be okay?"

"I'm sure he'll be fine. Charlotte will take care of him. Pippa, would you mind waiting here for a moment?" Ham asks politely. "There are a few things I need to discuss with Tenley about the attack."

"Like security stuff? What was that about?" I turn to Tenley. "And why *you*? Why were they after you?"

"I don't know." Tenley tries to sound convincing, but she can't meet my eyes.

"We won't be but a moment," Ham assures me.

"Sure." I cross the room, dutifully taking a seat on the black leather couch. "I don't want to be in the way. Can you check on Declan for me?"

"Of course." Ham ushers Tenley out of the room, leaving me alone and scanning the room for security cameras. Unless they're camouflaged in the corners, there's none.

I count to thirty after the door closes behind them.

It takes me twenty seconds to power up the computer. It's password protected, but *CharlotteDodd* opens it up. It takes me fifteen more to start rooting through the hard drive. My fingers fly over the keyboard as I search. What file would it be under? There's not a lot of information here.

Maybe it's not here. Maybe this really is just a simple security company. Maybe—

I search by name, then by date. Finally I find the list of names Tenley took from Revello's computer filed under R. It's not even encrypted.

With a quiet hum of elation, I pull out my keychain, which is a USB flash drive, cleverly hidden as a LEGO Princess Leia figure. I plug it into the computer and hit copy.

I hold my breath, keeping my gaze on the door. My fingers tap anxiously on the desk, the only sound in the room.

A quiet beep lets me know it's finished.

It takes me forty seconds to pull out the flash and stuff it back in my pocket and close the files.

"All good," I whisper as I enable sleep mode on the computer. "Nighty night, now."

I'm back on the couch, in the same position in exactly four minutes.

I'm that good.

But for the first time, I don't feel good about it.

Fifteen

F IVE MINUTES LATER, ONE of the doors leading out of the
reception area opens and Seamus appears.

"Is he okay?" I demand, jumping to my feet and forgetting for a
moment about the illicit information in my pocket.

"Declan's fine. I'm going to take you home," he says in a voice
that doesn't bode well for protest.

"It's okay. I'll wait for Declan."

"It's late, and you'll be wanting to go home. Declan will be a
while longer, so I told him I'd look after you."

"Thanks, but I can look after myself just fine," I tell him firmly.
"Where is he?"

"He's fine, and he's talking to Lottie and Ham. Look, Pippa,
let's go. I'll take you home. You can see him tomorrow."

"Would you leave Tenley?" I demand. I can't explain it, but if I
leave without seeing Declan, I'm afraid it's going to be the last time
I'll ever see him.

Seamus gives a snort. "It's a little different. You don't even know
him. Look, Pippa, you shouldn't be here." I'm surprised at his

bluntness. "This is a private matter—family only. Declan will talk to you tomorrow."

"Tomorrow," I echo. I'm not faking my reluctance to leave, but I need to focus. Eugene needs this info.

I have to get out of here.

"Are you sure he's all right?" I ask Seamus with real concern in my voice. "They were really laying into him back there."

"Whoever set that up is going to pay," Seamus says with ice in his voice.

The threat isn't directed at me yet, but I have problems looking Seamus in the eye. "Stay here and I'll get a cab home."

Seamus looks surprised by my quick about-face.

The hidden flash drive digs into my pocket and I feel the prick of tears behind my eyes.

"I promised Declan I'd get you home," Seamus argues.

"I'm fine on my own. Stay with your brother—please." I touch Seamus' arm. "I get that this is family business, so it's better if you don't have to chauffeur me around."

Seamus gives me a long look, one I can't read. "Fair enough. He'll talk to you tomorrow." He presses the button for the elevator and the doors open automatically. "Do you want me to come out to the street with you?"

"I'm a big girl," I say, blinking quickly. "Take care of your brother. Tell him I'm sorry... that he got hurt."

And then the doors close behind me.

As soon as they do, I knead my forehead with shaky fingers, taking deep breaths to fight off the onslaught of guilt. My eyes burn with unshed tears. The last time I cried was when Henry...

This isn't the time to think about Henry.

I still have a job to do. Declan will be all right. He's trained to handle himself, to deal with the hard knocks.

I straighten my spine as the elevator bings its arrival and step into the main lobby.

Whatever Ham's pretend office is down there, it's sure not the head office for NIIA, or this country's in a whack of trouble.

The agent in me wants to look around more, but I know that someone, somewhere, is watching me on a video screen. Plus the flash drive suddenly feels like it's burning a hole in my pocket.

I just stole information from NIIA.

I just betrayed Declan.

It's a quick ride back to the hotel. During the cab ride, I Google Mutual Liberty Insurance, trying to find a connection between them and NIIA. Anything to stop thinking about Declan.

I pray to all the gods Declan will never know what I did. But maybe it's better if he did, since it's over. We're on opposite sides. We'll never be able to trust each other.

Maybe honesty is overrated. I've told the truth to exactly one person in my life and it got him killed, so why would being honest with Declan be a good idea?

The Dublin police ruled Henry's death an accident, a mugging gone horribly wrong, but I know better. Someone found out I told him who I worked for and killed him. Warning? Revenge? I'll never know.

My heart doesn't ache like it used to, but that dizzying feeling of regret and guilt when I think about Henry hasn't gone away. I do my best to push him from my thoughts.

Declan's never been part of the plan so I should leave him out of it, for both of our sakes.

The elevator in the hotel is notoriously slow and I don't wait for it. My feet are heavy as I climb the four floors. It's been a long day and I'm shattered. With every step, a new ache develops–my hip from where I hit the car, my shoulder from when I fell to the ground. My face missed out on the majority of the punches, but I definitely took some body blows.

The sharp edges of the LEGO figure dig into my palm as I clutch the USB in my hand. I need to get rid of this. Maybe the guilt will vanish once it's safely away to Eugene.

I could seriously murder a pint of Guinness about now.

At the top of the stairs, I push open the metal door with my shoulder and wince at the new ache that develops. Giving it a rub, I step into the hallway.

Something is wrong.

I grab the door before it slams, closing it with a quiet click.

There are no noises coming from behind the doors between my room and where I'm standing by the stairs. It's not surprising since it's late, but usually, I hear a television or voices or something. Tonight, everything is silent. It's so quiet that I can hear the hum of the overhead light above me.

Suspiciously, I peer down the hall. The maid had vacuumed earlier in the day yet there's a visible footprint on the fading yellow carpet before my room.

I pause between the options of heading back down the stairs or kicking the arse of whoever's broke into my room.

I decide on the arse-kicking and tiptoe forward.

The door to my room is open.

A tiny strip of light shines between the door and the frame.

I shove the USB back into the pocket of my jeans and slip off my boots. I have big feet and my Blundstones have a sturdy heel.

They're better than nothing.

I stand before the door, listening for any sound, but all I hear is the buzz of the light. With a boot in each hand, I raise my foot and kick in the door.

Sixteen

- -

"**B**LOODY HELL, PIPPA!"

My boots thump to the floor. "Lysander! What in holy hell are you doing here?"

The dingy room is lit by the bedside lamp, but it's enough light for me to see that Lysander has made himself at home, seated on the edge of my bed. There's a book on the floor. As I stand gaping, he picks up the book, giving it an affectionate brush to wipe it clean from any of the carpet critters that might be roaming the place.

He always has a book with him. Lysander reads more than any man I know.

Along with his ever-present book, he's brought his minions, Carl and Robbie. They tag along when he doesn't want to get his hands dirty.

The sight of the three of them in my room raises my hackles. "I'd invite you in, but it'd be biscuits to a bear," I say, instinctively lowering my tone as I shut the door. "Make yourselves at home."

Carl, the equalizer, resembles an ox in both size and smarts. He slowly flicks the channels of the television. There are only five working channels, and yet he seems to be completely oblivious to the rest of the room.

"Where have you been?" Lysander asks in a quiet voice, standing to greet me.

"And hello to you too." Dutifully, I take a step towards him, even though suddenly out of nowhere, every instinct is telling me to run.

It's *Lysander*.

I offer him my cheek and he brushes his thumb across the bruise that's beginning to show on my chin. "Where were you?"

Like he doesn't know. There's no way Lysander and his minions have shown up just in time for my deadline. He's been in the city for the day, at least.

Probably longer.

Which means he knows about Declan. Just because I haven't heard from him doesn't mean he hasn't been watching my every move.

The unease grows in the pit of my stomach, but I don't let on.

Instead, I pull the flash drive from my pocket. "Just picking up a prezzie for your da."

He plucks the drive from my fingers. "Where did you get this?"

"Where I said I'd get it from." I keep my tone light, piling on the confidence so Lysander can't tell I'm nervous.

I shouldn't be nervous. It's Lysander. He's practically my fiancé. Even so, I turn away to toss my coat over the only empty chair in the room. Robbie, minion number two, has taken the ladder-backed chair in the corner and turned it backward. His arms are folded along the back, his rat-like face lasciviously watching my every move.

Robbie's a wanker and gives me the creeps. He gives most women the creeps. Lysander keeps him around because, unlike Carl, Robbie has more brains than brawn and a sadistic streak that comes in handy.

I could probably kick his arse, but I'd be afraid of the retaliation.

"You got this from NIIA?" Lysander demands. No, *well done, Pippa*, from him. He hands out compliments as easily as others hand out hundred-pound notes. He examines the drive like it's about to tell him all its secrets.

"The computer had access to NIIA files, so sure."

"You found the head office?" His handsome face gleams with sudden excitement and my heart sinks when I remember who I left behind. I hope Declan is all right.

"I'm not really sure *where* I was..."

"But you can get back," he presses. "You have access to files, to information—"

"No."

I'm not sure who is more surprised.

"What do you mean, no?" His words are no more than a whisper.

I've known Lysander long enough to be able to read his tells. I know when his eyes shift to the left he's lying, and when his hands ball into a fist, he's guilty. And I know that when his voice gets quiet, he's very mad.

I take a step back. "I don't have access. It's under lock and key. I got what we needed, but that's it."

All I can think about is Declan.

I got the list for Eugene as promised. That was the mission. That was *all* I had to do. No need for me to push and break cover. Declan never needs to know who I work for.

"How long have you been here?" I change the subject. Robbie cocks his head at my tone. Even the minions can tell I'm hiding something, let alone Lysander, who has known me since I was fifteen.

"Here—in this manky kip?" He glances around the room with disdain. "Unfortunately, for a while. But you mean in the city. Why? I thought you wanted me to visit."

"Of course I did. I do."

"It seems you've kept yourself busy without me."

I stare into his brown eyes, so dark that it's hard to make out the pupil. He's the cat and I'm the mouse; there's no way I'm getting out of this without a few scratches.

"His name is Declan Dodd," I say in a quiet voice.

Lysander's lips curve into a Cheshire-cat smile. "Oh, I know exactly who he is. And how much time you've spent with him. You've spent a fair bit of time working with Tenley Scott, the new NIIA agent."

"You knew that because I told you. It was so I could get the list for Eugene." I try desperately to keep my voice strong and tough but facing down Lysander isn't like conning a stranger. There are emotions and memories involved.

"It seemed a cozy group at the movies tonight."

I don't even bother asking how he knows that. "He works for NIIA," I say in a tired voice, pushing past him to the bed. "It doesn't mean anything. It's just work."

Lysander smiles again. "Declan Dodd is the least of my worries." Arching his eyebrow, he picks a piece of lint off his jacket and flicks it.

"Then what's the problem? Can you tell your boys to feck off so I can get some sleep?" I fake a yawn as I sink onto the bed.

"Why don't you pack up your things, Pippa?" Lysander voice is still quiet. "We'll be leaving now."

"To go home?" I have to see Declan, to explain...

No, I don't.

"Not quite yet. There are a few things that need to be taken care of here first."

"I said I don't know how to get into NIIA."

"You're very talented, Pippa. I'm sure you'll think of something. Because until you do..."

I quiet my voice and still my heart. "Now, that sounds a wee bit like you're threatening me, Lysander, and that's not your style." I glance pointedly at Robbie. "You have people for that."

"It's not a threat, Pippa."

"Then what is it? Because I'm knackered, and it's time for bed."

"I may not be worried about Dodd, but I do find myself having a few questions about your loyalty."

"You—what? Don't be daft!"

Lysander cocks an eyebrow. "Really, Pippa? You failed to complete your mission and now refuse to consider infiltrating our enemy. I think you're blinded by your infatuation. I've never seen you like this."

"That's a load of horseshit." I grab my knapsack, needing to do something with my hands so he doesn't see them shaking. "Let's finish this up if that's what you want."

I keep my head down as I toss clothes into my bag, not wanting Lysander to be able to see what I'm really thinking.

Ten minutes later, my things are packed and a black Escalade pulls up to the curb. Carl is behind the wheel, his beefy hands resting on the leather-covered steering wheel, with Robbie riding shotgun, a creepy smile on his face. Lysander holds the back door open, an expression of tolerant amusement on his face, masking his annoyance.

Every inch of me screams not to get in, but I have no choice. If I balk, I've no doubt Lysander will tell Carl to physically shove me in the car, and I can't stand to have their hands on me.

Something's up, but it'd be worth my life to let them see me scramble to figure it out.

"Where are we going?" I ask as the SUV pulls away from the curb. Traffic is light this time of the night, the streetlights illuminating the road. If only Declan was sitting beside me. My fingers twitch as though longing to have him take my hand and hold it tight.

"To see a friend." Lysander's focus is on his phone.

Could I make a jump for it? Carl isn't driving that fast and there aren't many cars to worry about. But it's late and the shops along the street are dark and deserted. There might be some drinking hole open, but not in this area. I'd be running along the street like a chicken with his head cut off, waiting to get caught. I can—

Why am I thinking of escape? This is *Lysander*. Lysander would never hurt me. Would he?

"Didn't know you had any friends in Toronto." I stare unseeing out the window, trying to figure out a plan.

"No, but you do."

I close my eyes again. *Declan.*

Tenley.

I've made the colossal mistake of falling for a mark. Not just Declan, but Tenley too. This is why it was better with no friends outside the family. They just *fock* everything up.

"Why don't you tell me about your friends?" Lysander asks, finally putting down his phone.

"They're not exactly *friends*," I bluff but Lysander knows me as well as I know him, and laughs at my attempt at deception.

"Nice try, Pippa. I know that you've been spending a lot of time with Declan Dodd. I know that you're working with Tenley Scott. I know that you met with both Charlotte Dodd and Ham Short tonight. Brilliant job in getting close to the NIIA family."

Every name hits me like a kick to the stomach and I fight not to flinch.

"I hope you've kept things on a professional level," he adds.

"I did what needed to be done."

"Really?" On the seat between us is an envelope. Lysander picks it up and hands it to me. I open it with fingers as stiff as blocks of ice.

Inside are pictures of Declan and I holding hands. Of me through the window of the cafe, laughing with Tenley.

"I didn't think you were that good an actress."

I hand the pictures back to him. "Think again."

"Well, we'll soon find out."

That's the last of our conversation. I keep waiting for Lysander to say something else, but he keeps his focus on his phone.

I spend the twenty-minute trip counting the ways I can trust Lysander. I know he cares about me in his own way. He'd never hurt me.

He would never hurt *me*.

But the cracks of doubt are quickly opening as wide as the Gap of Dunloe Gorge and for once I don't know what to do.

I hate not knowing what to do.

We finally pull into a subdivision outside the city. The other houses have matching paint and trim and look like they're made from a set of cookie cutters.

"Do you really need me for this?" I ask as Carl pulls into the short drive. The headlights flash on the garage door, which is an ugly teal colour, clashing with the yellow of the house.

This is the only one that stands out.

"Of course I need you." Lysander's voice softens, and he touches my cheek with warm fingers. "Now, more than ever."

I stare into his brown eyes, trying to read his expression, trying to guess his intentions, but they're blank.

Lysander isn't a good person. He's done things I know are wrong. Immoral. Illegal. And I've done things with him—for him—that makes me one of the bad guys.

But I'm not sure I want to be.

That's a scary feeling. Lysander and Eugene are my family. They're the only one I have. They took me in when no one else would, fed me, taught me. Eugene loves me like a daughter. And Lysander... loves me in his own way.

Lysander opens the car door and I slide out after him, reluctance making my feet drag. Unlike the neighbouring houses, this one is ablaze with light. Carl leads us to the front door. It swings open and my heart sinks.

"Lysander, sir, so nice to finally meet you in person," Benjy says, his arms wide in greeting. "And Pippa—glad to see that you're still in one piece."

"*Fock* off," I mutter.

Minka is the next person I see, her height filling the small hallway. "Long time, no see." She smirks. "Was that good for you?"

I ignore her and follow Lysander into the kitchen, frantically trying to figure out what the devil is going on.

Another man sits at the round table nursing a beer. I recognize him as one of the goons, and I'm satisfied by the bruises on his face.

"You remember Mikhail, don't you, Pippa?" Benjy hovers in the doorway. "The other boys have gone home, but they said it was fun, or would have been if you'd gone easy on them. You weren't holding back much, were you?" He smirks. "Protecting your boyfriend, were you?"

"Shut your gob!" I take a step forward and Benjy backs into Minka, standing in the doorway. "I asked for a favour, and you pull some kidnapping crap! What was that shite?" I poke a finger into his chest.

"Pippa! Such hostility," Benjy cries, his arms wide with pretend surrender. Mikhail still seated at the table, laughs into his beer.

"I'm goin' give you a kickin' like I did before if you don't shut your hole," I snarl at Mikhail.

"I'd like to see you try," Minka says, her voice surprisingly sweet.

I glance up at Minka, back at Mikhail. It might be best to figure out what's going on before going another round with her.

"Hey, hey," Benjy says jovially, sensing I've backed down. "Water under the bridge. Everybody's friends, everything's cool." He glances at Lysander standing behind me. "Hang on to your pit bull, will you? Pippa, sweetstuff, if I remember correctly—and I would, because I was watching pretty closely—you got out of the little ambush with your pride and your pretty face intact."

"But you didn't have to—" I cut myself off just in time. Benjy gives me a knowing smile.

"Didn't have to focus on Declan Dodd? Why would that bother you, Pippa?"

"It doesn't," I growl.

"I'm sure." Benjy offers Lysander a chair and then sits down himself. "Look, sweetstuff, I decided to kill a few birds with one very big stone. I've wanted to get my hands on terrific Tenley for a while now, ever since she slipped through my fingers last time. And whose fault is that?" He turns to Minka.

"Seamus Dodd," Minka supplies.

"You calling out of the blue was a godsend, and I really have to thank you," Benjy continues. "I had a bit of a score to settle with Seamus. Unfortunately, the boys got him mixed up with Declan. You know those Dodd boys; they all look the same."

My fist clenches at the remembrance of Declan on the ground. "No, I don't know that. You should have told me," I say sullenly. "I don't like going in blind."

"Well, then I'm sorry." Benjy give me a fake smile. "But maybe you didn't have to try quite so hard to protect Tenley. If you'd have let us get away with her before Charlotte and the cavalry showed up, we'd all be a lot better off."

"This was my game, not yours."

"Yes, but in the big picture, my needs are more important." Benjy's eyes are suddenly cold and dangerous, like a snake ready to strike.

I'm not afraid of snakes. "I don't think so. My game was for Eugene. Remember him—head of Mielson?"

"He's not top gun yet, and won't be if you keep messing up," Benjy says with an ugly expression on his face. "Sit yourself down, Pippa; I'm done with you. We're going to talk about our next move now."

"I'm not talking about anything with you," I say, taking an angry step towards the door.

Lysander stands. "Oh, I think you will," he says quietly.

Seventeen

I GLARE AT LYSANDER. "Why are listening to him blather on so? He's such a wanker; you can't trust him."

"Sit down, Pippa."

I feel the heat of my cheeks as my face flames at the dismissive tone. I pull out a chair, scraping it along the linoleum floor with a screech that breaks the ugly silence and sit down without another word.

Settle down, Pippa.

I've given too much away already. Now's the time to figure out what's going on and how to get out of it.

"Now that's dealt with, this is what I think," Benjy begins without another glance at me.

Carl and Robbie join the discussion. I stew in my anger. I've been in this situation too many times to count. Not the being angry at Benjy, but the gathering before the op. The planning. The debrief—men sitting around arguing about what's to be done or congratulating themselves on a job well done. Women might well be invisible.

"Charlotte is the Agency's prized possession," Benjy says impassively.

"She's not a possession," I interrupt through gritted teeth.

Benjy stares at me with cold eyes. "Don't you know it's rude to interrupt?"

"Don't you know it's rude to be such a bloody big *arse*?"

"Pippa." There's a warning in Lysander's voice that I've not heard directed at me before.

"Now, then." Benjy smirks. "I've given Mielson all I know about the Agency, but there's so much out there. Files and files and if we have that..." He rubs his hands greedily at the power the knowledge could give him. "I bet Charlotte knows everything. There's no hope of getting my hands on her, but Tenley—now, Tenley is a distinct possibility, because your girl Pippa's here giving us the inside scope. I'm the one who downloaded all of Charlotte's lovely memories into her head, but before I had the chance to ask her anything, Seamus Dodd stormed out with her. Him and that Colin Darcy."

My ears perk up at Colin's name. He didn't tell me that.

"Your father, the esteemed Eugene Mochrie, would love the info Tenley's got packed in her head," Benjy continues. "And it would be easy peasy to get it out. Tenley's got a kid, you know, and all we need is to—"

My blood runs cold. "No." The others look up at my outburst.

"C'mon, Pippa, I'm not about to *hurt* her," Benjy wheedles. "It's just insurance that everything will go smoothly."

"Pippa will do whatever needs to be done," Lysander says in a smooth voice. "There's no worry here."

They keep talking about where and when, and I stare at Lysander in disbelief. How can he even think that of me?

He can. He wouldn't have any qualms about using Tenley's little girl, or Seamus to get what he wants. And he clearly doesn't have a problem using me.

Lysander wants to take down NIIA for his father. One less watchguard in the world means more power for Eugene, and for him. And once Benjy hands him Tenley with her head full of Charlotte's memories, he thinks nothing will stop him.

"We need to move fast," Benjy says.

"Of course." Lysander gestures to the small television on the counter. "And we'll come up with a plan. But right now, the boys need to watch the game."

"You—what?" Benjy's shoulders sag with disbelief. "I thought—"

"The football match. There's quite a bit of money riding on this game," Lysander explains smoothly. "Pippa? You'll be watching footy with us?"

"Do I ever watch footy with you?" He knows I hate the sport. He knows I hate him making bets, but that does nothing to stop him. Lysander's one vice is gambling and I'm one of the few who realize that. It's the one thing he manages to keep from his father.

I wonder how much he's got riding on this match.

A sandwich on a plate is set down before me. I glance up to see Minka. "You look like you could use some sustenance," she says with what passes for a smile.

"Are you daft? You expect me to eat this?"

Minka raises her hands in defence. "Suit yourself."

"Why don't you go make friends?" Lysander suggests. "After all, you're on the same team now."

My heart sinks. He's completely serious. I'm being dismissed.

I pick up the plate and follow Minka out of the room.

She's sitting in a living room, or what would pass for a living room if there was more furniture. A brown and orange couch is propped against the wall with one of the legs broken off. A card table with folding chairs is in the corner of the room, and the only thing that doesn't look like it came from a thrift store is the fifty-inch television mounted on the wall.

Apparently, Benjy has his priorities.

"You have the puppet act down pat," Minka says, holding up her glass.

"What's that supposed to mean?"

She holds up her hands. "No offense. Just that Lysander thinks he's running the show, but I'm not sure if that's the case." She shrugs. "But maybe it is."

I'm torn between storming out of the room and finding out more about Minka. Since she's the lesser of two evils, I gingerly sink down beside her, only to land on a broken spring. Wincing, I shift closer to Minka. "I report to Eugene, not Lysander."

"Same thing these days. You've been out on your own for a while."

"What's going on?"

I've always kept to myself among Eugene's other agents, looking for Eugene to tell me what I need to know. If there's something that Eugene doesn't know...

Minka shrugs. "You played well tonight."

"That was playing?"

She takes a mouthful of beer and wipes her mouth. "The whole thing is a big game, isn't it?"

"Not for me."

"That's your problem, then. I see you sitting there, trying to figure out what's going on, what's good for you. I just go where the money is."

"So none of this matters to you?" I poke at the sandwich she gave me. It looks like ham and cheese, but the light in here is dim and I can't be sure. But Minka is right—I could use some food. I take a tiny bite from the corner.

It's bologna. With mayonnaise. I take a bigger bite.

"Why should it matter to me? Look at them in there." Minka waves her hand in the direction of the kitchen. "Those boys sitting around the table. They're playing a game, like a video game."

"Why did you leave NIIA?" I ask around a mouthful of processed meat.

Minka sighs. "They call it the Agency. Great group of people, but Mielson pays better. Simple as that. They came calling and made me an offer I couldn't refuse." Minka rests her arm on the back of the couch and sits facing me.

Her camaraderie isn't something I'm used to. I'm the only female in Eugene's inner circle, a position I have always guarded carefully.

For the first time, I wonder why. What has it gotten me? Yes, Eugene has treated me like a daughter, but for what? He's made me into this—this person, willing to kidnap a woman and use her child against her.

Whomever Eugene made me into is a bit of a wanker.

"Is it just the money for you? That's all you care about?" I ask Minka.

"Yep. My father is in a nursing home—a very nice one, thanks to Mielson. I only care about making him comfortable and happy."

"I didn't know my Da," I muse. "And even if I did, I don't think I'd care much if he was happy or not."

"Dad raised me on his own," Minka says proudly. "He's the one who got me into the Ultimate Fighting—"

"You did that?" My mouth drops open. "The mixed martial arts stuff in a ring?"

"For almost five years, until Ham Short recruited me."

"No wonder you're so bloody scary!" I laugh.

"You're not much of a helpless damsel yourself. I remember you from when you were starting out—that op in Monte Carlo? I was still with the Agency then. It was one of my last missions with them," she adds wistfully.

I smile smugly. "I kicked your butt and only my second time out."

"I wouldn't go that far. There were extenuating circumstances, but you did okay."

"Better than okay."

"I see you're with Declan Dodd." Minka raises her eyebrows with approval. "I was... fond... of Caleb when I was with the Agency. Declan's a cutie."

I can't help but giggle at Minka's words. Maybe she's more girl than they give her credit for.

"I haven't met Caleb yet."

"What did you think of Charlotte?" I roll my eyes in response to Minka's question. "She's a piece of work, isn't she?" But the way Minka smiles makes me think she approves of Charlotte's feistiness.

I spend the rest of the evening on the couch with Minka. It's strange but strangely nice. I eat my sandwich and we drink our beer. I even slip back into the kitchen to get a refill and am greeted by stone-faced expressions that make me more than a little uneasy. Robbie has taken my place at the table.

I return to Minka without a word.

More than an hour later, Lysander appears in the living room. "Pippa, love, Benjy has shown me to our room."

"We're staying *here* tonight?"

"It's best, since we move on Tenley tomorrow morning."

I glance at Minka, whose face has lost her earlier animation and now looks like a blank mask. "I guess I missed that part."

"I noticed you didn't feel the need to concern yourself with the details. Benjy has asked for our help with retrieving the memories from Tenley Scott. He thought having you along might make the procedure less stressful for her."

"What procedure?"

Lysander shrugged. "I don't really know much about it. And I don't really care. Once Benjy gets what he wants, we're moving on NIIA. It's time to take over from Ham. I'm afraid your boyfriend will be out of a job."

I drop my eyes. "He's not my boyfriend."

"We'll discuss that later. Time for bed." Without waiting for my response, Lysander turns and heads up the stairs.

I exhale wearily. How did this all go so wrong?

"You can't make her go through with it," Minka says in a low voice.

"Tenley?"

"I was there when they downloaded Charlotte's memories into her. The way she screamed and fought—no one should have someone's mind forced into theirs." Minka leans closer. "My father has Alzheimer's. I have to watch him losing his memories. No one should have to be forced into that."

I keep my gaze on the stairs. There's no telling when Lysander will return to fetch me. "How do I stop it?"

"Get to Tenley first."

I don't respond. I don't know if I can trust Minka. She could run back to Benjy and Lysander for all I know.

"Two houses to the left, on the street behind this one," she continues. "The garage is always unlocked."

I know what she's suggesting, but I'm not sure why. "Why are you telling me this?"

"You're not like the others. I can tell—I was watching you with Declan."

"I must be if I didn't notice you hanging about."

"You know they won't let you have him," she says urgently.

Declan? I mouth, my heart sinking.

"Get to him after Tenley," Minka urges. I follow her gaze up the stairs. "I like Declan, and I've heard stories."

"What stories?"

"Mochrie's made a name for himself. He doesn't like to be crossed, and that's exactly what you did."

"What did Eugene do?" I whisper, my voice hoarse with fear.

Minka gestures with her chin to the stairs. "It's not Eugene you have to worry about."

Eighteen

I S LYSANDER MY ENEMY?

I want to stay downstairs and find out more from Minka, but Lysander wants me with him, in a creepy, *keep-an-eye-on-me* closeness rather than anything romantic.

Romance is the last thing on my mind right now.

There's one closed door upstairs, and with a deep breath, I open it.

The room is lit only by a lamp, but I see Lysander lying on the bed as soon as I push open the door. He's fully dressed, missing only his tailored suit jacket, which is lying on the end of the bed. "Tell me about Declan Dodd."

I don't know what to expect, but it's not this.

"There's not much to tell." Taking a moment to compose myself, I slip my boots off by the door.

"You're dating him." Lysander shifts, propping himself up against the pillows. "You must know him."

"I've seen him socially a few times," I agree. "Much like you've been with other women. Or not really—Declan and I haven't..." I toss my jacket on the floor beside my boots. Cursing to myself, I realize I've left my bag in the car.

Lysander snorts. It's an odd response from someone who prides himself on his sophistication and decorum. "Pippa, don't assume I'm jealous. I don't care who you date right now. The problem is that you have created an extra obstacle. You know very well I've been tasked to take over NIIA."

"I thought Niall had." This must be new. The last thing I heard was Niall would be in Toronto in a month's time with his own agents. I'd be long gone back to Belfast by then.

"In light of the situation you've created, Da has told me to take it. And I'm to do it now."

"What's this I've done?" I move around to the right side of the bed. Lysander always takes the left side, regardless of where and what we're sleeping in. I once fell asleep next to him in the cargo hold of a plane and he woke me up to change positions just so he could sleep on the left side.

"Where's your loyalty, Pippa?"

"Where it's always been, Lysander." My voice is steady and firm, incredulous that I've been asked such a thing.

He stares at me as if he's trying to read my very soul. I look away, unnerved.

"Your da took me off the streets, fed me. He made me who I am today. No reason you should wonder about anything," I say.

Without waiting for his response, I stand and slip off my jeans. I leave on my shirt and crawl under the covers.

Lysander sits stiffly on the side of the bed for a moment before he gets up and heads to the washroom in the hall. As soon as he leaves, I let out my breath in a shaky exhale.

My cell chimes as a text arrives. With a heavy heart, I pick it off the floor.

> Are you okay? Seamus said you wouldn't let him take you home.

Declan. The simple text sends a thrill through me. As much as I want to ignore him, I can't.

> I'm fine. He needed to stay with you. Really tired now. Talk tomorrow.

His response is instantaneous.

> Sleep well. xo

I feel like crying.

I delete the messages. It won't take Lysander much to find them, but I'm not going to make it easy for him.

When Lysander comes back in the room, I pretend I'm asleep. And I think I do fall asleep for a while, but most of the night, I lay in the bed awake, listening to Lysander's breathing and wondering how I can fix this.

If it's even fixable.

At four-thirty, I pull myself out of bed.

Putting on my pants would make too much noise, so I sling them around my neck. With a last, longing look at my phone, I leave it on the floor beside the bed.

I set up the tracking system that Lysander uses on my phone. If I take it, he'll know my every move.

The door creaks quietly as I pull it open. Holding my breath, I glance over my shoulder, but Lysander doesn't stir. I'm about to slip through when Lysander inhales sharply before exhaling with a rumbling snore. I grab my jacket and boots and tiptoe out.

Shutting the door is just as difficult.

In the bathroom, I take a moment to tuck my boots into my jeans and then tie the legs together, before wrapping them around my waist like some sort of ugly denim fanny pack. When I'm all trussed up, it's time for the window. I'm assuming Benjy set the alarm, but I don't know for sure. The sensor is easy to take care of; earlier when I got a beer from the kitchen, I swiped a CN Tower magnet off the refrigerator. And during a bathroom visit, I found a pair of nail scissors to cut a strip off.

This little strip goes against the sensor to fool it. And it works perfectly—no alarm when I open the window. A gust of cold air rushes into the bathroom, making me wish I took the time to put on my pants. No time for that now.

After I crawl through, it takes a little maneuvering to close the window. At one point, I cling to the windowsill by my fingers while I slide the window closed with the palm of my hand. It's only a short drop to the flat roof of the garage.

This isn't one of those houses with noses, the ones that have the garage out front. This has it attached to the side, with the door from the kitchen. Maybe I could have made it downstairs and out the door, but who knows if anyone is still hanging about?

Out the window is always a good bet.

During my sulk in the kitchen, a bunny hopped across the lawn and lights flooded the backyard, same as at Mutual Liberty. It was overkill at a big company building, but it's a sure sign of paranoia for a house in a sleepy suburb. Benjy must have had problems with breaking and enter and got the idea about lighting things from Ham.

He has no creativity.

At the edge of the roof, I peer down until my eyes adjust to the darkness. Then I hang off the edge, careful not to grab onto the eaves trough, and stretch out my legs until the tips of my toes feel the wooden fence below. I feel a wee bit silly dangling in my drawers, but with a deep breath and a quick prayer to whatever god is in charge of good balance, I drop, landing on the top of the fence.

This is why I left my shoes off.

Keeping my arms wide, I crouch for long seconds before standing upright. Slowly, resisting the urge to grab the side of the garage, I turn to face the far corner of the backyard.

Here's hoping I'm still as good on the balance beam as I used to be.

I carefully walk along the top of the fence, like a cat hoping to stay out of the dog's way.

There's a bad moment right near the end, but I make it. Turning left, I continue along the back of the next fence. The lots are long, rather than wide, and this time it takes me no time to make my way across.

With a big smile, I hop down from the fence and hide in the shadows as I put my jeans and boots on.

I think this is the right house. Minka said it was two houses down on the street behind Benjy's. Let's hope she was right.

I peek around the corner of the garage and pull back with a gasp. Headlights on the road are coming closer, driving slowly, like they're looking for someone.

How could they know I'm gone so quickly?

Barely breathing, I press against the side of the garage and wait for the car to pass.

It stops on the street almost directly in front of me.

It's not the SUV that Carl drove us here in and I have no idea what kind of car Benjy and his goons have. Do I run? Stay and fight my way out of it?

There's not even a stick in the grass for me to use. I'm about to step out of my boots again when the car moves, only to stop in front of the next house.

I dart across the strip of lawn to peer around the corner in time to see something fly out of the window of the car.

It's the newspaper delivery.

My body sags with relief as the car continues down the street. I wait until it turns the corner before I return to the garage.

It's a manual door, which means I use the handle to push/pull it open. It's a pain, but at least it's quiet.

And Minka was right. It's not locked.

Inside is a blue minivan.

My lock-picking kit includes everything I need to break into a car or house, but it's in my backpack, which is in the SUV, back in Benjy's driveway.

"Bloody hell," I hiss.

There has to be something I can use. This is a garage for god's sake.

Hotwiring a car may be one of my skills, but the van looks like a 2006 model, which means old-school hotwiring is practically impossible. If I had my files to jimmy the ignition, however...

Or the keys.

At the back of the garage is a workbench, and it's been left in a tip. Running my hands along the surface, it doesn't take long for me to find a few pieces of wire.

It takes even less time for me to use the wire to unlock the door to the house.

Even though everyone knows it's a stupid thing to do, most homeowners leave the keys to their vehicles within easy reach from the garage. Minivan family has done the same thing, so all I need to do is step into their kitchen and the keys are right there on the counter, practically inviting me to take them.

It's a minivan, though. It means kids, kids that will have to be taken to school in the morning. If I take their only car...

The light over the stove has been left on, and from the dim light, I quickly find a receipt and a pen on the counter. Scribbling an address on the back of the receipt, I swap it for the keys and back out of the kitchen the way I came.

It's not until I'm in the van, on the way back to the city, that I start to breathe again.

Nineteen

- -

L YSANDER IS GOING TO be livid when he sees I'm gone, but there's nothing I can do about it. He's the kind that carries a slow, cold-burning anger deep inside, but I've seen first-hand how easily it ignites into a red-hot fury. The thought of it being directed at me is terrifying, but it's too late. I've gone too far to stop now.

I slow my breakneck speed when I get close to the address of the parking lot I left on my note. I hope they get the car back in time to get the kids to school, but if they don't, there's nothing I can do about that, either. Fear of what Lysander is capable of doing to Tenley in retaliation for my defection makes my hands shake so badly that I don't know if they'll be able to read the quickly scribbled note of apology I've left on the dash.

It's only a block from Tenley's café and I hot-tail it over there. I wait, huddling in the alley, shivering beside the garbage bins in the alley, wishing I'd thought to bring another jumper.

It's difficult to understand how Tenley's pretty head can be filled with Charlotte's memories. I've never been one for science fiction, or even regular science, so I've no idea how it could have happened or why. Tenley seems normal...

I haven't burned my bridges yet. I can go back, figure out something to tell Lysander. Do I really want to go against the organization for someone I don't even know?

You knew her well enough to use her.

I'll warn her that Benjy is coming to grab her, and that's it. Benjy will be hopping mad but Lysander—

Tenley hurries past the entrance of the alley so quickly I almost miss her. She's already at the door and turns at the sound of my footsteps.

The fear in her expression quickly turning to anger when she sees it's me. "What are you doing here?" Her keys are in her hand, sticking out between her fingers.

"You okay? I mean, how are you? I wanted to check in, see if everything—" My words rush out and I see from Tenley's expression she's having problems understanding me. I take a breath. "The fight in the garage, they didn't get you but—"

"No thanks to you."

She knows. She knows who I am, what I did.

It's like my legs have been kicked out from under me. I stagger backwards, trying to regain my balance. "Oh. Well. That's not important right now. You need to—"

"I think it's very important," she cuts off in anger, gesturing with a hand still holding her keys. "Did you see Declan? Do you know what they did to him? He's got a busted rib and two broken fingers! He doesn't have the training for this, Pippa! You put him in danger—you put all of us in danger and all for what? Did you get what you wanted?"

I gape at her like a fish out of water.

"Don't bother being worried about him now," she continues, her scorn burning me with its intensity. She turns back to the door and puts her key in the lock. "Go back where you came from and leave him alone. Leave all of us alone."

"I'm trying to warn you—"

Tenley rounds on me, her face red with anger. For a moment, I expect her to follow through with a fast fist. "You set Benjy up. You lied to me—to all of us. I let you work for me, for god's sake. I can't believe I trusted you."

A siren suddenly cuts through the morning quiet, reminding me this isn't safe for either of us. "Maybe so, but you need to trust me now." My words smash together in my haste to make her understand. "Tenley, please. You need to take me to the NIIA headquarters."

"There's no way in hell I'm taking you anywhere."

"Please," I plead. "Benjy's coming for you. I came to warn you."

Her eyes widen with alarm before her mask settles back onto her face. "Go away, Pippa. You're done here." She opens the door and punches the code of the security system with the intensity of a nun shaking her finger at a naughty student. For the first time, I notice her security is more high tech than the usual run-of-the-mill restaurants.

I wrestle to hold the door open. "Tenley, please. He's coming for you. He wants the memories."

"Tell him I don't have them." She manages to shove my hand off and slams the door in my face. I hear the click of the lock and Tenley disappears from view in the dark cafe.

"Tenley," I cry, banging on the door. "I'm sorry! I made a bloody hash of it. *Focking* hell." I rest my head on the cool glass door.

Maybe I can fix it.

A movement in a pile of blankets on the sidewalk makes me jump. "Got any change?" the homeless man asks, his face still creased with sleep.

"I got nothing," I say as I walk away.

"Sorry about your luck," he grumbles and burrows back down into his nest.

Literally, I have nothing. No phone, no wallet, no laptop. No friends.

For the first time in years, no one knows where I am.

I stand on the sidewalk and look around the quiet city like I'm seeing it for the first time. A bus thunders by, followed by a few cars. It's still now, but soon the chaos will start. I've been in the city long enough to know mornings are loud and busy, with streets packed with cars rushing and sidewalks full of pushing people headed to work.

For once, I don't have anywhere to go.

Since I was fifteen, I've been under Eugene's control, afraid he'd turn me in to the *garda*, afraid he'd turn me out of his house. Afraid of losing the security I'd worked for.

I've thrown it away because I feel *bad* for Tenley.

What's gotten into me?

I've done a long con on a politician's family without an ounce of guilt. I've stolen all kinds of things, including piggy banks, without feeling *bad*. What's with the sudden conscience?

"Bloody hell," I mutter.

Lysander won't understand my sudden turn from the dark side. This is bad. This is stomach-tied-in-knots, ready to hurl, bad. At least he doesn't know where I am. Toronto is huge, teeming with people. It will be nothing to fade into the crowds and wait for Lysander to be in a better mood.

Do I want to wait?

Leaving Benjy's is akin to cutting ties to my life. Do I want to wait for Lysander to reel me back in?

I always imagined that as a child, Lysander being a small-minded, grasping bully who hated to be thwarted in anything, whether it be losing a rugby game or his best girl. He hasn't changed much, only grown taller and more brutal in his getting what he wants.

And then it hits me like a slap in the face. Minka tried to warn me, but I didn't make the connection. Or didn't want to make the connection. Falling in love with Henry took me away from Lysander. He stole Lysander's toy, and there's nothing worse than a jealous little boy.

Lysander killed Henry to get me back.

Declan.

I break into a run as I weave around dog walkers and those stupid enough to be up so early. Thankfully, I had stalked Declan enough to know exactly how to get to his building. I make it there in record time, breathing hard and cramping from the run. The outside door is open, and I rush into the foyer with relief.

Of course, the inside doors are locked. It's five-thirty in the bloody morning. Why did I leave my phone behind?

I run my finger over the list of residents, hover over the button marked *D. Dodd.* My finger hovers over it. Declan can buzz me in and I can tell him everything.

I don't push the button.

Stalking to the corner of the foyer, the hood of my jumper pulled over my head, my thoughts race quicker than Declan drives. For once, I don't know what to do. If I go to Declan, that's it. I can't turn back from that. Lysander would never let me back in, and all my hard work over the years will be for nothing. My security, my family—gone. And for what?

There's nothing left for me. Declan will be safe—for now. Tenley won't trust me again, so I can't help her. There's nothing in this for me. All this worry and uncertainty is messing with my mind. Would it be better to slip away and –?

A man with a cap pulled low and clutching a *Starbucks* coffee pulls open the door. A tickle of fear brushes the back of my neck as he swipes a card to unlock the inside door.

Starbucks isn't open this early.

I'm a second too late. My fingers scrabble on the door, but it locks with a click. The man strides across the lobby like he belongs there. Maybe he does.

I punch the button beside Declan's name, again and again. The man in the cap vanishes into the elevator. When there's no answer from Declan, I run my hand down the row of black buttons, hearing the buzz, giving the occupants a wake-up call that no one's going to appreciate.

"I'm sorry, people! I've got to get in," I cry, trying Declan's button again.

The door unlocks with a click and I pull it open. "Ta!" I call as I sprint to the stairs.

Declan's apartment is on the sixth floor and I race up the stairs like there's a banshee on my heels.

I ease open the door with my shoulder and peer out. Declan's apartment is 618, just around the corner.

The man with the hat is standing outside the door.

Twenty

- -

"WHAT'S THAT YOU'RE DOING?" I cry, hustling down the hall. The hat jerks up and I stop short.

It's Robbie. He takes two steps toward me.

"Bloody hell." Without a thought, I rush straight for him, at freight train speed, and clothesline him with a strong arm to the neck. He goes down like a sack of bricks.

"What the *fock* are you doing here?" I kick his leg with the toe of my boot.

Robbie coughs as he gets slowly to his feet. "The boss wants to talk to him," he says, one hand rubbing his neck where my arm caught him, the other on the wall for support.

"Bollocks. Lysander only sends you to do his dirty work, not to pick up. What're you planning?" I surge to my full height, my fingers stabbing at his chest.

With a swift move, Robbie swats away my hand, catching me full in the face with a hard right. I stagger back.

"You'll have to take that up with the boss, Pippa, *love*." Robbie grins, showing a mouthful of coffee-stained teeth.

A door opens, surprising both of us. "What's going on out here?" An older man pokes his head out into the hall, his face still creased with sleep.

"I think you should go back to bed," I tell him. His eyes widen as he takes in Robbie and I. The door slams behind him and Robbie moves with a dirty uppercut that knocks the wind out of me with a whoosh.

He blocks my first punch and the next, but my third right hook finds the perfect spot against his jaw that sends his head banging against the wall.

When he stands upright, he's got a small knife in his hand. I see a bit of a red leather handle—it's *my* knife. The thought of his dirty hands rifling through my bag makes me see red.

"*Sonofabitch*!" A sharp kick sends the knife flying out of his hand. I follow it up with a knee to the groin that sends Robbie to his knees. But as I dance around him in an attempt to reach Declan's door, Robbie catches hold of my ankle. I land on my face in the hallway.

Robbie is on me before I can catch my breath. He flips me over and delivers a stinging punch followed by a backhand to the mouth, sends my head crashing against the thin carpet. My eyes fill with water at the force of the blows. I think he cracked my cheekbone.

"You should leave well enough alone," Robbie says, bringing his face close to mine as he presses his forearm against my neck.

"*Fock* you, you bloody bastard," I cry in a hoarse whisper as Robbie's arm blocks my windpipe. This isn't what's supposed to happen. I yank frantically at Robbie's arm between slaps at his head. Black dots dance before my eyes as my breath is cut off.

Enough of this *shite*. I buck up with my hips, using my core to raise my legs enough to smash Robbie in the shoulder with my knee, and slam my palm against his nose.

It works. He loosens his grip and I push him off into the wall.

He gets to his feet just in time for me to kick him in the face as I cartwheel by. A strong roundhouse kick sends him flying.

I'm torn between chasing him down and finishing him off and seeing Declan. With a muttered curse, I bang on Declan's apartment, leaving Robbie to stumble down the hall back to the elevators.

"Pippa?" The happiness in Declan's voice when he opens the door warms my heart, the smile on his face makes my eyes prickle with disappointed tears. "What are you doing here? Are you hurt?"

"Get inside," I huff, pushing him back into the apartment before he's finished. "He might have sent more."

"What's going on? You're hurt. Pippa, you're bleeding."

Oh, lord, he sleeps in red flannel pants and a T-shirt. How bloody adorable, with his blond hair standing on end, and with a day's worth of stubble. I can't help myself and throw my arms around him, burrowing my head into his shoulder and getting blood all over him. I breathe in his scent—sweet and sleepy and Declan.

His arms tighten around my waist, and I slip my hands under the thin cotton shirt, feeling the bandages around his ribs. Tenley was right. He is hurt.

I did this. I choke back a sob.

"Pippa? I'm glad you're here, but why—what's going on?"

I take another moment to enjoy being close to him before I pull away with all the willpower I can muster. "I'm sorry, Declan.

You have to call Ham. Tell him Lysander Mochrie is coming after you." Declan's expression is still one of confusion. "He works for Mielson."

"I don't understand."

"I just... in the hallway... he sent someone."

I can't tell him. I really can't.

"Was that you in the hall? I heard something, but I thought—"

I take a deep breath. This is the hardest thing I've ever had to say, but might as well do it, like ripping off a Band-Aid—in one fell swoop.

But worse.

"Declan, *I* work for Mielson."

It's so much worse than I expected. Bewilderment and disappointment flash across his face before understanding sets in, hardening his handsome countenance into granite. He steps away from me, only a few feet, but the distance seems forever. "Seamus said something last night, but I didn't believe him. I said you wouldn't..."

"I'm sorry. I never wanted you to find out."

"Seamus was telling the truth?" Declan shakes his head like he's rid himself of a horrible thought. "This was just a job for you, wasn't it? A way to take down the Agency."

I can't look at him.

"It wasn't that, I just needed this file—Tenley got it first, and I was trying to get it back. I didn't know about anything else—"

"I'm supposed to believe what you say? I'm just a mark to you. A way in to get the information, a way to get into the Agency."

"No. *No*, Declan, you're not. I really—" I stop myself because I'm about to tell him that I love him.

Love him.

"This is real for me," I say instead. Declan snorts in derision. "It is. Declan, I—"

"That was you last night? You set it up." His words puncture me like bullets. "You told Benjy where to jump us."

"I can explain..." The anguish in my voice is real, and pain clutches at my throat, hurting more than Robbie trying to choke me. "I never meant—"

He shakes his head. "I don't want to hear it. Get out. Go tell your boss everything he needs to know."

"Declan..."

"Piss off, Pippa." His voice is low and harsh and cuts right through me. "I don't appreciate being used."

There's nothing I can say, nothing I can do but wipe away the tears trickling down my cheeks. "I didn't use you. It wasn't like that."

"Is it the language causing the problem? You screwed me over. And Tenley. Don't forget about her. I thought she was your friend, but I was wrong about that too. That's what I call being used."

I don't have the heart to argue because he's right. I did use him and Tenley. "It was my job, but not anymore. I've been with them since I was fifteen, and I've done things I'm not proud of. But I can't let him hurt you," I say simply. "Lysander killed someone I loved and I can't let that happen to you, too."

Declan studies me, his face tense with anger, but at least he's listening.

"Will you call someone?" I beg, turning away. "So you're safe? Lysander's coming after you. Robbie was just the first."

Declan gives a bark of humourless laughter. "I don't need you to take care of me."

"Please, Declan... I know it's my fault. I'm sorry."

"You're damn right it's your fault. How could you do that to Tenley?" Declan's voice rises, but I cut him off. The threat to her shines like a beacon. If Robbie was here, then when—

"Tenley! They're going after her too," I say urgently, backing towards the door. "I tried to warn her, but I didn't think they'd move so quick. They know I left... I've got to go."

"Stay away from Tenley," Declan cries as I yank open the door. "And me."

I can't speak. Taking one last look at his perfect face, I run out of the apartment.

Twenty-One

I TAKE THE STAIRS two at a time. I have to force myself to stop
crying because I won't have enough breath to make it to the
bottom.

Is Benjy already at Tenley's cafe? Did she tell Ham she was in
trouble? Did she believe me?

I run faster, glad it's still early so there aren't many people to
dodge.

Declan was a distraction. Lysander took a chance that's where
I'd go. Maybe I can make it there before—

An arm sticks out of the alley I had hid in earlier, catching me
around the neck in the same move I used on Robbie.

And like Robbie, I end up flat on my back, gasping for air.

Charlotte leans over me, blocking out the weak morning sun.
"What do you think you're doing here?"

"Came... to warn...Tenley... to help..."

"No one needs your help, Pippa. Haven't you done enough?"

Massaging my throat, I push her aside with my free hand so I can get to my feet. As soon as I stand upright, Charlotte punches me in the mouth.

I stand there and take it. She hits me again. A perfect right jab that feels like she's pushed my eye socket into my skull.

"You done now?" I ask when she pauses.

"Maybe."

"Bloody hell." I touch my lip with a finger and find it covered in blood. "Do you have to hit so hard?"

"That's nothing."

"Look, you can kick my arse later, but you need to get Tenley out. Hide her."

"Before your big bad boyfriend shows up?"

The bell over the door to Tenley's cafe tinkles. I turn to see Ham. He doesn't look surprised to see me, but there is a deep frown on his face. "Charlotte—sixty seconds," he says without taking his eyes from me.

Charlotte shoulders me aside. For a short girl, it's pretty effective. "Get Tenley out of here. Go through the alley; Seamus will meet you on the next street over," she barks at Ham.

"Hello, Pippa," Ham says in a cold voice, blocking my way into the cafe. The lights are on, but there's no comforting smell of coffee and scones drifting out.

Even this early in the morning, Ham is dressed impeccably in starched khakis and a pristine white button-down shirt with a tie. He doesn't say anything about the fresh bruises marking my face.

"You'll make sure she's safe?" I demand. I crane my neck to see past his solid shoulders, relieved to see Tenley by the kitchen door, a bag in her arms. "And her daughter?"

"They wouldn't dare," Charlotte says as Tenley's face loses all colour.

Ham steps aside to let me in the door. "What do you know?"

"Not enough. This is Benjy's idea, but he's not running it. It's all Lysander. And..." I pause, cracking my knuckles on my right hand. They're cut and bruised from last night and swollen from hitting Robbie. "You need to watch out for him. Please. He's dangerous. And you have to make sure Declan's safe. They've already been there."

"What do you want for this?" Ham asks, his voice cool and abrupt.

"What do I want—what do you mean?"

"For providing us with information about Mielson?"

I back away. I've done what I need to do and now I can disappear. But while the thought of a life free from Lysander is a heady one, I know I'll always be looking over my shoulder. Lysander won't forget this. "I—I don't want anything. Just make sure Tenley is okay. Declan, too."

Ham gazes at me, expressions of distaste and admiration warring on his face. He catches me by the shoulder before I turn to leave. "You didn't have to come back."

"Yes, I did." As soon as I found out what Lysander planned, there was no other option. Tenley is—was—my friend. I need to fix the mess I made.

"Charlotte, bring her in when this is over," Ham calls. "Seamus won't take kindly to her coming with us now. But keep her hidden—we'll have more use for her if they don't know whose side she's on."

His words spark a warmth deep inside me. Somewhere to go. Somewhere safe, even though it's more of a demand than an invitation.

"What's this crap?" Charlotte asks in bewilderment. "Ham, she's nothing but a liar."

"She was doing her job. She'll be good as backup."

"Or she won't be!"

I stand flabbergasted as Ham strides across the cafe, his authority fitting him as well as his clothes. The door is open but still I don't leave. Am I a prisoner or a willing participant?

"We'll discuss this later. Be safe." With a last long glance at Charlotte over his shoulder, he ducks into the kitchen.

Tenley stands by the door into the kitchen with a forlorn expression on her face. "Try not to..." She looks around the cafe with a hopeful shrug. "Please."

Another woman with short, spiky dark hair and numerous piercings steps out from the swinging door. "Don't worry, Ten, we'll keep the place safe."

"Safe isn't the issue. It's the inevitable trashing of my place that I'm worried about," Tenley says.

"Simon has Lucy?" Charlotte asks, peering out the front door.

The relief is evident on her face. "It's really good timing that they're at Disney," Tenley says with a ghost of a smile.

"Good. Get out of here. Seamus is like an old worried woman when you're in trouble."

Tenley flicks her gaze at me but I don't drop my eyes. "This isn't me. I didn't know any of this was going to happen."

She turns without another word. I hear the kitchen door leading to the alley slam shut, leaving me alone in the cafe with Charlotte and the dark-haired girl, who is staring at me with curiousity.

She jerks her chin towards me. "Who're you?"

"That's Pippa. The reason we're all here on this bright, early morn," Charlotte says with mock cheerfulness. "Apparently she works for Mielson."

"You don't say?" Dark hair looks me up and down with a disdainful smile.

"We're supposed to *hide* her." Charlotte uses her fingers as quotations around the word.

"Don't do me any favours," I tell Charlotte.

"Don't think you're getting out of here that easily." Charlotte stands before the door with her arms crossed. "Ham wants me to bring you in when this is over, and I always obey Ham."

The dark-haired girl chortles with laughter and Charlotte joins in. "Yeah, not really. Look, duck behind the counter there," she gestures. "And keep quiet. I don't expect any trouble. That's Alessia." She turns and peers through the smoked glass door.

"No trouble?" Alessia demands sadly.

"Well, not too much. I've no doubt they're going to be a little disappointed when they find us here and Tenley's flown the coop."

"You have to watch out for Lysander's minions," I tell her as I head behind the counter. Should I stay in the kitchen? Out here? Run like hell? Lysander won't be expecting trouble, and I doubt he'll bring a full crew. Maybe he won't even come himself.

Alessia frowns. "Is that what he calls them?"

"That's what I call them."

"Trouble walking down the street," Charlotte announces as I crawl into a space between the now empty display case and the wall. A set of shelves blocks me from the sight of anyone on the other side of the counter. I don't mind a fight, and have gone looking for one more than once, but this time, I'm in no hurry to face Lysander.

"Small, rat-faced guy," I hiss at Alessia, standing before the kitchen door. "Be careful of him more than the big guy. He had a knife."

Alessia nods without turning her gaze from the door.

The bell over the door tinkles. "Good morning and welcome to *Soup du Jour*," Charlotte says in a cheerful voice. "Unfortunately, we have no specials this morning because our boss isn't here."

"Where is she, Charlie?" Benjy. Good. Maybe he's taking charge of this, and Lysander stayed home in bed.

"That's rude," Charlotte says. "Aren't you going to say good morning?"

"Say good morning to the lassie."

My breath catches. It's Lysander. I pull my knees to my chest, trying to make myself invisible.

I hear the shuffle of feet, a fist hitting a body. A gasp, distinctly male.

"And that's rude," Charlotte reprimands. "Don't they teach you in Scotland not to hit girls?"

"Ireland." I can picture Lysander grinding his teeth. He hates it when someone gets the accent wrong. "Robbie, check the kitchen."

"Got it, boss."

"Customers aren't allowed in the kitchen," Alessia drawls. I don't know where she's standing, but it sounds close. I resist the urge to peek out.

"Do I look like a customer?" Robbie demands. "Now, get out of my way, *soith.*"

"I don't know what that is, but you look like an ass," Alessia retorts. "Sorry—*arse.*"

Robbie's response is drowned out by the scuffle of fists.

She's good, I decide, finally peeking out from my spot. Graceful and strong; she's holding her own against the wily Robbie.

Until she knocks him down behind the counter and Robbie catches sight of me crouching there.

Twenty-Two

---

*P*OG MO THOIN!

    I'm not sure if it's me or Robbie who says it. But Alessia quickly realizes he's seen me and gives him a sharp jab in the face to keep him quiet.

He pulls her down and they wrestle on the floor. Robbie throws her against the counter close to me and it takes her more than a moment to rebound.

I make a move to crawl out from my hiding spot, but Alessia holds up her hand. *I got this*, she mouths.

Bounding to her feet, she gets Robbie in the prime position beside the end of the counter and, with a ferocious front kick, sends him flying. A table crashes.

A shrill scream fills the air. "Alessia!" Charlotte cries.

That's enough for me. I leap to my feet and over the counter like it's a pommel horse. Mikhail is the first one I see, and I give him a kick to the side of the knees before he has a chance to react.

Alessia is down, clutching her shoulder, and before I can get there, Robbie kicks her in the stomach. Two strides get me to her just as he pulls back his leg for another kick, but I drop into a crouch, and with a sliding side-sweep of my leg, knock him off his feet.

Robbie is back on his feet as quickly as I am. "*Soith.*" He pulls out his knife—my knife—again and lunges towards me.

I jump away from his slash and grab a nearby chair. With a mighty swing, I hit Robbie across the head and shoulders. The vibrations ring up my arms, but Robbie goes down beside Alessia. She grabs his head and slams it on the floor until his eyes roll back.

Alessia grins at me as she gets to her feet. "This how you treat the guys you work with?"

I snatch up the knife that fell out of Robbie's hand. "Mine."

"Pippa, love, what do you think you're doing?"

I turn in slow motion at the sound of Lysander's voice. He has Charlotte in a headlock, his arm pressed tightly against her throat. Carl and Mikhail flank him, and Benjy stands off to the side, nursing a bloody nose and a foul expression.

A trickle of blood drips from Charlotte's forehead, but other than that, she looks unhurt. She's not even struggling against Lysander's hold and when I meet her gaze, I have a feeling she can break free whenever she wants to.

"This is mine," I say. "You know better than to take my things." I hold the knife out in front of me. My voice is cool and controlled, but inside my jumble of nerves pop and jump like a cut wire.

"*Your* things?" Lysander's eyes are dark and cold. "You're nothing without us, Pippa. My father made you."

"He's charming," Alessia says scornfully.

"Give the knife over," Lysander demands in a quiet voice. "You nae belong here."

It's not even a choice. "No." I see the vein pop in Lysander's forehead, his face flush red with fury. I've never seen him so angry. I'm afraid he might snap Charlotte's neck. "Leave her be."

"Are you telling me what to do?" His voice is a whisper, his words ominously measured.

I take a step back on shaky legs.

"Your girlfriend did a great job warning us," Charlotte gasps.

My jaw drops. What the holy hell is she doing? "I didn't!" I stammer. "I came but—"

Charlotte continues like I haven't spoken. "Tracking device on her coat. Good that she left it with you. We knew when you were coming."

"Is that so?" His jaw clenches and Charlotte gasps as his arm tightens around her neck. He doesn't take his eyes off of me.

There's no coming back now. Whatever kind of monster Lysander is, he's been *my* monster for the past fourteen years. Brother, lover, protector, boss... I swallow my fear of being alone, push down the regret. They'll be no showing any weakness.

"Benjy, Tenley's not here," Charlotte says in a whisper. "The memories are gone."

"No! You couldn't have come up with a way to take them out," Benjy cries, all but stamping his foot with frustration.

"No point in—she's no use to you." Her face is pale, and she gasps for breath, but she's still talking like there's nothing wrong. "Something special you want to find?"

Even being held by a man twice her size, with an arm pressing her windpipe, Charlotte is a smart-ass. A glimmer of admiration surfaces.

"Maybe he wants to wipe out any memory that he's been nothing but an arsehole." Alessia steps over Robbie's still-unconscious form to stand beside me. "But you can't, so why bother? I think we should call it even and you head out on your merry way? Or we can keep going." She glances at me with a smug smile. "I'm pretty sure Irish is on our side now."

Lysander sniffs. "Three girls? Is that supposed to frighten me?"

"Those three? I'm out of here," Benjy says, heading for the door. Mikhail is right behind him.

"Good choice," Alessia calls after him.

Lysander holds firm, still with Charlotte at his mercy. Her face is slowly turning blue, but she doesn't struggle. I meet Lysander's gaze and take another instinctive step back. I'm used to his calm composure, so to see him so close to losing control is brutal. If he wants to continue this, I know he's coming after me. My stomach twists with fear. "Lysander... don't..."

"My father will hear about this." His voice snaps like ice.

"Tell your da I'm truly sorry." I swallow against the lump in my throat. "He gave me everything and I'll never forget this. I didn't want to disappoint him, but I can't—"

"You'll pay for this." Lysander's glowering glare is as ominous as his words. He nods at Carl, who helps the dazed Robbie to his feet. Lysander waits until his minions are at the door, before backing up, dragging Charlotte along.

"Hang on there..." Alessia stalks after him. I follow, filled with dread at what he's going to do with Charlotte, still holding my knife.

Can I use it against Lysander?

But after another glare at me, Lysander shoves Charlotte into Alessia's arms and disappears out the door.

I heave a shaking breath, and then another. He's gone.

He left me behind.

After working side by side with him for half my life, he left me without a word. "He *focking* left me," I say incredulously.

"Don't let the door hit you on the *arse* if you want to chase after him." Charlotte says in a hoarse voice, rubbing her neck.

She stalks through the cafe. There's not much damage other than the tables knocked over, and the chair I hit Robbie with looks a bit out of shape.

"Well, that ended well," Alessia says. "Tenley will be happy we saved her place."

"All right?" I ask Alessia, noticing her arm hanging stiffly by her side.

She winces. "No biggie. I think he dislocated my shoulder."

"Robbie's little trick. Here." I set the knife I'm still clutching on a nearby chair and take Alessia by the shoulder. It's easy enough to find the socket and bone. "It's a simple fix—" With a jerk and an answering squeal from Alessia, I reset her shoulder.

"Jesus! A warning next time might be nice," Alessia cries.

The tinkle of the bell over the door almost sends me into the ceiling with shock. An older man walks into the cafe tapping his watch with a frown. "You should have been open thirteen minutes ago."

"I am not watching this cafe for her this morning," Charlotte mutters.

"I apologize, sir," I say, stepping forward with a cheery smile. "As you can see, the place is in a bit of a tip. We had a break-in last night, and Tenley's gone off to deal with it. I'm afraid we're going to have to close up today." I give him mournful expression.

"Oh," the man says, with a frown. "No coffee, then."

"Coffee maker's broken," I lie.

Muttering under his breath, he stomps away, the mirror image of Benjy.

"We're getting good at disappointing people today," Charlotte says cheerily, as I lock the door after him.

I do my part to make sure the cafe is left the way we found it, but don't join in with Charlotte and Alessia's conversation. There's too much running through my mind.

I'm alone.

I haven't felt fear like this since I was fifteen. When my mother died, things moved fast and before I even had time to begin to grieve, I had been shipped from the outskirts of London to my uncle's place in Belfast. I barely lasted a year before his wandering hands and bad temper forced me to leave in the dead of night.

I found myself on the streets, friendless, with only a few quid to my name. Alone.

It was a bad time and the dreams of those nights spent running from shadows, hungry and afraid and huddled in doorways trying to stay warm, still jerk me awake at night.

I was on my own for three months and seventeen days before I stole Eugene Mochrie's wallet from the pocket of his suit jacket. It had been stupid to try, but I hadn't eaten in days. I still remember the way Eugene looked, walking through those streets like he owned them. They were *my* streets. What was such a nancy boy doing here?

At the time, I'd thought it was the smartest, stupidest decision I'd ever made. Eugene took me in and the fear of being alone slowly faded, but I never forgot.

I know I can survive if I run, but I don't want to live with that fear again.

"Let's go," Charlotte says after she tapes a note on the door that the cafe will be closed for the day. "We're done here."

Both she and Alessia have bruises beginning to blossom on their faces. Charlotte's forehead has stopped bleeding, but there is still dried blood on her cheek.

I remember my first fight.

I had fought on the streets, but that was for survival, for food or money. Eugene had sent me into the house of a business rival to pick up money that he was owed.

The money had been locked in the safe in the man's office, and his twenty-year-old son had tried to stop me.

I found out later the son had been taken to the hospital with a broken collarbone after I shoved him down the stairs.

Bruised and bloody, I had shown up at Eugene's house with a bag of money, shaking with exhaustion.

"I'm proud of you, girlie," he had told me. He had cleaned the blood from my hands and face and fed me bangers and mash.

Why I am thinking about that now?

Alessia turns off the lights and Charlotte waits for us by the door. When I don't respond, Charlotte frowns. "Don't even think of making a run for it."

"Her legs are short, but she's fast," Alessia points out.

I stay where I am. "What does he want with me?"

Charlotte shrugs. "Got me. Same thing you want probably—information." She takes a moment to study me. I think I look okay on the outside—calm and cool. But inside I'm shaking from the mess of emotions tangling me into knots. "Is it better if we take you by force? Does that make it easier?"

"Why would you want to do that? Make it easier, I mean."

"The guy's a douchebag, but he was your douchebag."

I snort. How is it that with a simple sentence, Charlotte lets me know she gets it? She can't know everything, but it's enough. "Yeah, that would be better."

Twenty-Three

C HARLOTTE AND ALESSIA TAKE me back to Mutual Liberty Insurance.

"Back to Ham's security firm?" I say sarcastically as Charlotte punches in a code to get into the parking garage.

Any friendliness from Charlotte and Alessia, as little as it might have been, disappears as soon as we enter the building. On the drive from Tenley's cafe, both were civil. Alessia even asked me a few questions while Charlotte pretended to glower. I have a feeling Charlotte Dodd is not normally the glowering type.

But everything changes once we enter the building. I'm not restrained, but the way Alessia and Charlotte flank me, it feels like I am. Both of them get serious faced and the hard knot in the pit of my stomach grows.

I don't know how to fix this.

In the lobby of the building, Charlotte leads us across the marble floor to a door set away from the banks of elevators and swipes a key card to open in. Inside is another bank of elevators. Charlotte places her palm on a computerized screen jutting out of the wall and leans closer to scan her eyeball.

"Charlotte Dodd," a robotic voice says as the elevator doors slide open. "Good morning, Charlotte."

I look around wildly for the source of the voice. "What's that?"

Alessia smirks as she jerks me forward by the arm into the elevator. "Guess you're not as high tech back home in Scotland."

"Ireland." I study the car. It looks normal, with mirrors and a gleaming white floor.

"Hi, Agatha," Charlotte says to the wall as the doors slide closed. "Could you have Ham meet me at his office?"

"Of course, Charlotte. You will arrive in sixteen point nine seconds."

"You have a talking elevator?" I ask. My stomach gives a lurch as we drop at a dizzying speed. "Bloody hell, that's fast."

"We are descending at a speed of .895 floors per second."

"We're what? How far down?"

"The offices are two hundred feet below the surface," the voice retorts. "Approximately twenty floors."

"Who are you?" I ask in bewilderment. Eugene has a good setup back home, but his secretary, Siobhan, barely acknowledges me when I come in, let alone gives me chatty fun facts.

At least I can see Siobhan.

"I am AG416, otherwise known as Agatha," the voice reports. "I'm here to service all your needs."

She sounds downright perky. I fight the urge to introduce myself.

"The upgrade sounds the same," Alessia points out, peering at herself in the mirror. "Why didn't Perry change the voice? Maybe a nice Australian guy. Wouldn't you like an Aussie mate telling you g'day?"

Alessia does a horrible Australian accent. It's no wonder she can't tell the difference between Ireland and Scotland.

"Perry prefers my soothing, informative voice," Agatha says.

"It is a nice voice," I add.

"Stop talking," Charlotte says irritably. "You don't need to know any of this. You're not staying."

I want to ask why I'm even here if I'm not staying, but the elevator comes to a stop. I glance at the mirrored ceiling, seeing my worried reflection. "This is really underground."

"Way underground," Alessia agrees. "You get used to it."

The doors slide open and Charlotte grabs my arm to lead me into an all-white hallway with the same spotless floor as the elevator. She marches me down the hall with Alessia trailing behind.

I've been to many countries, doing odd jobs for Eugene, acquiring certain things, but never has a place seemed so foreign to me. If I was walking around the International Space Station, I don't think it would feel as strange. And I can't put my finger on *why*. I've been to offices of high-ranking government officials, law enforcement, drug lords and a madam operating a brothel in Indonesia, but being in the bowels of the Agency beast is throwing me off my game.

I have no game. Maybe that's what's throwing me.

Charlotte has a tight grip on my arm, but I could get loose if I wanted to. I can tell from Alessia's face that her shoulder hurts, even with me popping it back into place, so she wouldn't give me any trouble.

Why did I pop her shoulder back in? And why did I help them? I would have been easy to take off from the cafe during the fight. Or here—turn around and hot-foot it back to Elevator Agatha and she'll get me out.

I glance over my shoulder, gauging the distance back to the elevator.

"Declan!" Charlotte exclaims.

My head swivels at the word. "Declan. Your face..."

I reach out instinctively to touch him, but yank my arm back when he looks at me like I'm a snake ready to strike. It hurts my heart to see him. The bruises weren't noticeable earlier in his darkened apartment, but under the bright fluorescents in the hallway, the purple-red blooms on his face are unmistakable and look painful.

"Thanks to your friends," he says.

"I didn't mean for you to be hurt."

"What about Lottie and Seamus? Was it okay if they took a beating? And Tenley?"

Nothing hurt as much as seeing the scowl on his face. "Declan, I'm—"

"What's she doing here?" he snaps, turning to Charlotte.

"Ham has some questions," Charlotte says, sounding bored.

"All she's going to do is lie."

I take a deep, shuddering breath that cuts me to the quick but it sets me straight. I gave up my spot with Eugene for nothing.

I'm really on my own.

"Thank you for coming in," Ham says politely, ushering me to a chair across from his desk.

"There wasn't much of a choice."

I look around. The room is a mixture of what I would imagine a CEO's office would look like, all big desk and files, and the lab of one of the geeky geniuses from *The Big Bang Theory*. Computers and technical-looking equipment cover every surface, along with scraps of paper, and empty coffee cups. I hope that's a fake sword hanging beside a mini basketball net affixed to the wall. There's a wee bit of everything in here. Instead of giving me insight about Hamilton Short, ruler of the Agency, his office makes me even more confused. I don't know if he's going to punish me or pat me on the head.

Charlotte sits beside me, looking like she wants to be anywhere else. Alessia, whom I thought of as my potential ally, deserted me in the hall. She went off with Declan, and I had to force myself not to follow. Declan clearly sees me as enemy number one, and I'm not about to chase after him like a wounded puppy.

Wondering where he went is different than chasing after him, but doesn't make me feel any better.

Joining the party is a woman with dark hair and vaguely Southeast Asian features who stands behind Ham and gives the impression of a being a watchdog. Her expression is even less welcoming than Charlotte's.

Ham appraises me from across the desk. I stare back at him, willing my expression to go blank, trying to hide the hurt of seeing Declan.

Ham steeples his fingers, resting his elbows on the desk. There's a red file on the desk before him.

I decide to strike first. "So what's that in your wee file there?"

Ham picks up a file on his desk and begins to leaf through it. "Pippa McGovern-Stock, agent of the Irish Intelligence Party."

"Guess a girl can't keep her secrets in here."

"We're an *intelligence* agency," Charlotte says scornfully. "Your disguise wasn't all that good. Or maybe I'm better at seeing through it."

"If you have something else to do..." Ham says to Charlotte, the suggestion clear in his voice.

Charlotte holds her ground. "Is there something Pippa's going to tell you that I shouldn't hear?"

"No."

"Then I'll stay."

The quick exchange is enough to allow me to grab on tight to my composure. No sense letting them see how rattled I am. I've been through interrogations before, and this isn't it. I'm not sure what this is. A chat over tea? If that's the case, they forgot my cuppa.

"The name's Pippa Katherine Felicia McGovern Stock," I tell them. "Named after my great-aunties. Although I've been thinking of dropping the Stock. It's the only thing my da ever gave me, but I'm not sure I need it."

Ham gives a barely perceptible nod and continues. "You work closely with Eugene Mochrie. Strong ties to Lysander Mochrie." He pauses with a glance at me. "You're aware the Mochries work for Mielson?"

"Yes." That was an easy question. No harm there.

"You're aware the Mielson has been responsible for the instability in the intelligence community? That they are trying to take over individual organizations and combine them, which would mean no country's secrets will be safe? That these actions would lead to wars and assassinations of leaders and dictatorships?"

That's a little more difficult. "Well... that's not how it was explained to me," I hedge.

"And how was it explained to you?" Charlotte asks in an icy voice.

"It wasn't," I admit. "Eugene sent me out, told me what he needed, and I got it. He left me out of the big-picture discussions."

"I take it Lysander was part of these discussions."

"You'll have to ask him."

"Just how close are you to Lysander?"

"That's none of your business."

"It's Declan's business," Charlotte says sharply. She crosses her arms and looks away with a huff. Ham raises his eyebrows but says nothing. His eyes are such a dark blue they look almost black, which makes it difficult to read him. I can't really see him with Charlotte.

"How long have you known who I am?" I ask, moving the conversation away from Declan. I have no desire to talk about Declan and Lysander in the same sentence.

"We did some research on you after Revello's party," Ham continues. "You've made quite the name for yourself in Europe. Impressive."

"It's not that impressive," Charlotte mutters. "A couple heists. She's a common thief."

"I once got something out of the red box going into Buck House. There's naught simple about that." I grin at her scowl.

"Like I said, Pippa, your victories have been impressive, and I'm sure they've helped cement your spot in the organization. What

I've learned about Eugene Mochrie is that he prefers to work with family. You're one of the few outsiders he's brought into the fold."

I don't respond. I know full well Eugene thinks of me like a daughter and here I am singing to Ham like a canary. There's loyalty for you.

"When you came into Tenley's cafe, we came to the conclusion you were working on Mochrie's orders, trying to infiltrate the Agency," Ham continues.

"I wasn't trying to infiltrate anything." I wish I had a plan. I wish I'd thought it out more because now that I'm here, I haven't got a clue what I'm doing. I may be good at solo missions, but as I sit across from the head of the Canadian intelligence organization, I've been taking orders from others.

But now, whatever I tell Ham is up to me. It's a heady sensation, but it also makes my stomach knot. With my luck, I'll end up with any ulcer.

"You were trying to get Robert Revello's list of beta testers for his new search engine," Charlotte says. "All the information that was collected from his tests. The info that Tenley got away with."

I try to look innocent. "Is that what that was?"

Charlotte shakes her head with disgust. "Why did you want to bring her in? She's not going to tell us anything."

"Why don't you go check on how Alessia is?" Ham invites. "I can take it from here."

"You're trying to get rid of me," Charlotte accuses.

"You're not exactly objective," the woman behind Ham says in a patronizing voice.

"Payton and I can take it from here." Ham is polite, but even I know there's no point in Charlotte arguing with him.

With a martyred sigh, Charlotte gets to her feet. "Don't even think about nosing around my brother while you're here," she snaps.

"I don't plan on being here that long."

"Good." The door closes louder than necessary and I don't miss Ham's sigh of resignation.

"Charlotte's very protective of her family," Ham says.

"No shit, Sherlock," I snort.

"Why are you in Toronto, Pippa?"

"To see the sights," I reply blithely.

This would be easier if they locked me up. Or tied me down. Answering Ham's questions is like giving a baby medicine. You can tell them it's good for them, but it still doesn't make it taste any better.

The realization that I've cut myself off from Eugene's organization has sunk in, but I won't know the ramifications for a while and until then I'd like to keep from jumping into bed with Ham and his crew.

Even though jumping over that counter to clock Robbie was akin to getting ready to go to bed.

"Am I wrong that you had the same mission as Charlotte—Revello's list?" I keep my gaze trained on Ham's desk. "We gave you the opportunity to complete it."

"No, I made the opportunity. That was what Benjy was for—to get me inside." I bite my lip as the truth spills out. It's not so bad. They knew about that.

"Do you honestly think we leave computers sitting around for guests to hack into?" Ham raises an eyebrow. "We knew who you were, Pippa, and as soon as Benjy showed up in that parking garage, we knew what you had planned. You were just doing your job. It's unfortunate but... we know you passed the information on to Eugene Mochrie." Ham pauses. "Apparently he has a buyer—Jacqueline Robineau. A meeting has been scheduled."

Maybe the Agency is better than I gave them credit for.

"Why are you telling me this?" I ask. "What do you want from me?"

Ham leans forward, his dark gaze searching. "What I'd like to know, Pippa, is what you're still doing here. You could have been long gone by now. What do you want from us?"

What am I supposed to say to that?

Twenty-Four

"I 'LL MAKE THIS EASY for you, Pippa," Ham continues. "We have a file on you, a fairly extensive file. We know Eugene Mochrie got you off the streets when you were fifteen and molded you into his personal thief. There isn't a lot you can't—or won't—acquire for him. We know of your close relationship with Lysander Mochrie. You seem to be his right-hand woman."

"I wouldn't say that."

"What would you say?"

I don't say anything. I stare at my hands in my lap, my fingers twisting.

"You have no family, and consider the Mochrie's as your own. They've had your complete and utter loyalty for the past fourteen years."

"Has it been that long?" I mutter.

"And to repay you for your indiscretion with Declan Dodd, they've put a contract out on you."

My head jerks up and I grip my fingers so tightly they crack. "That's a bloody lie."

A contract. As in a contract for someone to kill me.

Me.

"You weren't aware of that," Ham continues relentlessly. "But I'm sure you knew what would happen when you turned against them."

As much as I pretend otherwise, I know Ham's telling me the truth. Lysander is being petty and nasty.

I can't seem to breathe properly. I knew Lysander was angry about Declan. I knew he would be furious when he learned I was taken into Agency headquarters. It didn't matter if I was a prisoner, or went willingly—to Lysander, I should have never let it happen.

I was captured by a Mossad agent once in Egypt. Lysander didn't even bother trying to get me out, although with Eugene's reach, it would have been easy to arrange a ransom. No, Lysander left me to suffer all the indignities of being held prisoner. In his mind, I had allowed myself to be caught, the same as if I had willingly given them information.

Which I didn't.

It took me six weeks to get myself out of there, and another three months until Lysander felt like he could trust me again. That time was bad enough; I never imagined that he would take things even further.

But it's not the thought of a contract being put on me that sends me into a tailspin. "What about Declan?" I whisper, my voice straining with unasked questions.

That's when I realize I have got it so *bad* for Declan. Much worse than I ever imagined.

Why the *fock* did I ever put myself in this position? How could I be so stupid? I've prided myself on being the ultimate professional, and now, after snogging a few times, I've thrown everything away, including my bloody life.

"Declan." The chair squeaks as Ham leans back. I can tell right away that he knows what I'm feeling. I never thought I was so bloody easy to read, but after Charlotte knowing too much about me, all I want to know is how they learned that bloody mind-reading trick. It must be a Canadian thing.

"Therein lies your problem," Ham continues. "Tenley was your mark, and you played her perfectly. But Declan was different. I sensed that the moment I met you, and I'm sure Lysander Mochrie did too. He's a dangerous man," Ham says, sympathy, whether it be real or pretend, evident in his voice.

"I'm not worried about me." Even I think I sound worried. "But Declan..."

"Is fully protected," Ham is quick to assure me. "I can offer the same to you, Pippa."

I meet his gaze and hold it. "No, you can't."

"I think you can stop underestimating us."

"You say you can, but really, what can you do? And what do you want from me?"

Ham shrugs. "Information. A few chats like this."

"I won't help you take them down."

"That's what you've been trained to say," Ham points out. "But your behaviour this morning tells me differently."

"I didn't like what they were doing. With Tenley. They threatened to use her daughter. That's it. Everything else—it's not my fight."

"What is your fight?"

"I don't have a fight."

"I think you do. You knew a man named Henry Wallace?"

I close my eyes. Please don't talk about Henry...

"He was killed seven years ago, in an apparent robbery gone wrong. Our files show Lysander Mochrie had him murdered."

A giant hand clutches my heart and squeezes so tightly that it's hard to breathe. I open my eyes to find Ham watching me. "You knew that, didn't you?"

"No... maybe... I don't know." I take a shaky breath, and then another. "I didn't know for sure."

"Consider it confirmed. Like Charlotte said, we're an intelligence agency, and a very good one. I realize what I'm asking is difficult for you, Pippa. I understand the ties of a family. It was the same for me. My uncle might have helped create NIIA, but it was the senior Seamus Dodd who took me under his wing and taught me everything. Declan's grandfather."

I don't say anything. My mind is reeling. Lysander did have Henry killed. Part of me knew it, all of me suspected it, but I never did anything about it. I told myself Lysander wasn't capable of it, but I forgot that he was perfectly capable of giving Robbie the order to deal with Henry.

Robbie would have taken a knife... my knife.

He would have done the same to Declan.

"Help us save Declan," Ham says quietly. "I know it's a lot to ask. I'll give you time to think about it."

"I don't need time," I tell him in a choked voice. "Do you know how Seamus Dodd was killed?"

"It was an accident..." Ham trails off.

"I met him once," I say, my voice unemotional, like I'm reporting a news story. "Nice man, scary as *fock*. He came to supper at Eugene's, drank his brandy, smoked his cigars. I remember Eugene called him a *wily cat*. And when he left, I'm fairly certain Lysander was given the order to take him out and make it look like an accident."

Payton gives a gasp, the only sound she's made since Charlotte left. Ham looks at me with a shocked gaze that he doesn't even bother trying to hide.

"You didn't know about that little tidbit, did you? I'm not just a thief, you see; I'm good at keeping secrets. I think that bit of information makes us even. I'll help you make sure Lysander doesn't come near Declan. But I'm not telling you anything else about Eugene. That's off-limits."

"We need to stop them."

"I've no doubt you will, but it won't be with my help. Once Lysander is out of the way—locked up in a small cage, preferably, I'll be on my way. I just want to make sure Declan is safe."

"He will be."

"He better be. Your head's up your arse if you think this'll be a piece of piss."

After my chat with Ham, Payton takes me to a room that is a half step up from a prison cell, but still cleaner than my latest digs. "This looks comfy," I say sarcastically, flopping down on the thin mattress.

"It could be worse." Payton stands by the door with her arms crossed and a frown on her face.

"Oh, don't tell me you've got a hate on for me, too." I tuck my arms beneath my head. "I just met you. Usually it takes a wee bit to turn someone to the dark side."

"I seriously doubt that."

"You don't even have the authority to keep me here. It's not like you're the *garda*. I'm doing you a favour."

"You should keep thinking that." Without another word, Payton leaves. Despite the lack of authority, the door locks with a click, leaving me alone.

I've never minded being alone before.

Until now.

I've got no one.

Somewhere in this hole in the ground is Declan. He's in hiding because of me. He wants nothing to do with me because of what I've done—lying, cheating, stealing...

Technically, I didn't cheat.

What did I expect? I work for a man who is trying to take over the intelligence community and make a tidy profit from it. No one will ever be safe again, especially not the agents here. They're Declan's family.

But Eugene is my family.

He must have known about Henry.

For a moment, I let my rage towards Lysander build and bubble. It's easier to be mad at him than scared silly.

And I am scared. Curling up into a ball, I let my thoughts lead me to Declan and fall into an uneasy sleep.

A soft knock on the door wakes me. When I open my eyes, the sudden brightness of the white hall is just as effective as sunlight pouring into the room. I squint at the figure standing by my bed.

"Lunchtime," Tenley says. From the expression on her face, she hasn't come to fetch me out of the goodness of her heart.

I'm getting tired of this pariah act.

"Look, Tenley," I begin, swinging my legs over the side of the bed. "I need—who are you?" I demand as a man steps into the room, one who looks vaguely familiar.

"Perry Dodd. I'm here to make sure you get fed."

I study his face. Declan's brother, with the same blond hair and handsome features. Under his glasses, Perry's eyes are darker, more grey than blue, but it's still easy for them to pass as brothers. "Oh."

"Ham said you'd be hungry." Perry speaks more formally than Declan. Frankly, he sounds a bit like an arse.

I stand up; regardless of what he sounds like, my tummy is hollow and anything sounds good right about now. "Starving."

And then I glance down at myself. I'm still wearing the same clothes I wore to the movies last night. There's blood on my shirt and stains on my jeans from rolling around the parking garage. I surreptitiously sniff my armpit. Do I smell?

It feels like forever since Declan picked me up, and I slid into the car and kissed him...

"As you can see, I'm not looking my best," I say. "Hope you're not taking me anywhere fancier than the local McDick's. Anything but poutine."

"How's the local cafeteria sound?" Perry asks.

"Sounds schoolgirlish, and I forgot my uniform."

Tenley shakes her head with disgust at my flippant tone. "Eat, and then you can have a shower. There should be some clothes around that will fit you until we can pick up yours."

"I don't have anything," I admit, the sudden vulnerability making me feel like I'm standing naked in front of a pack of rugger buggers. "I left my pack with Lysander, and I don't think he'll be hurrying to get it back to me."

"Everything?"

"Every stitch. Plus my laptop and my wallet. And my toothbrush." I hold out my hands. "All you've got is me. I haven't got a quid to my name. Here, anyway. I've got things back home, but again, they're not going to be pleased when I show up to collect my last paycheck."

"We'll deal with it," Tenley mutters, leading me into the hall without another word.

"You know what would be nice? One of those scones from your little cafe." She glances over at me with a raised eyebrow. I smile apologetically. "Too soon?"

She doesn't answer.

"Look, Tenley," I try again. "I'm, well, I'm sorry if you think I meant anything. I didn't. It was just my job."

She glances at me, eyes narrowed. "Do they not teach you how to apologize in Ireland?"

"I'm not that good at it. But I'm sorry if I—that I..." I shrug ruefully. "I didn't like doing it. I mean, I liked hanging out with you. It was fun working in your place. You're the first friend I've had in a long time, and I'm sorry I made a hash of it."

Tenley's expression thaws slightly and she nods.

That's all she gives me.

Tenley and Perry escort me to what looks like a high school cafeteria, or what I imagine one would look like, had I gone to a proper school. Living on the streets, and then with Eugene, meant no proper schools for me.

I did get my high school diploma, though. You can get anything online these days.

A laughing group sits at one of the tables. This place smells better than I expected. My stomach rumbles a reminder to feed it.

Tenley leads me to a door into a kitchen. Steam rises from trays, mixing the aromas and making my mouth water. I don't remember the last time I ate—possibly the popcorn at the movies last night?

Minka gave me a sandwich at Benjy's. The memory makes me feel even guiltier.

"What'll it be?" the man behind the counter asks with a grin.

There are trays of already made sandwiches, oozing with thinly sliced meat and cheese, looking better than any deli, hamburgers, fries, mac and cheese.

"How many agents do you have here?" I ask in amazement. "This is a ton of food."

"We're a big organization," Tenley says. "It surprises everyone."

"Yeah, cuz Canada..." I trail off.

"Leads the world in intelligence and information-gathering techniques. Not to mention the technologies we've developed."

"You sound like you're giving me the spiel."

"Do you think I want you to work here?" she snaps.

"Look, I said I'm sorry!" I turn to the server. "I think I'll have the mac n'cheese." There's no sense wasting time arguing when I could be eating.

Perry and Tenley sit with me. When I see Tenley's burger, I regret taking the pasta until the first bite. They talk in quiet voices as I wolf down my lunch.

"So here's the double agent." I look up at the sound of Alessia's voice standing by the table with a handsome, dark-haired man behind her.

"Hi, Tyler," Tenley says. The two words have more welcome than what she's given to me all day.

"Double agents usually have two teams to work for. Last count, I had zip," I explain to Alessia as she takes the seat beside me.

"So you're not planning on hanging around? Tyler, this is Irish. Irish, this is Tyler Dunn." The way Alessia smiles at him suggests more than simple coworkers.

"Pippa." I correct.

"Have we met before?" Tyler frowns like he's trying to remember me.

"I don't know. Maybe?" He's older, with greying hair at the temple and tired eyes, but there are laugh lines etched into his face that tells me he was once more light-hearted than his appearance suggests.

Something about him triggers a warning in the back of my mind, but I keep it to myself.

Tyler frowns and Alessia pats his hand. "I'm sure you haven't seen her before." She meets my confused stare. "Tyler lost his memories a while back and they're slow coming back."

"Is that anything like...?" I turn slowly to Tenley, recalling what Colin and Minka had said.

Tenley rolls her eyes at Alessia. "Tyler and Charlotte had their memories of the Agency removed to go undercover. That way, no one could talk if they were caught."

"That's... hardcore," I stammer.

"It's something," she says with a frown. "Long story short, the device that puts the memories back in is broken and Peyton hasn't been able to fix it, so Tyler's memories are stuck on a computer disc."

"Except the ones you have," I say slowly. Her eyes widen. "Colin Darcy is a friend of mine. And Benjy said some stuff. So did Minka."

"Minka?"

"She's the one who helped me get away from Lysander. She said no one should go through what you did."

"Minka said that?" Tenley asks with amazement.

"She's not bad, except when she's beating the crap out of you." Alessia steals a handful of Tenley's fries.

"Minka..." Tyler's brow furrows. "She's a big girl, isn't she? Tall."

"You could say that," Tenley and I say in unison.

Twenty-Five

Aᶠᵗᵉʳ ʟᴜɴᴄʜ, Tᴇɴʟᴇʏ ᴛᴀᴋᴇs me with her when she stops by the lab. I meet Ida, a purple-haired sprite with tattoos and piercings and the coolest gadgets this side of a James Bond movie. Apparently she invents the tech for the agents, like this cream that melts glass and special batons that give a good jolt. For the first time, I have a desire to park my shoes at the Agency doorstep just so I can play with the toys.

I start to wander the room, my eyes wide with awe, until Ida snaps not to touch anything.

After the quick visit, Tenley escorts me back to my room, and I'm happy to see a pile of clothes waiting for me on the bed. They're not mine, but at least they're clean. She points out the shower before she leaves. Food, a shower and something clean to wear helps to feel more like myself, but it doesn't do anything for my growing uncertainty.

What am I doing here? It's clear I'm not a prisoner, but I'm definitely not an invited guest.

What would Eugene want me to do?

The thought pops unbidden into my head. I've been drinking the Eugene Kool-Aid for so long it's hard to think for myself.

What do *I* want to do?

I have to admit, NIIA has a pretty sweet setup. Bigger than I thought, more efficient than I imagined. They caught on to me from day one, and I'm good.

They may be better.

May? They are better. Or they better be if they want to keep one step ahead of Lysander.

I spend most of the afternoon, fresh and clean and lying on the uncomfortable bed, staring up at the ceiling and wondering what I can do to call off Lysander.

Alessia finally shows up for escort duty. Ham has summoned me back to his office.

"How's the shoulder?" I ask as she leads me down the endless white corridor.

"They gave me nice drugs," she says with a grin. "Scotty says you did good at popping it back into place. The worst thing about it is that it's the same arm that I got shot in."

"You got shot?" In all the years with Eugene, I've been in danger countless times but avoided serious injuries like being shot or stabbed or gotten any broken bones. Eugene used to say it was because I was so flexible.

I've been thinking about him a lot today.

"It's how I met Tenley." Alessia brings me back from my memories.

"The thing with the memory swap. Tell me about Tyler," I invite.

"He has some memories, and more come back every day," she says as if reciting a passage.

"That's tough. What about Charlotte?"

"Same. Her memories mainly come back as dreams. I pity Ham for having to sleep next to her. When he does sleep, that is."

"So she doesn't remember being a spy? How can she do the stuff she does?" Should Alessia be telling me this? Should she be walking down this creepy long hall with me like we're on the way to the pub?

But she is, and we are. It's no wonder I'm confused. What do they want with me?

"Peyton says it's muscle memory," Alessia says. "Like riding a bike or having sex after a *really* long time. Charlie's got talents that she'll never forget. Same as you and me. We'll always be spies."

I think of myself as more of a thief than a spy. My CV would list me as Professional Intelligence-gathering Thief.

I guess that makes me a spy, then.

"What about Tenley?" For once, I ask out of simple curiousity, not to gather info to use against her. "They put Charlotte's memories in her head, so does she know everything Charlotte does?"

"Pretty much. That's what makes her so good. She's only been working here for six months or so, and you've seen her in a fight. She's pretty awesome. Not as good as me, but pretty awesome."

Alessia and I will get along just fine. If there's a need for me to get along with anyone.

"Thanks for coming," Ham says as we enter, gesturing us to chairs. The space seems neater than my earlier visit, even with the row of straight-backed chairs lined up before his desk. Charlotte,

Tenley, and Perry are already seated. They turn to stare at me as I take a seat.

Alessia shivers as she turns a chair around and sits, resting her arms on the back. "Brings me back to all my trips to the principal's office."

"I don't like being so outnumbered by women," Perry frowns.

"Thanks for being so misogynist," Charlotte says.

"You think *you're* outnumbered?" I mutter.

"We're just waiting for Declan to get here," Ham continues like we haven't spoken.

My heart leaps at the thought. "Is he okay?" I ask hesitantly.

"Ask him yourself," Charlotte retorts. "Actually, don't bother, because he doesn't want to speak to you."

"Charlotte," Ham chides in a low voice. "Declan can make his own decisions and fight his own battles."

There's a decision to be made? Do I have a chance to make this up to him?

But when Declan walks in a moment later, any hope plummets like a broken elevator. He doesn't even glance at me as he takes a seat the furthest away from me. In my defence, Ham is the only one Declan acknowledges.

I try not to make it obvious that I'm staring at him.

"Thanks for coming in," Ham says to Declan. "You normally aren't a part of operation meetings, but I wanted you here since you're directly impacted."

Out of the corner of my eye, I see Declan glance over at me.

"Eugene Mochrie has been arrested," Ham announces.

"What?" My shock rings through the room. "How?"

"Thanks to you, actually," Perry says, his gaze on the data pad in his hand. "Or because of you. After you passed on Revello's list of names, Mochrie met with his buyer, who is affiliated with Interpol."

I sit back, a whoosh of air escaping. "That can't be true."

Perry passes me the data pad. On the screen is a video of Eugene being led to a car, his hands cuffed behind him.

It could be a fake.

I recognize the house as Eugene's.

I did this. I brought Eugene down. All the years I've tried to make him proud of me, all the times I've competed for his attention, his respect, and I'm the one who brought him down.

There's no pride in this, only shame. I close my eyes. If he thinks I'm responsible...

"I'm not sure of the actual charges..." Ham glances at Perry for confirmation.

"Industrial espionage," Perry supplies. "He's been disavowed by every country he's been affiliated with, so he's on his own. Interpol has located Niall Mochrie in France and is working on bringing him in."

"And Lysander?" My voice is hoarse with fear—for myself, not Lysander.

But of course Charlotte doesn't realize that, and she gives a great snort of disgust at my question.

"Still at large." Ham frowns at a pile of papers before him. "And that leads us to this meeting. Pippa, you know him best. What do you think Lysander will do?"

"I don't know."

"I told you she wouldn't help us," Charlotte explodes.

"I can't help, because I *don't know*." I round on her. "I never thought he'd kill Henry, but he did. And he sent Robbie to Declan's, so..." I trail off and meet Declan's gaze, holding tight to my heart. "This is my mess. I'll fix it. There's no sense you doing this dance. Send me back and I'll fix it. Declan was part of the plan, nothing more than a mark. Means nothing to me. That oughta do it."

Charlotte snorts. "You're not that good of an actress. You're hung up on my brother. That's obvious. So, you manage to convince him that you're not—what's the Big Bad going to do then?" She pantomimes handing me a gun. "He means nothing—take him out. How're you going to get out of that?"

"What do you suggest, then?" I don't mean to sound so harsh, but I can't help it. This is the only plan I've come up with.

"You say he's going to try and take me out?" Declan asks. For once he's not scowling at me. He's not smiling either, but it's a start. He looks...

Excited.

"I've no idea what he's going to do," I admit. "Right now, I don't think he's the full shilling."

"Let's catch him in the act," Declan says. "Stop him and then take him out, so neither of us ever has to worry again."

"You're not being bait!" Charlotte bursts out.

"Bait?" It takes a moment for Declan's suggestion to sink in, but the instant it does, I shake my head with enough vehemence to send my hair flying every which way.

"It's not a bad idea," Perry muses, stroking his chin. For a moment, he looks like Declan. They have the same expression of stupid determination.

"No way," Charlotte cries. She has a similar expression, only more intense, with flashing blue eyes and a clenched jaw. For once, she doesn't look like a kid playacting at being an adult.

The debate between the siblings goes back and forth for several minutes, with the non-Dodds wisely staying out of it. At one point, Charlotte leaps to her feet. I think she's ready to take a swat at Perry, until Declan tugs her arm.

"Lottie, it's all good," Declan soothes. "Let this Lysudder guy give it his best shot." I think he's mispronouncing Lysander's name on purpose, but I can't be sure, and I'm bloody well not going to correct him. "I know you'll stop him. You're better than him."

I'm afraid to comment on that too, because what if she isn't?

"Declan's right," I announce. "I think it's the only way."

"What do you propose?" Ham demands.

"Lysander will go for Declan somewhere it'll hurt me the most," I say, thinking fast. "Henry—Henry was killed outside a pub. It was where we first met. With Declan," I glance over to find him with his blue-eyed gaze locked on my face. I can't read his expression but it's not the cold indifference it had been earlier. "He'll go bigger. In Lysander's mind, Declan took away his favourite toy, and he wants revenge."

"You consider yourself a toy?" Disgust leaks out of Alessia's voice.

"No, but he does."

"How will he do it?" Ham asks in a low voice. "Attempt it."

"It'll be personal. An accident maybe, but it'll have to be where no one else will be hurt. He's got a bit of a soft spot for innocent bystanders."

"You're kidding me," Charlotte mutters with a roll of her eyes.

"So we pretend to go on a date?" Declan asks. "And he tries something and we stop him."

I frown, thinking it through. "I don't think it's enough. He knows he's wanted so it'll have to be something worth it. Something that would really mess me up." I stare at Declan, not wanting to say what I'm thinking.

The plan that's popped into my head, already fully formed.

It's crazy. Insane. Bigger than anything I've ever attempted.

And I think it will work.

"So what?" he demands. "You're thinking. I can tell."

Something inside me melts, because even after everything, Declan still gets me.

"Pippa? What is it?"

"We get married."

Twenty-Six

"**Y**OU ARE *NOT* MARRYING my brother!" Charlotte is back on her feet. If I had any reservations about the idea, seeing Charlotte shrieking like a banshee would set me straight. If there's one way to make me do something, it's telling me I can't.

"Charlotte, we're discussing things. We're looking at options," Ham says in a firm voice.

"This is not an option. And there's no discussion."

Charlotte's reaction doesn't surprise me. I probably wouldn't want me to marry my brother. And I honestly don't care what she thinks about it. As much as she might think differently, Ham is the one in charge here.

And Declan. This is his life, so he should have the last word.

"You want to marry me?" he asks me incredulously.

"I don't want—I mean, I don't think..." There is no good way to answer that question, so I finally stop trying and settle with a helpless shrug.

"It would give the opportunity to flush out Mochrie," Ham muses, tapping a finger on his desk. "But it's asking a lot of you, Declan."

What about me?

"It won't be a real wedding." It's Perry who makes the comment, but it cuts through me like a hot knife to butter. I don't want to marry Declan, but I don't want to *not* marry him, either.

Do I want to marry Declan? Maybe in a perfect world... I try to stop the giddy thrill that buzzes through me.

I have an image of me in a white dress, with Declan smiling down at me. It's a simple dream, like a teenage girl who writes *Mrs. So and So* in her notebook would dream, but it's nice. I've never had the image before, except with Henry. And after Henry, I pushed all the happy thoughts of the future deep down.

"Are you willing to do this?" I assume Ham is asking Declan, but when I glance up, he's looking at me.

"I want Declan safe, and Lysander put away. Whatever it takes. What do you say?" I turn to Declan, with a fake smile on my face. "Will you marry me?"

The discussion about my pseudo-wedding is relatively short.

Declan quickly agrees, and once Ham is on board, Charlotte's arguments fall on deaf ears. I sit back and let the others sort it out.

It's not a *real* wedding.

It's a trap, like Admiral Ackbar said in one of those Star Wars movies.

My head is telling me one thing, while my heart is a wee bit flummoxed. I see Declan sitting quietly and wonder what he's thinking about this. He's going to be my husband—not my real husband, of course. Only real enough to keep him safe, and that's what's important.

I still want to snog him senseless. But even if he'd let me, the cut on his lip would make it painful.

I did that.

Ham is starting in on logistical stuff when I stand up with an obnoxious scrap of my chair. "Mind if I take a break? You don't want me here for this."

"She probably shouldn't be here," Charlotte mutters.

Ham glances up at me. "That's fine. Can you find your way back to your room?"

My cell, you mean? "Sure, no problem. I'm knackered, so I'll try for a nap. Lots to do... planning a wedding." I flash a fake smile. "Which you're going to plan for me."

"Fine." Ham waves me towards the door. "I'll update you later."

"I'd appreciate that." As I turn to leave, I meet Declan's gaze. He looks like he's about to say something and I pause, but nothing is coming. Giving him a tight-lipped smile, I take my leave, feeling all eyes on my back as I slide out the door.

I'm sure most of them would like to stick a knife into me.

Two wrong turns, three requests for directions later, I finally break down to ask the mysterious Agatha-voice for help. I'm in my room for exactly sixteen minutes. Just long enough to make sure Declan isn't coming after me.

It's a lot easier to find my way out of head office than it is to navigate the maze of hallways inside. And I'm sure some alarm will go off when they realize I'm gone, but by that time I'll be out of here.

It's their own fault for leaving me alone.

I make it to the parking garage using a code stolen from Perry earlier and a fake excuse for Agatha. It's difficult to lie to the computer. I still don't know where the voice is coming from, so how do I know she doesn't have some secret power that can tell if I'm lying?

During the quick stop at Ida's lab earlier, there were enough little parts lying around for me to put together a decent lock-picking kit. Leaving like this wasn't part of the plan, but if I have the chance to venture outside, shouldn't I grab it?

I don't think about what might be waiting for me. Or who. Lysander might have put a contract on me, but it's only been a few hours. He'd have to call in favours from the Europe crew. Maybe some of the Americans. How many hitmen are in Canada?

I'll be back before anyone notices I'm gone.

My steps slow as I come to the pretty blue sports car. I'll be even quicker if I borrow this.

The security in Declan's car is good, but no match for me. Thanks to the wire and thin metal bar I swiped from Ida's, it takes no time to get the door unlocked and slide in. I never took the time to appreciate the vehicle before since I had been too busy appreciating Declan, but it's nice. Clean too, with nary a fingerprint or food wrapper in sight. The interior smells like him—musky with a hint of sweetness. I sink into the driver's seat, pretending the comfortable leather is Declan's arms around me.

I've got it so very bad.

The car quickly growls to life. Declan's going to hate me even more when he finds out I've stolen his car.

Borrowed. Borrowed sounds better.

The soothing voice of Adele asks hello from the speakers. I had expected music from another boy band from the 90s. If N'Sync is for when he's happy, what does it mean when he's listening to Adele?

Listening to Declan's music makes me feel strangely closer to him.

I ease Declan's car out of the parking garage. Employees of Mutual Liberty Insurance swarm the sidewalk in front of the building, completely oblivious to what's going on below them. Do they know there's a bunch of spies living under them, like a bloody mass of ant tunnels?

The car creeps down Bloor Street. Don't these people know I have somewhere to be? I keep my gaze on the rearview mirror, expecting to see Declan and Charlotte legging it down the street after me. And Perry—

That nancy boy's really going to have his knickers in a twist once he finds out how easy it was for me to leave. "You don't have the balls to drive this car like it should be driven," I mutter.

I've done my research, memorizing streets and landmarks; I know five different routes to take from that dingy hotel out of the city and all the major intersections with red light cameras. If Eugene taught me anything, it was how to thoroughly prepare for every outcome.

But nobody expected an outcome like this.

I bang my head onto the steering wheel with frustration at the five o'clock traffic. How does anyone get anywhere in this city? It's like the car *wants* me to go fast. But the other cars on the street won't let me.

I jump the light with a series of honks and angry fingers, turning onto Mount Pleasant Blvd and out of the congestion of Bloor. Jamming the car into third gear, and then fourth, I weave around the harried accountants and soccer moms trying to get home from work.

This car bloody well does want to go fast!

I don't slow down until the lights of St. Clair.

"*Fock* me," I mutter. There's a black SUV two vehicles back, the perfect distance for a tail. It caught my eye when I pulled onto Bloor, but I never thought—

I never believed Lysander would go through with it. And I honestly didn't believe Ham when he told me there was a contract on me.

It's a black generic SUV with tinted windows. It could be Carl and Robbie. It could be Papa Poutine for all I know.

When the light turns green, I bully my way to the right-hand lane. They're right behind me.

Who is it? I can take just about anyone in a fair fight, but this isn't fair. So let's play dirty. With a squeal of tires, I make the next right.

"*Focking* bloody hell!"

It's a dead-end road. A cul-de-sac, I think they're called. Stupid name.

The SUV is right there with me.

"You want to play, then let's play."

I hit seventy clicks bloody fast in Declan's sporty car. A dog walker shakes his fist at me as I race by. Just as I'm about to barrel up the driveway at the end of the street, I yank the parking brake, sending the car into an impossibly tight three sixty.

I speed towards the SUV. A game of chicken, then.

Declan's car seems really small compared to the SUV, especially when it's barrelling down the street towards me.

Am I really going to ram them? This car will put a wee dent in their great hulking truck.

For the first time, I wish I had a gun.

Closer... we're only two houses apart. I see the driver by now and it's no one I know. Maybe this isn't for me. Maybe this is only a coincidence...

I swerve right at the last moment, only inches from the bumper. The SUV over corrects, or the driver isn't as comfortable with road racing as I am, because with a screech of brakes, he jumps the curb and drives across a manicured lawn.

The man with the dog is running to the car, this time shouting as well as shaking his fist as I speed away.

I don't even stop at the end of the street but barrel straight onto Mount Pleasant Blvd. The luck of the Irish as well as the traffic gods are with me and I make it across all four lanes of traffic with a lot of horns and tires screeching, but not a scratch on me or Declan's car.

That was fun.

Twenty-Seven

MY HEARTBEAT HAS RESUMED its normal thump by the time I leave Declan's car in a lot a few blocks away from Tenley's cafe. I hurry along the sidewalk, trying to look inconspicuous as well as watch everything around me. There's nothing that triggers the danger sense, but the game with the SUV tells me they're out there, maybe more than one bunch.

Maybe this wasn't a good idea.

The sun hides behind the buildings and I shiver in my thin T-shirt. It's not my shirt; it's not even a shirt I'd buy for myself, and it's a little too tight, which calls attention to the puppies.

The third male I catch checking out my chest looks away in fear when I growl deep in my throat.

I know it's dangerous, but I need to know what's going on. Without my kit, the only change to my appearance is to pull my hair back into a messy bun. It does nothing to hide the colour, but it does disguise the amount of it. I wish I had one of my hats, or my fake glasses, but Lysander has all of that. I feel naked.

Ham may be telling the truth, but how am I supposed to know if I can trust him?

I don't know who I can trust.

The sign I left in the window of *Soup du Jour* this morning is still there. With the lights out, the place looks a little sad. I stand across the street and wait, trying to blend in.

Thankfully, I don't have to wait long.

"I'm surprised to see you." The British voice is a soft husk, almost like he's whispering in my ear.

"I'm not." I smile ruefully at Colin, still with the dark hair and without the glasses.

"What's happening?" he asks with a worried frown. "It's not like Tenley to close for the day."

"Let's go to that pub from last time," I suggest, and his frown deepens. "I'll fill you in, but it'll have to be inside."

Without another word, Colin turns and leads me to a pub half a block away. It's different from the one he took me to last time, less upscale, more me.

I find a table where I can face the door, all senses alert. Lysander may have acted quicker than I imagined, but he's not getting the jump on me again.

"Is Tenley all right?" Colin demands as I catch the waiter's gaze.

"A pint of Guinness, please," I tell him as he hovers by the table. "You?"

"Nothing. What happened?" he persists as the waiter departs.

"She's flying it," I assure him. "There was a little kerfuffle at the cafe this morning, but she's all good."

"Did Benjy try for her again?"

"With his new bestie, Lysander." Even as I talk to Colin, I keep my gaze fixed on the front door. "She's safe. The Tenley story is over, so you can go back across the pond. Nothing to worry about."

"Over... as in..." he trails off with an expectant air.

I shrug. "I don't know anything about that. But she seems all normal... nothing like anyone else."

I'm sure Colin will report what I say back to Benjy or Lysander, or both, but I'm not going to make it too easy on him. And I don't feel bad for lying to him. As far as Colin is concerned, he's better off thinking Tenley got rid of Charlotte's memories. Better for Tenley, too.

Colin smiles, an expression of relief on his face. "I'm glad."

The waiter appears and I must have the same relieved smile on my face as Colin does. "I can murder this," I say, taking the frothy pint glass and tipping it back for a welcome mouthful. "It's been a pisser of a day."

"What's going on?" Colin asks.

Taking another gulp of Guinness, I wipe the foam off my upper lip before answering. "You know, just pissed off the wrong people."

"Lysander."

"Mainly him."

Colin gives me a sympathetic smile. "Do you ever think getting involved with the Mochries was a mistake?"

"I think Lysander getting in bed with this Mielson thing caused the big stink. That was none of me." I sigh heavily. "I was having a *craic* being a thief."

"You're playing in the big leagues now, Pippa."

"No, I'm done. Wiping my hands of it all." I demonstrate for effect. "Time for a simple life for me."

"I can't see you settling down for the simple life, Pippa."

"You know what?" I give him a rueful grin. "Neither can I. Sounds good, though, doesn't it?"

Colin glances over his shoulder and leans closer. "You've heard about Eugene?"

"That'd be my fault, too. Or so they think. How's he making out?"

Despite everything, there's still a big part of me tied to Eugene. Prison isn't easy, and being a powerful man can make it worse. He's not as young as he used to be.

"He's being held without bail. Other than that, he's fine. Why are you here?" Colin asks bluntly. "This is dangerous for you."

"I knew you'd be around and I need to know what's going on. What news of Lysander? Do you know his plans? What have you heard?" When Colin remains silent, I lean across the table and grasp his hand. "You play both sides, but I'm asking you to stick with me right now. We've been friends a long time and I've no one I can trust. You're my only hope."

Colin smiles at my intentional *Star Wars* quote. "Honestly, Pippa, I'd tell you if I knew anything. It's gone dark. Whatever they've planned, they're not saying anything."

Which means Lysander either hasn't got a plan yet, or he's going to be doing a real number on me.

For a second, I want to tell Colin to deliver me to Lysander, in the hopes I can talk him down. Maybe he won't go after Declan if he's got me back in his clutches. The urge is there, like stealing the last slice of pizza when you've already had half a pie.

"What do you need?" Colin asks. "Are you safe?"

"For now." I toy with my glass.

Could I? Would it work?

"You're not that good of an actress."

Maybe Charlotte was right.

"You're with the Agency."

It's not a question and I don't hesitate with my answer. "I'm not with anyone. I'm looking out for me now." Part of my plan was to tell Colin that yes, I went with Charlotte willingly. Colin may be my friend, but he has a job as well, and he knows what side his bread is buttered.

"But they're keeping me safe," I admit. "For now."

I don't tell him about the wedding. Not yet.

I study his face. He looks tired. Colin has been on the job for almost ten years now, and feeding Eugene intel on the side for almost as long. Working both sides can't be easy. "I can't think why you don't go home."

"I will," he says heavily. "Just a few things to finish up."

He's not about to tell me what those things are. "Is there any way you could get a phone to me? I left mine behind. Along with everything else." I glance at my beer and then back at Colin with a winsome smile.

Colin nods. "I'll see what I can do."

"I don't know how you can get it to me. I doubt I'll be allowed out for another stroll."

"You shouldn't be out now. I'll find a way. A burner phone?"

"If you can. Tenley should be back tomorrow." I nod to the window even though *Soup du Jour* is no longer visible.

"Is her daughter safe?" Colin asks with a worried frown.

"She'll be enjoying rides with Mickey right about now."

"Good."

"She's a nice girl, but Colin..." I trail off. I want to tell him he has no hope with Tenley, but don't know how to say it without sounding like a right bitch.

"I know," he says with resignation. "I hope she's happy with him."

"You'd be my first choice," I tell him loyally. "But Tenley is smitten with Seamus."

"I'd probably be smitten with Seamus, too." With a wry smile, Colin pushes back his chair and stands. "Let me go first in case you were followed."

"I know the drill, Colin. I took care of the first wave, so it should be all clear."

Colin frowns down at me. "Don't underestimate him, Pippa. You're not as careful as you ought to be and I'd hate to see anything happen to you."

"I'd hate to see something happen to me, too." I stand and throw my arms around him. "*Ta*. You've been a good mate."

"Don't write me off yet." He pats me on the back, then pulls away. "Be safe."

"Always."

With one last smile, Colin disappears into the crowded street, leaving me to finish my pint alone.

Since he wasn't making a move to pay for my pint, I snatched his wallet when I hugged him.

Twenty-Eight

I stay put, watching the door to the pub swing open as people come and go. Colin's wallet makes an uncomfortable bulge in the waistband of my pants as I sip my Guinness. I smile as the figure slides into the chair next to me.

"I should have known you're not the type to follow orders."

"No one gave me any."

Charlotte pulls my glass towards her, takes a sip of the dark brown liquid, and grimaces. "This stuff is crap."

I snatch back my glass and take a healthy swallow. "The piss yellow water you call beer is crap."

"That's the American stuff. Canadian beer is good."

"I'll take your word for it."

I'm not surprised when Tenley joins us. I assumed they'd send Charlotte after me, but it was a toss-up whether it would be Tenley or Alessia to come with her.

"How do you know Colin?" Tenley asks, pulling out the chair across the table from us. Her cheeks are pink and eyes are bright.

"Who?" I feign ignorance.

"I saw him leaving."

"Did you follow?" Charlotte asks her.

"For a bit." Tenley's eyes slide away, so I know Colin gave her the slip. That must have been hard on him. I'm sure he would have loved a chat.

Charlotte turns to me. "So is this your idea of a nap? What's wrong—you didn't want to stick around and talk about your wedding?"

"It's hard to get excited when you're already talking about divorce." I wipe away the ring of condensation on the table left by my glass.

"Aw, Pippa got her feelings hurt? Do you blame us?"

"There's enough blame going around."

"What were you doing with Colin?" Tenley asks, going back to Colin like a dog with a bone. She picks up the drink menu lying on the table between us.

I pull my glass back and lift it up in a half salute. "I knew he'd buy me a pint of the black stuff." I finish the Guinness, watching Tenley's eyes widen over the rim of the glass as I chug it, gulping loudly. Setting it down with a flourish, I sigh with satisfaction. "Reminds me of home. You can take me back to your leader now," I say, even though the last thing I want is to go hide out underground.

The same waiter, now wearing the smile reserved for women out on the lash, hovers by the table and asks Tenley and Charlotte what they'd like to drink.

"I need a vodka tonic," Tenley says without hesitation, flipping the drink menu shut. "Actually make it a double. It's been a helluva day, and it's not over yet."

Charlotte glances at me. "Are you going to have another?"

The question throws me. "Are you buying?"

"She'll have another and I'll have one too," she tells the waiter, who smiles wider, no doubt with visions of a fat tip on his mind.

"You shouldn't be here," I hiss as the waiter walks away. "It's not safe."

Charlotte frowns at me. "I checked the perimeter. Do you really think he—?"

"I do, because he did. There was a car following me. I took care of it."

Charlotte eyes widen. "And Declan's car?"

"Is just as pretty as it was the first time I saw it."

"What happened?" Charlotte demands, sounding exactly like Perry.

It's because of her insistence that there's more than a little pride in my voice as I recap the end of the SUV. Maybe not the *end* end, but the end of their attempt to follow me. "I can take care of myself," I finish.

"Fine. Try it." Charlotte pushes back her chair and motions to stand up. Tenley grabs her arm.

"Stop it. We're on the same side—the Declan side," she adds as Charlotte opens her mouth to retort.

An uneasy silence falls on the table as the waiter approaches, balancing our drinks on his tray.

"You just said Guinness was crap," I say to Charlotte after he leaves.

Charlotte's smile is hidden by the rim of the glass as she takes a sip. "Like I'm going to admit I like it to you. How did you get Declan's car?"

I shift my gaze. "I borrowed it. Since we're to be married, I didn't think he'd mind."

"I think that's called stealing," Tenley puts in.

"No, how did you actually *drive* the car?" Charlotte insists. "Declan's got this anti-theft device... a few years ago, someone had the gall to steal his beloved Mustang, so he got Ida in the lab to fix it so this high-tech alarm goes off if anyone unauthorized gets behind the wheel. He allows Caleb and Seamus to drive it, but I don't know of anyone else. He won't even authorize me," she finishes with a little sister whine in her voice.

"Nothing happened when I drove away," I say with confusion. It had been a breeze to break in, and even easier to turn on the ignition. "No bells or whistles, not even a boo."

"Maybe Declan added her," Tenley suggests. "He was talking to Ida the other day."

"Huh." Charlotte gives me a steely glance but I see a little admiration there.

"So what you're saying is I'm the only one who can drive Declan's car back?" I gaze longingly at the Guinness. "I can't drink that. Or, I can, but not another."

Charlotte giggles, making her look about twelve. "Declan also has a tracking thing on his car. As soon as he figures out you took it, he'll come and get it. He can drive us back."

"But he'll be pissed something brutal."

"But not at me."

I grimace. Just when I think Charlotte might be on my side, she flips a switch.

"Well, I say we drink," Tenley announces. "This has been a *shitty* day." Her voice drops at the curse word. "Soup got trashed;

someone wants to kidnap me *again,* and my little girl is having the time of her life at Disney *without me.* So I really think this deserves a drink." To prove her point, she drains her glass and thumps it on the table.

"If you're sure no one saw you come in." I want nothing more than to forget my troubles for a bit, but the danger is still here. Can I put my trust in Charlotte and Tenley, not only that they've secured the area, but that they have my back in case someone gets in?

There's a long pause before I finally lift my glass. Tenley grins at me and waves for the waiter.

"I never do this," Charlotte says with a strange look at Tenley. "Go for drinks, I mean. I remember the first time Declan and Caleb took me out for a beer after an op. I got carded, and they refused to serve me because they couldn't believe I was over nineteen. I was twenty-two, for god's sake!

"You do look young," Tenley says with a tact I don't have. "It'll be a good thing when you're older."

"I'm old enough now."

"How old *are* you, babyface?" Without the latest comment, I'd peg her at twenty-two, maybe three, but no more. She looks like a baby with her smooth, round cheeks and ponytail. Maybe with some makeup...

"My birthday was a month ago. I turned twenty-eight."

I lift my glass to hide my surprise. "Happy belated."

"How old are *you*?" she demands.

"A wee bit older. Twenty-nine. Been doing this for a donkey's years." I take another sip. "The pubs, as well as the job."

"I'm the newby, then." Tenley clinks her glass with mine. "I'm twenty-seven, but haven't been in the *business* that long."

"I wish I could tell you to get out while you still can, but I love it," Charlotte confesses.

I wonder if the beer is already going to Charlotte's head. She's finished half her pint in a few mouthfuls.

"It's all I've known. Or at least it's all I've known from what I can remember. I know my grandpa Seamus recruited me and—" Charlotte continues before she's interrupted by Tenley giggling into her glass.

"It's funny thinking of Seamus as a grandfather," Tenley confesses.

Two hours later, after introducing them to some fine Irish whiskey, we're well on our way to being well fluthered.

Colin's wallet burns a hole in my pocket. He won't mind treating us.

I don't know what would happen if Lysander walked through the door of the pub right now. We'd get the job done, I suppose, but it'd be messy.

There are a lot of laughs. There's talk, a lot of it trash, but some fun stories too. I've not felt the weight of the world lifted off me like this for some time.

I've no doubt Charlotte will run straight to Ham with everything I say, but so what? Lysander gave me up for dead, and even if Eugene wasn't in Interpol custody, Ham's going to bring down

Mochrie and Mielson and everything in between. From the sounds of what Tenley and Charlotte tell me about him, I think he can do it, even without my help.

It doesn't seem like a bad idea to rid the world of the bad guys.

Tenley has a little girl, an ex-husband and a past that isn't about staying one step ahead of the *garda*. Charlotte's life has been like mine, earmarked for this life at an early age and trained as such. She didn't have a choice either.

"Did you ever want to do anything else?" I ask her, my accent sounding stronger even to my own booze-raddled hearing.

"I worked in an office. I didn't much like that." Her *much* sounds like *moch*. Charlotte's beginning to sound a wee bit Irish herself. It happens with accents and alcohol. Once in a Melbourne pub after too much tequila, I stumbled back to my hotel sounding more Aussie than Chris Hemsworth.

"When they took my memories, they made up a story that I was an aid worker for Citizens Seeking Safety for Humanity. I thought that might be fun to try. Helping the world, you know."

Tenley gives her a strange look. "Charlotte, you've *saved* the world. I think that's better than helping."

"But no one knows what I do," she points out. "Does anyone know about the Russian electrical plant I stopped from blowing up? Or the Columbian cartel that I took down? No."

"I do," Tenley grins and taps her forehead.

"What's the story?" I give my head a shake. The shared memories are too complicated for me on a good day, let alone after several pints. "You know all her secrets, including stuff about Ham? And you're dating her brother, but have memories of him in your head?

Not sure how it works here in Canada, but that sounds a wee bit incestuous, if you ask me."

"It's better now," Tenley assures me. "I can control it. At first, all these images of Charlotte would just pop into my head whenever, usually at the worst possible time. The first time Seamus kissed me..." she trails off with a frantic shake of her head.

"I don't need to know that," Charlotte says to her glass.

"I don't worry about it now," Tenley assures her. "It's like things from your past that you don't want to think of. Unless you make an effort to remember, most of it can stay buried."

"Most?" Charlotte raises an eyebrow.

Tenley grins mischievously at her. "For the longest time, I couldn't look at Ham without thinking about..." Her smile widens and Charlotte groans.

"Please, never tell him that. He'd be so embarrassed. I know he looks all buttoned-up and all, but inside he's a real softy."

"Except for the abs, which are rock hard," Tenley whispers.

The drinks had gone straight to her head.

"Stop talking about his abs! It's not fair because I can't talk that way about Seamus!"

"I know!" She slaps the table with a laugh.

These last two hours have been brilliant.

"Ham seems a wee bit tightly wound." I stop before I say he's got a stick shoved up his arse because that's not polite.

Tenley snorts. "I'd say so." She taps her forehead. "I know a little—a wee bit—too much about our Ham."

"He's my Ham." Charlotte pouts.

"Yes, he is."

"We have to go back soon." Charlotte sighs, her shoulders drooping. "My Ham will be worried. And I keep expecting Declan to show up and drag us off by the hair." She gives me a sideways glance. "Maybe just you."

"Might not be a bad thing," I say idly, thinking of Declan dragging me off to snog me senseless.

"You're getting married," Tenley announces, not even trying to hide the slurring. "That's so cool. I remember *my* wedding. We did it just so we could have sex because we were in the abstinence club at school, and sex before marriage was *wrong*."

"Welcome to the Catholic church," I say wryly.

"After the wedding, it was all *sex sex sex*." Tenley ignores my comment. "*Sex sex*, all the time. And then I got pregnant, and I was really sick, and no more sex. You call that shagging, don't you?"

"Shagging, yes. Poor Tenley."

"Simon was good at the shagging part," Tenley says with a fond smile. "And he was a good husband. Great father. But eighteen is too young to get married. It was never going to work. And I'm okay with that. But I wasn't okay with not being able to plan my own wedding. My mother-in-law took the whole thing over." She swept an arm for emphasis, almost knocking over Charlotte's glass. "I just had to show up in a pretty dress. One that *she* picked out."

"Ham hardly has time to talk to his mother," Charlotte says. "So I don't think I'll have to worry about that. If we're ever getting married."

"I know what we should do!" Tenley exclaims, slamming her glass down with enough force she shakes the table. "We should go try on wedding dresses."

Charlotte grins. "We totally should."

Twenty-Nine

A ND THAT'S HOW I find myself running down the sidewalk to Richard's Bridal, a few blocks away from the pub.

Charlotte takes point, with Tenley bringing up the rear, all of us laughing in a very unspy-like manner.

Maybe Colin was right about me not being as careful as I can be.

Tenley takes the lead as we tromp into the boutique, an elegant shop with grey walls and racks of wedding gowns.

"I don't think we should be in here," I say in a loud whisper to Charlotte, feeling like a bull in a china shop. "And why is it still open?"

"*She* needs a wedding dress," Tenley squeals, bouncing up and down with all the excitement of a teenager meeting her favourite boy band.

I gaze around the sea of white fabric as Tenley explains to saleslady Helen all about my upcoming wedding, how Charlotte is going to be my sister-in-law and the fact she, Tenley, is dating Declan's brother.

They expect me to fit into one of those dresses—me, with my curves, chest and enough junk in the trunk for a weekend of camping. Not going to happen. I may be a looker, but I'm no size two.

"Once this family gets started, everybody's going to want to get married." Tenley continues, nudging Helen with a theatrical nod at Charlotte.

"What style are we looking for?" Helen asks. I give her credit—her pained smile doesn't falter. The three of us smell a bit manky, and Charlotte has a smear of ketchup decorating her shirt.

Along with the drinks, we had burgers and chips, thanks to Colin's fat wallet.

I've never had a BFF, not even a close girlfriend. I've never been lonely, but that's because I didn't know what I was missing. Growing up, I was caught up with gymnastics and making my mum proud and never had time for friends. They say a girl's best friend is her mother, but not here. Felicia McGovern was a tightfisted, hard-faced woman convinced the world owed her more than anyone else.

I'm about to try on wedding dresses, which is something a mum should be there for. But she was never there for me when she was alive, so I don't know why I'm thinking about her when she's dead.

"What kind of styles do you have?" I ask politely.

Helen looks at me like I have three heads. I've come across her kind before—posh, with a stick as big as a paddle stuck up her arse. I don't handle them well.

Luckily Tenley is really good handling people with paddles. And wedding dresses.

"Pippa's not usually the dressy-dress type, but can't you just see her in a big, Cinderella type gown? I think we're going for a fairy tale wedding, with the horse-drawn carriage and the twinkling fairy lights..."

My jaw drops like a bucket of fish. Charlotte looks just as shocked, which means this idea isn't something they talked about in the wedding meeting.

Tenley's enthusiasm does the trick. Helen's face loses the snooty expression. "I think that would be lovely with her shape," she gushes. "And that hair." She tweaks one of my curls between two fingers. "I see her in a tiara with ruffles and lace..."

"No tiara," I snap.

"Of course not. Why don't you head to the change room and I'll bring you a selection. We're getting close to closing, so perhaps—"

"I'm sure this won't take long," Tenley assures her. "Pippa knows exactly what she wants."

"No, I don't," I hiss as Helen glides away.

"Tenley, what the hell?" Charlotte gasps.

"It'll be fun!"

"I don't know about that. I gotta tell you, I don't have a quid to my name," I show her Colin's wallet. "I knicked this from Colin because I'm skint. I've got nothing to pay for a dress."

"You stole Colin's wallet?" Tenley is aghast.

"He's got another one. Probably. But I don't."

Tenley turns to Charlotte. "I guess Ham can pay for it," Charlotte says uneasily. "He's got the money. At least the Agency does." She grins suddenly, looking like a mischievous teenager. "I guess that means Canada will be paying for your wedding."

"Yay, Canada." I raise my fist in a cheer, my smile weak and uncertain. I don't like this. If Ham pays for my wedding, what will he want in return?

Maybe having Lysander's head on a platter will be enough for him.

The fitting room is larger than my last two hotel rooms put together, with dark grey sofas and two different change cubicles, each big enough for a comfy chair. There's no mirror in the curtained cubicle—once the dress goes on, the bride-to-be climbs onto the raised platform in front of the full-length three-way mirror in the middle of the fitting room to get critiqued.

Tenley lounges on one of the sofas while Charlotte prowls around the fitting room, more out of curiousity than reconnaissance. I pace the floor, twisting my fingers so hard my knuckles crack. This time it's not Lysander who's scared me.

I've not even bought a prom dress, so how am I supposed to figure out the wedding gown? A few more episodes of *Say Yes to the Dress* would have been helpful.

I catch my breath when Helen appears, reverently holding a mini mountain of white satin and lace in her arms.

"This is it," Charlotte says, pushing me towards a cubicle. "Get naked."

I strip off the jeans and borrowed T-shirt and stand there in my granny panties and bra that's seen better days as Helen carefully holds the first dress for me to step into.

"Bloody hell," I whisper, as Helen settles the white lace on my shoulders before zipping it up.

I'm wearing a wedding dress.

At least most of one. The dress can't be zipped over my chest.

"We can fix that," Helen says, holding the dress closed against my back for me to get the full effect.

"Oh, Pippa," Tenley croons, her hand against her mouth.

"You're not *crying* are you?" Charlotte demands.

"She looks so pretty," Tenley argues, swiping a quick knuckle under her eye.

Even I think I look pretty. The way the taffeta bodice is draped around my waist is very flattering and the lace neckline is so pretty. I'm not sure if it's the run to the boutique or the cool air outside, but my cheeks are flushed pink.

It might be the Guinness.

"This is an A-line, which works for every figure," Helen explains. "Very nice, but let's try this one."

One by one, I try on the four dresses Helen brought out. She's complimentary about my curves and very good at her job. We're given a quick bio on each dress, which only Tenley listens to, and how the dress works best for my body type. I don't even have the third dress zipped up before she *tsk tskes* and makes me take it off.

"It's not *you*," she says, helping me out of the dress. "At least it should not be you."

She doesn't even know who I am, and she knows what's me?

"There weren't many for your measurements," Helen says ruefully. "Since your figure is quite... *abundant*... the options are somewhat limited."

"Because I have big boobs," I clarify. "And some junk in the trunk."

"Mainly because wedding dresses seem to be made for size two twigs with the chest measurements of prepubescent boys." Tenley pokes Charlotte with her elbow. "You shouldn't have any problem with that, Charlie."

Charlotte cups her tiny breasts as she lounges on the uncomfortable-looking sofa in the fitting room. "I love my girls, whatever size. They never get in the way and they never let me down."

"Mine get in the way of everything, including a gymnastics career," I say, inwardly marvelling at the exchange. This is—that was something friends say to each other.

Friends. Me, with friends. Who would have thought?

"We'll find the perfect dress for you," Helen assures me. Despite the confidence, Helen hasn't brought out anything that makes me cry with happiness. Her words, not mine. "Would you girls like to try on something as well?" she says in a sly voice as she heads back for another selection.

"Yes, please!" Tenley's answer rings out before Helen finishes the question.

I step into another dress and don't hear Charlotte's response over the rustle of the fabric. It's a towering confection of silk and lace, dwarfing me and my assets. I turn to look over my shoulder at myself in the mirror as Tenley zips me up. This one fits all the way up. "It has a big butt bow."

"But it doesn't make your butt big," Tenley promises.

Charlotte tugs at the offending bow. "It can come off. If I had my knife—"

"Here you go!" Helen trills, bustling into the room with another armful of white fabric. Tenley forgets all about me and hustles into a stall. Charlotte forgoes the privacy cubicle and stays with me on the platform, stripping off her clothes without a care.

If I had her body, I wouldn't have care either.

"I'm just going to go lock the front door," Helen calls over her shoulder as she heads for the door.

"Oh, you have to close?" Tenley calls, sticking her head out from behind the curtain. "I'm sorry we're taking so long. It'll just be1"

"Finish trying on your dresses," Helen says. "I can tell this is fun for you all. Such good friends!"

I meet Charlotte's eyes in the reflection of the mirror. "This is fun?" she murmurs.

"We're good friends?" I ask.

A pause and Charlotte shrugs. "Well, at least she knows what looks good on you."

Wearing only her bra and a pair of black boyshorts, Charlotte helps me out of the dress and into another one. I can't help but compare the two of us—Charlotte so slim and tiny and me, so not. Undressed, it's obvious Charlotte is all muscle. I didn't know such a small person could look so strong.

I wonder if I could take her.

"That looks nice," she says, nodding at my reflection. The dress is ivory, which Helen says is better for my pale complexion than pure white.

I smooth down the lace bodice, staring in the mirror. It's strapless, and there's no hiding the abundance of my chest measurements. The skirt is so pretty, with layers of floaty fabric. A jeweled belt slims my waist.

"I think I like this," I whisper, unable to stop the smile.

Charlotte tugs up her dress and stands before me so I can zip her up. "That's pretty," I tell her. Her dress is mermaid style, off the shoulder with a ruched bodice that makes her chest look bigger than her size A cups. It fits her petite frame perfectly.

"So's yours."

"Do you think Declan would like it?" I ask quietly.

"It's so pretty!" Tenley interrupts with a squeal as she bursts out of the fitting room wearing her own dress. She stops at the sight of me. "Oh, Pippa!"

"It's..." I stare at myself in the mirror.

"It's beautiful," Tenley says in a soft voice. "It's really big. It's..." She adjusts my skirt. "Fluffy."

"You look like a wedding cake!" Charlotte chortles.

"I kind of do." I can't take my eyes off my reflection. I gingerly pick up the hem.

It fits perfectly.

"It's like it's been made for you," Tenley marvels. The admiration in her eyes warms my suddenly cold feet.

The dress makes me feel beautiful. For the first time in my life, I feel pretty and feminine and beautiful. This is my wedding dress. Only it isn't my wedding. Not really. It's an elaborate hoax to draw Lysander out of hiding so Ham can take him down.

The thought spoils my happiness as the three of us preen in front of the mirror.

Tenley looks beautiful in the white satin, and Charlotte even more adorable in the mermaid dress, but I can't take my gaze off my own reflection. There's a lump in my throat and my eyes suddenly burn. Is this what Helen means when she says the dress should make the bride cry with happiness?

Or am I crying because this isn't real?

"This is so beautiful!" Tenley is teary-eyed, running her hands reverently along her dress. It's slim fitting, off the shoulder without much lace or bling. "This is the dress I would have wanted when I was eighteen."

"It looks amazing. I like that on you," I add, smiling at Charlotte.

"I can move in it, too." She hikes up the skirt and lets a side-kick loose that could knock a grown man down.

"I can't move in this one," Tenley complains.

"Do you think you'll be kicking in your wedding dress?" I laugh.

A scream cuts the air.

"You were saying?" Charlotte says scornfully.

Four men burst into the fitting room.

Thirty

"I THOUGHT YOU CHECKED the perimeter?" I demand, falling back into a fighting stance.

"It was clear." Charlotte is the first to move, jumping off the pedestal straight at the first man, fists poised. I hear the crunch of hand against nose and then she's rolling across the room to her next victim.

She's right—the dress does allow her to move.

Tenley is poised to attack; she has a black baton in her hand but my attention is caught by the two coming for me.

"I see Lysander is being pissy about this," I say, backing up to one of the cubicles. The heavy grey privacy curtains are held up by a rod, one that I hope is strong enough to hold my weight.

I jump for it, hanging for moment to make sure it holds before I start to swing. My bare feet catch the first man full in the chest, sending him stumbling backward. The second dodges him, but can't miss me when I let go of the bar and fly straight for him, feet first.

The dress practically covers his body as I straddle him. I give him a series of quick jabs which send his head smacking against the grey carpet. When his eyes roll back into his head, I give him a swift kick in the ribs, then jump to my feet to face another.

He backs away from me, right into Charlotte.

"You're not going anywhere," she tells him, twisting his arm behind his back. "Who sent you?"

He shakes his head and Charlotte twists harder. "Mochrie," he gasps.

"Lysander Mochrie?" The rage is there, simmering at the edges, but so is the vast disappointment—in Lysander and in myself.

"Yes," he howls as Charlotte twists his arm again. Tenley takes her baton and raps him smartly in the head with the handle and he goes down like a sack of potatoes.

"Your boyfriend is an arsehole," Charlotte proclaims, stepping back to let him fall to the ground. She swipes her hand under her nose, trying to catch the trickle of blood. "I've got to get out of this dress before I bleed all over it."

She stands before me to unzip. "And he's stupid," she continues. "Sending only four of them? For *us*?"

"Maybe they thought they'd catch me alone." I survey the mess of the fitting room. Unconscious bodies lay on the floor, with one of the couches overturned and a curtain hanging off the rod. "It's a bit of a waste."

"I hope Helen is okay." Tenley hurries from the fitting room, still in her dress.

"I want to know how they found us," Charlotte demands. "We were clear before we went into that pub."

"Colin probably ratted me out." Even saying the words makes my heart ache. I can't really blame Colin, but we were friends.

At least, I thought we had been.

Charlotte stares at me and I do what I can to mask my expression. "Are you okay?"

Hiding disappointment is getting harder to do.

"Just peachy." I sink onto the couch, my dress spreading out like a sea of foam. "But he's not going to give up. And maybe next time he won't send ones so daft."

"We'll stop him," Charlotte assures me, pulling her phone out of her bag. "I'll call Ham and get this fixed up."

"I didn't mean to make a such a mess." I glance up to see Tenley supporting a white-faced Helen. "Are you all right?"

"My shop," she gasps. "They just—I couldn't—are you—"

"I'll take the dress," I interrupt. "It's perfect for me."

Ham shows up in record time with a foursome of strangers wearing navy blue overalls who brush past us without a word and get to work removing the men.

Seamus is right behind Ham. My heart gives a series of funny little leaps, like I'm playing hopscotch when I see Declan. Seamus goes straight to Tenley, holding her at arm's length, while Declan shifts uneasily as he catches sight of me.

I'm still wearing the dress.

"You look..." he begins, with a hungry expression on his face, but then it vanishes, like turning a page. "You could have asked for the keys." He frowns. His bruises haven't gotten any better in the few hours since I've seen him last.

"You shouldn't be out," I chide.

"Neither should you." He glances around at the boutique, anywhere but at me. "You're buying a dress? I guess—yeah, you'll need one."

There's a pause.

"Do you like this one?" I burst out.

Declan's face explodes with eager excitement, like the teacher's pet being called on in class. "You look really pretty. I like the top part." He points awkwardly at my chest area and I sag with relief. "You're beautiful."

He smiles—a real, true smile, and it makes me catch my breath. It's warm and real and I want to see more of it.

"Thanks."

For a moment, for half a second, we're a normal couple sharing the excitement of our big day.

And then his face closes up again, like a door closing in my face, and we're not.

"Tenley thought it was a good idea to get a dress." I shift my weight, pulling at the skirt. "To make it more realistic."

"Probably a good idea," Declan agrees, shifting his gaze again.

"Declan..." I begin. He glances warily at me and my heart sinks. "Right. Well, I was about to apologize for the muck I made of things... again... but now I see there's no point. But I will say one thing: I like you. I like you more than I should, considering who you work for and who I worked with. Finding you was a bonus for *me*, not this mission. I made a right hash of things because of you. So maybe you should be saying you're sorry to *me*." I take a deep breath, keeping my voice level with difficulty. "That might have been more than one thing. I know this wedding means nothing to you. I've had some fun with it tonight, but that'll be the last of it. I'd like you to stay alive and so would everyone else, so we're going through with this farce."

It's one of my longer speeches and my face is red by the end of it because everyone is staring at me, including one of the navy-suited guys.

"She's right."

I don't know who seems more surprised to hear Charlotte say that; Declan, me or Ham.

"That's twice they've come for her in the last couple of hours and who knows what this Irish mob star has in store for you. Let's get back to Head Office and both of you need to stay put until this is over." With that, Charlotte marches out of the fitting room. "Let Pippa get out of that dress, and Ham, you need to come and pay for it," she tosses over her shoulder.

The room clears in a hurry, leaving only Declan and I.

I shake my head in disbelief. "She's had a few drinks. Plus she tried on a dress—that does something to a girl's head."

He meets my gaze, holding it tight with his blue eyes. Things start to tingle because the way he's looking at me doesn't say angry.

I'm not exactly sure what it says, but I'd like to find out.

"What did it do to you?"

"I shouldn't have—" What have I got to lose? "No. I meant everything I said. I like you, Declan, and I'm sorry about everything that's happened. Except meeting you. I'm as happy about that as I was when it first happened."

He nods and drops his gaze. "I'll let you get changed."

"Wait. Can you—I can't get out of this on my own."

Declan pauses, his eyes wary. Turning around, I stretch my arm back in an effort to reach the zipper.

"Sure."

The zipper moves in slow motion.

I feel the warmth of Declan's hand against my back as the inter-locking teeth slowly separate and his knuckles graze my bare skin.

I hold my breath as Declan pulls it lower and I'm not the only one. I hear the sharp intake of his breath as my back is bared.

The dress gapes open.

Declan's hand lingers.

I pause for a long moment before stepping away. Holding my arms close to my chest to keep the dress from sliding, I turn to face Declan. "I am sorry," I whisper. "I never meant to hurt you."

"You lied to me," he mutters.

"Just a few details. Nothing else." I hold his gaze for a moment longer, willing him to believe me. Then I grin. "Except that I really don't like the Backstreet Boys."

After a shocked silence, Declan laughs.

Thirty-One

I CHANGE OUT OF my dress, the dress Declan says is pretty, and hurry out of the fitting room.

"I'll see to all the repairs." Ham is saying to Helen, touching the older woman's shoulder to avert her attention from one of the blue overalls heading out the door with the last of the attackers thrown over his shoulder.

"But how... why...?"

Tenley brings her a cup of water. She's changed out of her dress and back into sensible pants and shirt. If it wasn't for the bruise blooming on her cheek, it would be like nothing happened.

"The girls work for a covert government organization," Ham explains to Helen. "These men were dangerous, but the girls saved your shop."

"But how—"

"I must ask you to keep this to yourself," he adds. "Please let me know if there's anything at all that you need. We'll be out of your way now."

"But... but..." she stammers.

"Again, I must insist that you keep this to yourself." Ham gazes deep into her eyes. "For your own safety."

"Of course," Helen gasps.

I have no doubt Helen won't ever say anything about this. Ham is pretty good at what he does.

Seamus and Charlotte escort Declan and me the few blocks back to the parking lot where I left his pretty blue car. The others take the van with the now conscious and handcuffed assailants. I wonder what Ham is going to do with them.

They're better off with him than reporting the failure back to Lysander.

"Ham told her what you do," I say to Charlotte as we hurry along the sidewalk, sticking to the shadows close to the stores. "Why?"

"He says sometimes truth is stranger than fiction, so he doubts many would believe him," Charlotte explains. "Saleslady Helen is scared, but in the morning, she'll convince herself it was just a robbery attempt. The Agency has kept so quiet for so long and no one believes Canada has any sort of covert spy organization."

That makes sense—sort of. At least as much sense as the rest of the night.

I can't believe Lysander has already sent two different groups after me. What was he trying to do—have me killed? Seriously? Because they were half-assed attempts at best.

Although Seamus doesn't seem to think so.

"How could you let her go out like that, Lottie? Don't you know how dangerous this guy is?" he rages at Charlotte as we hasten to the parking lot.

Helen presented me with the vast plastic bag with the Richard's Bridal etched in flowing letters like she was offering me something priceless, and I do my best to hold it carefully, but Seamus's walking speed is making it difficult.

"Tenley wasn't in any danger," Charlotte assures him with a roll of her eyes.

"And she didn't *let* me out. I left," I tell him, shifting the bag in my arms.

"Why? What was so important that you put Tenley and Lottie in danger?" he snaps at me.

I heft the bag. "I got a dress. And it's pretty."

Seamus huffs and stalks ahead. There's no sense telling him that I met Colin. He's so protective of Tenley that I'd be in for another tongue lashing for sure.

Suddenly Seamus stops. "How did you take the car?" he demands of me.

"I... very carefully," I say with a grin, before turning to Declan. "I *was* very careful with it. Didn't get a scratch on it."

I push the image of racing across four lanes of traffic out of my head. No one saw that; no one needs to know.

"Did you give her access?" Seamus asks Declan.

"I was wondering about that too." Charlotte gives me a sideways glance. "Because if you didn't, maybe you and Ida need to rethink the security system."

"It's all good." Declan keeps his gaze straight ahead.

"So you added her." The scorn drips off Charlotte's words. "You added *her* but not your sister."

"She's a better driver."

My snort of laughter quickly turns into a cough when Charlotte glares at me.

"At least, a better car thief," Declan adds.

"I can steal a car," Charlotte protests. "That time in Niagara when I grabbed the bike with Luke—I've stolen lots of cars!" She turns to me as if waiting for my approval.

I shrug. "I'm practically a professional."

"I can drive better than she can. Let me drive, Declan. I'll show you," she begs.

"No."

I've never heard such a firm finality in Declan's voice, and I hide my giggle with the rustle of the dress bag as we enter the parking lot.

Seamus holds up his hand. "I'm checking out the car first. Wait here."

"I tried to hide it," I call after him. Seamus ignores me as he hurries across the parking lot, the overhead lights creating pools and shadows easy to hide in.

"It's hard because it's flashy," Charlotte says disdainfully.

"At least I have a car," Declan says.

"That was Benjy's fault," Charlotte argues, dropping her voice. "He owes me."

"What did Benjy do to your car?" I ask, hugging my dress to me for warmth against the chilly evening.

"Drove it into the lake."

I nod. "My park job is better, then."

Seamus beckons us over to the car. "It's safe. I found a tracking device," he says, throwing the black device to the ground and grinding it with his heel. "Waste of tech. Everyone knows where

Head Office is now, thanks to Benjy. And once we get you in there, there's no breaking you out."

"Are you sure?"

Declan opens the door of the car for us and Charlotte scrambles into the backseat. I carefully pass her my dress before climbing in after her.

"It's only because I've taught Lysander a few things," I continue. "He'd give it a go to see."

"Do you think *you* could break into Head Office?" Charlotte demands. She raises her voice over the music that bursts out of the speakers as Declan starts the car.

"I think I could give it a good try. I got out, didn't I?" I gaze out of the window, watching for anything suspicious as Declan backs out.

"I knew you were gone."

"After the fact," Seamus points out. "Maybe Ham should talk to Ida."

No one says much else on the way back.

I can't stop thinking of how Declan's hand lingered against my back when he was unzipping me.

He said the dress was pretty. I smile, shifting my gaze when I see Declan's blue eyes in the rearview mirror. When I flash back, he's still looking.

Ham meets us in the parking garage. Lysander's hired guns are nowhere in sight, already taken away by the boys in navy blue.

"Pippa, I must insist you remain within Head Office for the next few days," he says immediately as I crawl out of the car.

"Sure."

"You're not a prisoner; this is for your own safety and that of my agents," he continues as if I didn't respond. "Mochrie was quick to act. It might not be so easy to escape him next time."

"That's fine. I don't want to put anyone in danger. Sorry about the joyride and thanks for the pickup."

"Thank you," he says, a frown on his forehead at my easy acquiescence. "We'll move you to a different room, get you everything you need."

There's only one thing I need.

I've never minded being alone, but another day being confined begins to send me a wee bit batty. I miss the outdoors—birds singing, wind blowing, the sounds of traffic outside my hotel room window. Being stuck underground takes some getting used to. There's no windows, the air is cool, but it's been breathed by the hundred or so other agents down here with me, and it's so quiet that it gives me the creeps.

I honestly don't know how many agents there are in the Agency. I may be hiding out at the head office of Canada's spy organization, but nobody's saying much to me. Conversations stop when I walk by. Meetings are held about me, but without me.

The room they assign me doesn't have much, but it's more comfortable than the hotel. I don't miss the cobwebs festooning the corners of the ceiling. I give a list of sizes to Alessia, who returned with a variety of clothes for me. The food is good and I get eight hours of sleep at night, but I'm still stuck here.

There's no word from Colin, nor any secret package slipped to me over my breakfast burritos. It's like the world has forgotten me.

On the second day, Ham allows me into the gymnasium.

I think he only meant to have me use the facilities, but I end up joining a training session given by Declan's brother, Caleb.

There are twelve new recruits; I don't know if they're new agents or still trying to make the cut. Seven women in their twenties, an older woman who is pushing forty and four men—one who seems a cocky arse. I take great pleasure in flipping him onto the mat several times.

Caleb finds me at the end of the session.

"So you're Pippa." Taller than Declan, Caleb towers over me, but his smile is warm, much warmer than any of the other members of the family. He has the Dodd family good looks—sandy blond hair curling around his neck and sky blue eyes like Charlotte. If I had to rate them, I'd put Caleb ahead of Seamus and Perry.

Declan is first, of course.

"Guilty as charged." Caleb nods his head slowly, and I let him appraise me for a moment before I put a stop to it. "Any questions? Concerns? Accusations?"

"Not really. I guess I can see what the fuss is all about."

"There's a fuss?" I slap my hand on my chest. "About mc?"

"I've never known my brother to be so hung up over a girl."

My smile instantly blooms. "How hung up are we talking about?"

"He's marrying you, isn't it? He was always allergic to the word."

"It's a bloody word to spell. I always get mixed up with the *a* and the *i*."

Caleb grins, showing even white teeth. The Dodd family dental bills must have been atrocious. "How're you doing in here? Ham says you're under house arrest."

"He told *me* I *wasn't* a prisoner."

"Why would he tell you if you were? So you can make another escape attempt?"

"I wasn't escaping. I just had things to do."

"Busy woman," Caleb says, heading to the change room.

"Not anymore," I say ruefully.

Later that afternoon, Tenley comes by my room carrying a box.

"Helen from Richard's Bridal dropped this by the cafe," she says, setting the box on my bed. "She says it's a veil that would go perfectly with your dress."

"A veil?" I parrot, staring at the box like it's going to bite me.

"Open it," Tenley urges. "Let's see what it looks like."

"You didn't look at it?"

Tenley gives me a withering look. "It's *your* veil, not mine."

"I just thought..." Without finishing the thought, I pick off the tape and flip up the lid. I thrust my hands into the mass of tissue.

I feel the tulle of the veil, but I also something hard. I don't mention that to Tenley. Instead, I pull out the delicate fabric.

"It's beautiful," Tenley sighs.

The veil is a long piece of tulle, the same ivory colour as my dress, with matching lace along the sides and the end. Helen included a matching headpiece, a pearl-encrusted comb that I can tuck into my curls.

"Bloody hell." I hold up the fabric so Tenley can better admire it. "Did you pay for this?"

She shook her head. "Helen only said that it *had* to go with the dress."

This makes me instantly suspicious. "What's wrong with it, then?" I study the lace on the edges, touching every inch of the veil before taking the comb in my fingers.

"There's nothing wrong with it."

"There is if it's from Lysander."

"You don't know that it is." She starts her own investigation and after a few minutes of intensive searching, neither of us can come up with anything wrong. "I think it's okay. Maybe Ida can scan it."

"It's good." I set the comb back on the bed and stare at it. "I'm a bit paranoid."

"I think you have a right to be. Being locked in here and knowing..." she trails off. "Anyway, you've got your veil. And I've confirmed that we can hold it at Thrice." Tenley notices my confused expression. "The wedding. I know the owners. It's a really nice restaurant, and they said we can have it there. No sit-down dinner, but definitely food. I worked out the menu with Cooper."

"Menu? So this is like a *real* wedding? Like with food and flowers?"

"I thought you said it needed to be."

"But I thought we'd go to City Hall?"

Tenley pulls out her phone and types in a note. "Marriage license. I've got to go to city hall tomorrow. Maybe Declan can do that."

"You're *organizing* my wedding?"

From her expression, Tenley seems offended at my question. "I don't have to."

"*Ta* very much." My mind explodes with happiness and I reach out to touch Tenley's arm. "I never expected this. How can you—you have the cafe, not to mention Lucy..."

I can't finish a sentence. This might be a phony wedding, but it seems so real. And for Tenley to put so much effort into it...

"You don't have to do this," I finish. "But thank you so much."

"Lucy's still in Florida. And this is fun," Tenley admits, shifting her gaze back to the veil. She picks it up and attaches the headpiece, then hands it to me. "I was so young when I got married and Simon's mother took care of most of it. I never got to enjoy how much fun it is to plan a wedding. And it's even more fun when I'm planning someone else's and Ham's paying the bills!"

My hair is pulled back into a Charlotte-like ponytail, and I tuck the comb into the hair above it, draping the veil over my shoulders.

Tenley smiles her approval. "Nice."

"Do you think you'll get married again?" I ask.

"I don't know." The way Tenley shifts her eyes away from Charlotte suggests to me that she has thought about it quite a bit. And probably with Seamus.

"Does Lucy like him?"

Tenley nods. "Sometimes I think she likes him more than I do. It's going to be horrible if something happens..."

Now it's Tenley who trails off. "What's going to happen?" I ask, admiring myself in the tiny mirror on the wall. "You're like two peas."

She smiles but changes the subject, telling me about the menu. "I'm making the cake. It won't be big, but you don't need one because there aren't many guests."

I sigh nervously. "This feels like what a real wedding would feel like."

"Lysander will never know the difference. It's the perfect trap." Her comment brings both of us out of the haze of pre-wedding excitement. "About Declan—is this the only reason you're doing this?"

I sit down heavily on the bed, the veil pooling around me. "I dunno. I came up with what would piss off Lysander the most, what he would most want to spoil. If he knows I'm to have a wedding, he's going to want to ruin it. And then you all can catch him, and Declan won't have to worry."

"He likes you. Declan, that is. He likes you a lot."

"I like him too. Getting married seems a big step for this one thing, but it doesn't feel... wrong. Like if I was to marry someone else, that would feel wrong. Does that make sense?"

"To me. Maybe not to Charlotte yet."

I chat with Tenley for a few more minutes before she takes her leave. To go home, I assume, even though she's nice enough not to mention it to me.

It's not until after she leaves and I'm carefully folding the veil back into the tissue that I remember there's something more in the box.

It's a phone.

I snatch it out of the box and hug it to me. "Colin—*ta* very much. I'll get you an invite to the wedding for this."

Thirty-Two

I'LL BE A MARRIED woman by the end of the day. I'm not sure how long I'll be married for, but for a while at least, my name will be Pippa Dodd.

Pippa McGovern-Dodd.

Unless Lysander stops it. But if he manages to do that, chances are I'll be dead. And Declan too. Or maybe Lysander'll try, and Ham will stop him, but I won't be Mrs. Dodd and Declan will run for the hills.

It's no wonder I hardly sleep a wink.

Ham shows up at my door as I'm on my way to the cafeteria for a wedding day breakfast and a much needed cuppa. "Good morning, Pippa."

Once again, Ham is impeccably dressed in a three-piece charcoal suit with a cherry-red tie. I rouse myself from my funk long enough to notice how smart he looks in the waistcoat, then sink back into the depths when I compare my jogging pants and jumper.

I'm going to need a fair bit of work to look good for the wedding.

The thought sends a nervous tingle through me, enough that I only manage a muttered, "Morning."

"Any wedding nerves this morning?" Ham asks.

"Not really," I lie. "It's no big deal."

He raises an eyebrow. "Please don't say that in front of Tenley. She's really thrown herself in the preparations."

"She didn't have to," I retort in a sullen voice. "But it was nice of her. If I ever have a real wedding, I'd want her to plan it. If I couldn't, like now."

Ham glances around my room. I don't have much, but what I do have is strewn across every surface. But I've seen his office, and I'm not worried about him seeing my mess. What's he going to do, ground me until I clean my room?

"I realize being here is less than ideal. I hope you understand that we're only looking out for your safety," Ham says stiffly.

"I know. It's... fine." I stop myself from listing how very *not fine* being stuck down here is. But it's not Ham's fault.

It's mine. Mine and that bloody possessive, mad as a box of frogs, Lysander Mochrie.

I'm going to give him a good piece of my mind when I see him next. But that's a big if. Thanks to Colin's phone, yesterday I was able to drop off the grid. Pippa McGovern is no longer in the employ of the Mochrie family, or the Mielson organization. End of that chapter in my life.

I was also able to safeguard my nest egg in a new bank in Grand Cayman and make inquires about selling my flat in Belfast.

I should be happy to close the doors of my life as a bad guy. Maybe I would be if I knew what was in store for me.

Instead, I feel a little lost.

"Would you mind joining me in my office for a few minutes?" Ham asks.

I've never met a man as polite as Ham Short. There has to be a way to make him unbutton, pull the stick out of his arse, but I've yet to see it. Normally, the priss and prude type of guy is not for me, but I just love the way he looks at Charlotte. It gives me hope that true love is really out there.

"Sure," I tell him. "What's up?"

He doesn't answer until we're on the way to his office. A different office, if I have my directions right. Other than the hours I've spent on Colin's phone, reading every online Irish newspaper I can find, my stay here has been my mission.

I've wandered the halls of the different floors, found my way into places I probably don't have authorization for, and observed everyone and everything. In just the few days I've been here, routines are falling into place and I can get from Point A to Point B without asking for help.

Research, reconnaissance, reward. Only I don't know what the reward is yet.

Ham pulls me aside to let a group of new recruits by us in the hall. A few of them nod to me. I worked with them again yesterday. Caleb invited me to the front of the class to use me as an example, showing off my sparring skills.

At least one of the Dodds like me.

"I'd like you to speak to Eugene Mochrie," Ham says after they pass.

"You want—what?" I stammer, caught flat-footed. "I thought he was the Big Bad."

"Actually, Lysander Mochrie is the more dangerous of the Mielson agents. At least the ones we've tangled with."

I bite my tongue so I don't mention how I've "tangled" with a few of them and think Ham is absolutely correct.

"Why?" I ask instead.

Ham jerks his head and I follow him to a small room. This isn't the lab/office where he has meetings and works on projects and prepares ops, and where Payton hangs out. This one is a tiny little cubicle so close to the cafeteria that I can smell the eggs cooking.

My stomach rumbles a reminder.

He shuts the door behind me and gestures to the chair before his desk. "I've set up a face-to-face call to Mochrie, he says, sitting across from me. It's a small room, with a smaller desk, and it feels intimate being here with Ham. Like we share a secret. "He's in a British prison, awaiting sentencing. I thought you could tell him about the wedding."

I perch on the edge of the chair. "Why? Wouldn't that be like throwing fat on the fire?"

Ham pushes the laptop on the desk aside and leans on his elbows. "Not exactly. I want you to tell him you'd like to come home. Convince him you're trying to get him out of prison."

"But I'm not... am I?"

"Pippa, I agree with your plan to flush out Lysander. It's necessary. But I wouldn't be a good leader if I didn't do everything I could to ensure my agents escape without injury. If Eugene believes you're interested in returning to the fold, then perhaps Lysander won't target you."

"Me—you're doing this for me?" I can't begin to hide my shock, and Ham smiles at my response.

"Don't be so surprised. I've been watching you since you've been staying with us. You've got quite a bit of potential. Talents that haven't been utilized."

"I'm a thief," I say, my voice small.

"Is that all? I think you could be much more than the simple thief you believe yourself to be."

"What do you believe I am?"

Ham smiles at me. "I'd like the opportunity to find out. Caleb told me you've joined his training class—"

"Twice. That's not joining."

"It's a good start. After this is over, I'd like you to spend some time with Charlotte."

"Are you trying to *recruit* me?"

"Are you comfortable with that?"

"How do you know I won't jump ship the first time I see daylight?"

Ham studies me with dark blue eyes that are impossible to read. "I don't. You've got a good heart, Pippa. Circumstances have thrown you into a certain role. I don't believe your lot in life is to be a third-rate thief with Mielson, scrambling for an ounce of respect from the powers that be."

"Well, when you put it like that..."

"I know enough about who we're up against to realize that you don't exactly fit their mold. I'm offering you an out."

"Thank you." I pause for a moment to consider my words. "I know of someone else who doesn't fit into Mielson, someone who would fit in here." Ham raises his eyebrows for me to continue. "Minka Grace."

Ham leans back in his chair as if he's putting distance between my suggestions. "I don't think so."

"She's the one who got me out of Benjy's," I say in a rush. "Or at least she told me how. She warned me about Lysander. She's in it for the money—that's it."

"Minka had her chance with the Agency and decided it wasn't to her liking," Ham says stiffly.

"No, the pay wasn't to her liking. At least, Mielson paid more and, like I said, that's all she wants. Her father is in a home and she has to take care of him. That's all that matters to her, making sure he's happy. She'll go with whatever side will help her with that."

Ham doesn't say anything, but for once, I can tell the wheels are moving under that inscrutable expression.

"At least check it out," I urge. "It shouldn't be hard to confirm her story. You need agents, and Minka is a good one. At least she's good in a fight. I should know."

Ham makes a sound that might be a chuckle, but I can't be sure.

Time to get down to business. "So—Eugene. You want me to grovel, beg him to take me back?"

"No need for such theatrics. I thought you might extend an olive branch, suggest vaguely that you might have a way to get him released."

"That's not possible, though, right?"

"I don't think he's going anywhere for a good long time." He checks his watch. "Are you ready to do this? I have Eugene coming online in two minutes."

"Ok. It's just..." I trail off, unsure of what to say.

Ham gives me a sympathetic smile. "I realize how difficult this whole situation is for you. I want to make it as easy as possible."

"You really want me as an agent?" I blurt.

"We could use your experience and talents, Pippa."

"But I was a bad guy. Tenley might never forgive me and Charlotte wants to rip my head off because of Declan. And then there's Declan." I drop my gaze so he won't see the sadness in my eyes.

"Tenley and Charlotte both encouraged me to bring you aboard. They were very impressed with your commitment to the task that night at Revello's. And even though you were working against us, I was impressed by your tenacity to recover the list."

"Yeah. Sorry about that."

"Not at all. I suspected you would try for it."

"But I was a bad guy for doing it."

"Is that how you see yourself?" His laptop *bings*. "Pippa, as enlightening as this discussion has been, could we table it for a moment? Eugene is available."

I glance at the laptop with horror. "Is this like video chat? I have to see him? He can see me?"

"Is this a problem?"

"No. But—no." I take a deep breath. "Let's do this. Are you hanging around?"

"I thought I might. He won't know I'm here."

He gives me another smile as he turns the laptop to face me. I only have time for another deep breath before Eugene's image shows up on the screen.

He looks tired. And old. Eugene Mochrie's first priority was always his organization, but coming in at a close second was himself, which included proper grooming and attire. To see him with grey-flecked stubble, mussed hair and wearing the bright-orange prison jumpsuit is painful.

But I don't let him see it. "*How're ya*, Eugene," I say in a low voice. Contrite. Apologetic.

"Pippa." He frowns, the movement carving a furrow into his brow. "I see you're hooked into NIIA now."

"Hooked—I don't know if I'd call it that." I stop myself from glancing at Ham. Eugene will be watching my every move. "But I'm involved with one of their agents."

Eugene shakes his head. "I expected more of you."

"It just happened," I plead. "I never thought... Eugene, we're getting married. I wanted to be the one to tell you."

As close as he may be watching me, I'm doing the same and I notice he doesn't look all that surprised. "I'm sorry to hear that."

"Really? I know what you wanted for me and Lysander, but don't you want me to be happy?"

"I want to see you and my son together and running things," Eugene says in a gruff voice. "I've raised you like my own, and this is how you repay me?"

Oh, the guilt! Eugene has always played the guilt card better than an Italian mother. But I can play my games too.

I lean closer to the screen, glancing over my shoulder. "I want you out of there, and I think I've got a way to do it," I say softly. "Declan knows some people."

Eugene leans forward, the frown vanishing. "Keep talking."

"I don't know who's listening, but just so you know, things are in the works. I'm trying, Eugene. I haven't forgotten you."

He sniffed with disgust. "Unlike my son. He's got his own agenda and he won't even discuss it with me."

That means I'm his agenda. "That's Lysander," I say with a forced smile. "He likes being the lone wolf."

"He's going to get his lone wolf self killed or thrown in a prison like me."

"It's not forever." I give him a tremulous smile. "I hate seeing you in there."

"It ain't that bad," Eugene assures me. "Three square meals and I've got some friends with me."

"At least you're not alone."

"Doesn't mean I want to hang out longer than I have to." He gives me a pointed stare. "Do what you have to do to get me out of this bloody place."

"I will."

"And as for your wedding..." Eugene pauses, swipes a hand over his forehead. "You've been like a daughter to me, Pippa, lass, especially since I lost my Daniella. Lysander isn't the easiest man to live with, but you'd be a part of the family. Maybe I didn't need to go that far. I wish I could walk you down that aisle, lassie."

A sob rises in my throat, choking me. "I wish that too." For a moment I feel my arm tucked into Eugene's, smell the cigars he smokes. A wave of nostalgia crashes over me, and if this was a real wedding, I'd be in tears by now.

"Well." He nods, grimaces a little. "Behave yourself now. And get back to me about you know what."

"As soon as I can." I don't have to fake the tears that well up in my eyes. "Be careful in there, please."

"Who's going to mess with me?" Eugene guffaws. Then, with a grin, the picture vanishes.

I suck back my sobs, wipe away any tears as Ham closes the laptop. "Thank you, Pippa," he says.

What am I supposed to say to that?

Thirty-Three

H AM SUGGESTS I GO back to my room without continuing
our discussion. I forget about breakfast.

My surrogate father is in prison, waiting for me to orga-
nize an escape that's never going to happen. I need some
curl-up-in-a-dark-corner time right about now.

Ham offered me a job.

My thoughts bounce like a game of ping-pong, back and forth.
Eugene–Ham–Lysander–Declan.

Lysander wants me gone, Ham wants me to stay. Charlotte hates
me one minute, seems to tolerate me the next. Suggested I be
brought on board.

I lie in the dark room, wondering what my next move should
be. I'm on my own now. I didn't like it when I was younger and it
hasn't gotten any better. Who do I trust?

Like a sign, a knock sounds on the door.

"Go away," I mutter, burrowing my head into the pillow. For a
moment I think whoever is there has been listening to me, but then
there's another knock, louder this time.

"Pippa, I know you're in there."

I bolt upright. Is that...?

"Declan?"

He stands in the hall outside my door, in faded jeans and a long-sleeve T-shirt, about as far from wedding attire as you can get. Still, he looks good, so much that I want to touch him to make sure he's real.

"Got a minute?" He seems nervous—quick speech, eyes darting and without a smile.

My heart slowly sinks at the sight of the furrow on his forehead. Serious Declan. Unhappy Declan. Something-wrong Declan. "Sure." Pasting a smile on my face, I hold the door open for him to come in. There's no need for him to know my knees are quaking.

I have no idea what he's going to tell me. I only assume it's bad news.

Everything's bad news since I got to Toronto.

"You okay?" Declan asks.

"Why wouldn't I be?" I take a seat on the bed, the sheets still twisted from my restless night. It's the only furniture to sit on and after a moment, Declan joins me. Part of me wants to make a joke about being alone together just hours before our wedding, but nothing is funny about it.

"Is it the wedding?" he begins, turning to face me. He's close enough for our knees to touch, so close I can smell him. The nice Declan smell. Maybe if he hugs my pillow long enough, I'll be able to keep it around.

I can't meet his eyes. Or lie to him. "I told Eugene I'd get him out of prison. Or, *you* could get him out."

Declan nods. "I suggested that. Do you think he bought it?"

My mouth drops open. "You suggested it?"

"I thought it was worth a shot. I know you were close to him, so it couldn't have been easy." He puts a hand on my knee.

Shaking my head in disbelief, I brush off his hand and jump off the bed. "What do you want from me?" I start to pace the tiny room. Anything to avoid being close to him. As much as I want him to touch me, I don't think I can handle the sympathy right now.

"I want you to be safe."

Why does he have to sound so nice? Like he cares?

"Why?" I whirl to face him, still sitting on the bed still warm from my body, looking impossibly cute and smelling a little like heaven. All I want to do is snog him senseless, but I can't let myself within an arm's length of him until I understand this. "Why are you doing anything for me? And it's not just you—Ham and Tenley, and even Caleb's being nice to me."

"Caleb's a nice guy."

I hit my chest hard enough to hurt. "But I'm not, Declan. I'm one of the bad guys, and you're being nice to me. A week ago, we were opposite sides and now—I don't know what's going on."

Declan reaches out and puts his hands on my hips. "What did they do to you?" he murmurs.

I allow him to draw me closer, so that I'm standing between his legs. "No one did anything. This is who I am."

"No, it's not."

I stare at him in disbelief. "You know who I work for. Lysander is the reason you're stuck hiding out, and he wasn't just my boss, he was my friend—sort of."

"Sort of more?"

"Sort of complicated."

"I can handle complicated."

"Why would you want to?"

Declan smiles. "Sit down, will you? You're eye level and it's kind of making it difficult to concentrate."

His eyes level is my chest level. I choke back a laugh, and the tension in the room dials back a thousandfold as I sit beside him.

"Look, Pippa, you're a cool girl who seems all tough, but is really a big marshmallow inside."

"I'm not a marshmallow," I mutter.

"You're sweet and soft, and I like you," he admits. "I like you a lot."

"Why?" I whisper as he tugs one of my curls, his fingers brushing my jaw.

"You sound like a broken record. Or a two-year-old. *Why why why.*" His smile reaches his eyes, reaches inside me as something deep down wakes up with a hungry yawn.

"You should be wanting to get as far away from me as possible, but instead you're sitting on my bed." My hand itches to touch him, but I wait.

"You don't make your bed."

"I suppose you do?"

Declan shrugs. "I'm a bit of a neat freak."

"I'm only a plain freak—no neatness involved. I don't see the point of making my bed because I'm only going to get back into it later."

"Fair point. Do you wear pyjamas?"

"Why—?" I begin, but Declan rolls his eyes. "—would you want to know that?"

"If I'm imagining you crawling into an unmade bed, I'd like to know what I should be imagining you wearing. It might make the messy bed easier to take."

I swallow against the sudden dryness of my throat. "I, um, a T-shirt." I shrug, wishing I had a more flirtatious answer, but I'm struck dumb. "Whatever's handy."

"Like, my shirt." He moves closer, his hand now tangled in my hair.

"That'd be all right."

"I could handle it too." His other hand touches my knee. I wish I was wearing something more flattering than a pair of baggy joggers.

His hand is warm. The bruises on his knuckles have faded, the cuts beginning to heal. I lift a shaky hand to his cheek. His jaw is a purplish-blue, but the swelling from his nose is gone. "What are you doing, Declan?" I ask in a soft voice as he moves even closer.

"Do I have to spell it out? I thought you were a spy?"

"I'm a thief."

"Well, you've stolen my heart."

I laugh out loud, and Declan joins me. "That's cheesy."

"I like cheesy. I like the Backstreet Boys. You know I'm going to try to convert you."

"It might take a while."

"We've got lots of time."

We don't. We might not.

Or—we might have all the time in the world. Right now, it feels like we do.

"Do you want to marry me?" Declan asks in a husky voice.

How can I tell him that I want nothing more? But I want it to be *our* wedding where he wants to marry me because he loves me, not because it might be the only way to keep him alive. "Yes," I say automatically, thinking he means the plan, the trap to catch Lysander in the act. Because Declan doesn't mean anything else. Right? "I've given up everything to keep you safe."

"I mean, aside from that. I'm trying to ask if this is real for you." Declan sounds unsure, uncertain and completely adorable.

I've had enough of tiptoeing around.

"*Yes*! Everything is real for me." My words trip over each other, all the emotions that I've bottled up spilling out at once. "I didn't mean to fall for you; I knew I shouldn't have, but I couldn't help it. I never thought of you as a mark. You were just a really cute guy I wanted to snog."

"You thought I was cute?"

"I still think it."

"Do you still want to snog me?"

Is it my imagination or is Declan leaning even closer to me? "Declan." I put a hand on his chest that is quite a bit closer than it was only a moment before. "What are you doing?"

"I'm trying to snog my bride. Is that how you say it?"

"But we're not married yet."

"I don't think I can wait that long."

We do more than snog in that little bed.

After, we lie under the covers that Declan has straightened, I trace the tattoo of a shamrock on his chest.

"I'm Irish too," Declan says. "My great-grandfather came to Canada after the potato famine."

I laugh. "You're about as Irish as a box of Lucky Charms."

"But I am," he protests. "Maybe one-fourth."

"I'm half English," I say. "My mum met my da in London."

"Where—I don't know anything about you." Declan turns serious. "I'm going to marry you and I don't even know what your parents are like."

I'm going to marry you.

The words produce a tingle through my body, even the parts that weren't already tingling. "They're dead," I say bluntly, Declan's words still ringing in my ears.

He seems shocked. "What? I'm sorry."

"Happened a long time ago." I resume tracing the tattoo. "Mum had cancer and before that she had a chip on her shoulder the size of the White Cliffs of Dover. We might have been close if she hadn't been forcing me to turn my body into a pretzel for years. It's all good. I'm over it. Don't know about my da. He left when I was but a baby."

"My parents are gone too. And my grandfather."

Now *is not* the time to tell Declan how I know Eugene and Lysander were responsible for his grandfather's death. I will tell him, but not now.

"I know." My voice softens, much more than when I told him about my mother. "You Dodds are a wee bit famous."

"What else do you know about me?" Declan rolls onto his side with a smile on his face.

"I know you're one-fourth Irish. And I know you have a tattoo." I lean in and brush his lips with mine. "Verra sexy."

"I got it after my granddad died. My gran hated it. How was I supposed to know she hated tattoos?"

"I'll have to remember not to show her mine," I say, willing the conversation to go elsewhere but his grandfather.

"You have a tattoo? I thought I checked you all over."

I smack my palm against my arse. "I'm going to get *Declan Dodd* right here."

"So only I can see it?"

"That's the plan."

"I'm very jealous, you know, when it comes to my women."

"Well, you don't want to see how jealous I can be if you keep referring to your 'women'. *Woman*. Just one. Just me."

"Just you."

He kisses me. I'm very good with that. But before I let things go any further, I push away from him with a sigh. "You have to go. I've got to get dressed."

"You don't have to. I like you undressed."

"Dressed might be better, since there's this wedding I have to go to. That's what brought you here in the first place, isn't it?"

"I wanted to see you."

"I've wanted to see you before I even met you." My heart feels ready to burst. Declan is incredible, everything I've ever wanted before I even knew I wanted it. He—

Lysander is going to kill him.

It's as if a bucket of ice is thrown over me.

"What's the matter?" Declan asks urgently. "Your face—it's like you've seen a ghost."

"I don't want to lose you," I whisper, tears suddenly welling up in my eyes. "I just found you."

He leans over and kisses my nose. "I'm not going anywhere."

"But Lysander—"

"Isn't going to get anywhere near you. Or me. Or us. The only thing that's going to happen is we're going to get married. To each other." He grins. "I can't believe I'm this excited about it."

"I'm scared," I admit. Being like this with Declan has let all my vulnerabilities out into the open, as well as my insecurities. I'm so scared that I can't think straight. If Lysander burst through the door right now, I wouldn't even know what to do first.

Maybe cry.

I hate crying.

"Stop it," he says with a frown. "I can see all those thoughts going through your head. Nothing is going to happen."

"Promise?" I shake my head. "You can't promise."

"Yes, I can, and I will. *Nothing*, Pippa. He won't get close to either one of us."

He doesn't have to get close.

"You get dressed," Declan says, climbing out of bed. I let the sight of his nakedness distract me from my thoughts. "That'll make you feel better."

I don't know if it will.

It's not like me to be like this—needy and scared, more of a wimp than a bathering stook. I don't like it. I take a deep breath, and then another, clearing my head.

I sit up in bed, pulling up the sheet. "I'll see you in a couple of hours," I tell him, reaching up for one last kiss. "I'll be the one in the big dress."

"The pretty dress."

"You shouldn't have seen it. It's bad luck."

"We got all the luck we needed when you blew your mission to get Revello's list." He laughs and I join in.

"I've never been so glad to fail at anything," I admit.

"One last kiss," Declan says. "I love you, Pippa."

My lips freeze less than an inch from his mouth. "You do?"

"I do. I didn't want our wedding to be the first time I told you."

"Oh." I touch my fingers to my lips. "Oh. I didn't know."

"No, I guess not," he says awkwardly.

"I love you too!" I burst out, and his face creased into a smile. "I love you a whole lot."

"I love you a whole lot too."

I finally push him out the door, his declaration making me even more nervous.

Thirty-Four

T HE NEXT FEW HOURS feel like a dream, or maybe one of those out-of-body experiences where you see your body lying there and you're hovering above it. I see myself being driven to the restaurant by Caleb, with Tenley beside me, talking about mundane things like extra security and a hidden cache of weapons, but get the sense it's not really me sitting there.

It's so *weird* that this is my wedding day. Wedding evening. The sun is low in the sky, and the air is beginning to chill. The service is to begin promptly at seven, Tenley told me several times. She seems more nervous than I am.

I feel numb.

It's wrong. It's all wrong. And then I think of Declan, and I smile, because he is the only thing that feels right.

I twist my hands in my lap, staring at the ivory fabric. Organza, Tenley tells me it's called.

She's wearing a dress of vivid, hot pink with short sleeves and a short, tight skirt. Perfect to run in.

Tenley, with Charlotte and Alessia in tow, showed up in my room while I was still in the shower. Seeing the three of them lounging on my bed, only minutes after Declan had shared it with me, was enough to wipe the smile off my face.

But the bottle of champagne Alessia passed around had been enough to wipe away some of the nerves.

"Everything's good to go," Charlotte had said, taking the bottle from my hands. "Ham's secured the restaurant with a six-block perimeter around it. If that bloody Irish wanker puts a toe over the line, we'll grab him." Her voice was no-nonsense, but her appearance was anything but; her dress was bright blue, short and sleeveless, with a fuller skirt. I suspect she'd be quick to demonstrate how easily she can kick in this one as well. Her hair hung down her back in a wave of white-gold. It's the first time I'd seen her with her hair loose.

Then they proceeded to get me ready. Hair, makeup, nails—almost two hours of personal pampering. Normally, that's not my thing, but I kind of enjoyed it. I'm sure the champagne helped.

"I don't know how I'm supposed to feel," I admit to Tenley as Caleb slows to park. A spot has been blocked off in front of the restaurant. "I'm excited, but scared, like *really* scared. Like jumping out of a plane scared."

"I remember the first time I did that," Tenley muses.

"I think I might throw up."

"Maybe not in the dress. Or on me, please." She straightens her skirt as Caleb stops the car.

I glance wildly out the window. The sidewalk is full, couples going for dinner, groups out for a night at the pub. And me, sitting here scared like *shite* in my wedding dress.

"Ready?" Caleb asks as he steps out of the car, hurrying around to open the door for us.

"I can't believe this is really," I gasp, on the verge of tears—and not the *good, I'm getting married* kind of crying.

Tenley looks at me, grasping how close I am to losing it. "It'll be fine, Pippa. We'll get him."

"I'm sorry if something—if they..."

"Stop apologizing. You were only doing your job. And now you're going to do your new job. All right? Let's get this over with. Sorry—let's celebrate this blessed event!"

I laugh at her fake smile.

Caleb helps me from the car with a warm hand and a reassuring smile. "My little brother's a lucky man," he says.

I steel my nerves as I follow the pink of Tenley's skirt into the restaurant. The tables are pushed back with rows of chairs set up. There's an aisle.

That's all I see because Declan waits near the bar, with Seamus beside him, and a big grin on his face.

"We're doing this *now*?" I can't pull my gaze away from Declan and his smile.

"Do you have something else to do?" Caleb jokes. He takes my arm and someone hands me a bouquet. We wait until Tenley slowly walks between the crowd. There are more people than I expected. Agents, I assume.

"Your turn," Caleb whispers.

This is real. What started as a ruse, a way to lure Lysander into a trap, is now a real wedding.

I can't breathe, and I still feel like I'm about to hurl, like the morning after I last went off the rails, but I let Caleb doggedly lead me down the aisle.

I stare wide-eyed at the guests.

They're excited for me. They're not watching the doors to check for Lysander, but smiling at me. How did this become so real?

And then I get to the end of the aisle. Declan.

"Hey." His smile lights up his face as he takes my hand.

Suddenly, everything relaxes, like waves stilling into a place of calm after a storm. I'm getting married.

For real.

I wouldn't be able to describe the justice of the peace if you paid me. He's the voice telling me about love and kindness, the words blending into white noise as I gaze at Declan.

The flower in his lapel matches the pink roses in my bouquet. I smell his cologne over the flowers—the musky, sexy, Declan smell.

He looks so confident and relaxed standing there, like there's no place he'd rather be. His hand holding mine warm but not sweaty.

I fight the urge to giggle, and Declan raises his eyebrows. "I can't bloody believe I'm doing this."

I meant for it to be a whisper for Declan's ears only, but it comes out louder than I expect. Those closest to us titter with laughter.

"Well, you won't be doing anything if you don't let me finish," the justice of the peace says with a smile. "Do you take Declan Cornelius Dodd as your lawful wedded husband?"

Cornelius? I mouth. Declan shrugs. "I do."

"And do you, Declan, take Pippa Felicia Katherine McGovern as your lawful wedding wife?"

Wife. I'm about to be someone's wife.

"I do."

"I now pronounce you husband and wife."

Declan kisses me, on and on. I hear the cheers.

"Pippa, this is Gran," Declan says proudly, leading me over to an older woman with white hair and a radiant smile.

Amelia Dodd is dwarfed by her grandson. She's Charlotte's size, with Charlotte's round cheeks and blue eyes.

This is who Charlotte will look like when she's old.

Gran hugs me tightly, and I feel like I'm home.

More guests flock to us, names and faces gone in a flash, too many for me to comprehend. Music plays and someone hands me a glass of water. I keep smiling, holding tight to Declan's hand. At first, I thought there would be Declan's family, Tenley and Alessia, but Ham fills the restaurant with quite a few of the new recruits.

It makes me feel better that there are so many agents here.

My cheeks ache from smiling, my toes beginning to feel crushed by the shoes, but there are still more who want to congratulate us. I'm separated from Declan as he makes the rounds, thanking those for coming with his easygoing charm.

My husband.

I see Charlotte's worried face by the door, Alessia standing guard by the window and the reality of what this is hits me with a swat to the face. It doesn't matter how many agents there are. It only takes one bad guy to get to Declan.

I stand tall, scanning the guests for anyone who doesn't belong, who looks the slightest bit suspicious.

Everyone looks happy and smiling and glad to be there.

Tenley comes over to me and pulls me off to the side. "Have you checked the kitchen?" I demand. "Or the basement? There are storage rooms someone could be hiding in. Let me go look." I hike up my voluminous skirt, but Tenley grabs my arm before I can move away.

"We have agents in the kitchen, and the basement was swept just before the ceremony. Everything's good," she assures me. "There's no sign of him."

"You don't need a sign. The bloody bastard can be waiting anywhere. There might be someone else. They could be anywhere—" My voice raises, the nerves swooping back with a vengeance.

"Pippa."

I take a deep breath. "What?"

"Stop. It'll be fine. This is your wedding—enjoy it."

"It's a bit difficult to do, considering." I scan the crowd, looking for Declan with his grandmother, surrounded by his brothers. Caleb stands a head taller, blond head tipped back, laughing at something Seamus is saying. Even Perry has a smile on his face, his almost cheerful expression at war with his formal black suit, all tightly buttoned and tied. He holds the hand of his wife, Annaliese.

I have a sister-in-law.

Tenley follows my gaze. "He looks so happy."

"They all do."

"They won't let anything happen to him. Declan's not an agent; they'll protect him."

"They better." I notice Charlotte staring at me. She gives me a nod.

"Like I was saying, things are moving along. They'll bring out the food soon, after you have your dance, and cut the cake."

"My dance?"

"The first dance? Don't they do that in Ireland?"

"The last wedding I went to was in a pub and everyone was dancing. Mostly on the tables. I dance with Declan?"

Tenley laughs. "Did you have someone else in mind?"

"No, that works." My gaze is drawn back to Declan, bending his head to his gran's white one with a smile on his face. He looks so good in his suit, the navy bringing out the blue of his eyes, his shoulders wide under the jacket.

The tattoo on his chest that I've already seen.

"Dancing is nice," I say with a smile.

"Then we'll cut the cake." She motions to it sitting on a table near the bar. I knew Tenley could bake, but I had no idea she was so talented. The cake is three layers, each with icing of a different colour—green, pink and yellow, and decorated with flowers and curlicues. It's beautiful and fun, and more me than anything here.

I turn to Tenley. "Thank you." I hope she hears the sincerity in my voice. "For the cake, and everything you've done. I really appreciate it. You've made this so special for me." My voice cracks on the last word.

"I tried."

"You did good."

"Look, Pippa, I know we didn't start out on the right foot..."

With a wave of my hand, I pull her into a hug. "Don't be getting sappy on me now. I only have this cheap waterproof mascara on, and I'm not about to be testing it out."

"Fair enough," Tenley says with a laugh, squeezing me tight.

Somehow I ended up with friends and a husband. A real family.

I excuse myself to visit the washroom before I test out the quality of my mascara.

After I calm myself, after Colin finds me in the washroom, I fix my smile and sweep out to the little area Tenley marked off for dancing. Declan steps forward to claim me.

"Hello, Mrs. Dodd," he says, his smile lighting up his eyes. His gaze sweeps over me, admiring, adoring, and sending a tingle through me. "Have I told you how beautiful you look?"

An area opens for us, with the guests circling us, their cries of congratulations still ringing in my ears. Declan slips his arm around my waist, tucking me close and taking my hand in his.

"Hello, Mr. McGovern." I smile. "Have I told you how handsome you look?"

"Not in a few minutes. And Mrs. Dodd—guess we haven't had that talk yet." He laughs.

"We haven't had much of a talk about anything yet. Not even where we'll be spending the night." I drop my voice flirtatiously.

"Oh, you think I'm that easy, do you? Put a ring on it, and I'll fall right into bed with you?"

My smile widens. "It didn't take a ring this afternoon."

"It was the morning."

"Well, the second time was this afternoon."

Declan pulls me closer, his laughter sending a rumble through his chest. His hand drops to the small of my back. We sway together, oblivious to the music, the guests smiling at us. Declan fills my head, my senses. I rest my head on his shoulder, not minding how the pins containing my hair dig into my scalp.

The hair pins were Ida's gift. I can pick any lock around with them. For once, I'm not thinking of how soon I can put them to use.

I'm not thinking of anything but Declan.

"I love you," I whisper into his jacket.

"I told you everything would be fine," Declan says.

Lysander is long gone. He can't hurt me now. Declan is safe and protected and—

The cake blows up.

Thirty-Five

C AKE FLIES EVERYWHERE, COLOURFUL icing slapping
against suit jackets and dresses, the little bride and groom
figure perched on top of the cake shooting through the room like
a cannon ball.

A smoke bomb is tossed into the restaurant, breaking the front
window with a medley of breaking glass.

"He blew up my cake?" Tenley cries into the sudden chaos.

There's a scream as a dozen men storm through the door. As
I'm yanked away from Declan, I recognize Carl, Mikhail and Benjy
among them, dressed all in black. One of the new recruits pulls me
behind the bar. Lights glint off the bottles lined on the shelf as we
crouch low.

"What is this *shite*?" I cry. "Declan?"

Pushing away from the recruit holding me, I slam into Caleb,
bounce off Seamus, who is already deep into the fight with one of
the minions, and trip over Perry, who is crouched under a table.

Suddenly, out of the smoke, Gran Dodd appears in her smart
pink suit. One of the black-clad minions towers threateningly over

her. I'm about to grab Gran and hustle her to safety when she does a perfect crotch shot, sending the minion to his knees.

And then she smacks him on the head with her matching pink leather handbag.

My jaw drops.

"Get out of here," she instructs, catching me staring. 'You'll ruin that dress." She uses her handbag on another minion, tries for a third as he rushes past her.

Eyes wide with awe, I obey and stumble away, leaving Gran with a huge smile on her face.

"Declan?"

"Pippa!" My head whips around at my name, but it's Charlotte waving to me by the bar. Hiking my billowing skirt up around my knees, I slide back through the chunks of cake to her.

"I've got Declan," she says, grabbing a knife from behind the bar, and slicing a slit in her pretty dress from hem to upper thigh. "He's in the kitchen."

There's a window; it's an open kitchen where customers can watch the chef prepare their meals. I look to the back of the restaurant but see no sign of Declan. "Good, but I don't see Lysander anywhere."

One of his minions comes too close as he grapples with one of the new recruits, and I kick the back of his knee. He falls into the arms of the recruit, who flips him over the bar as easily as tossing a bag of rubbish into the bin. Bottles shake and one falls, the sound of the tinkle of broken glass masked in the fight.

"You said he wouldn't be in the thick of things," Charlotte points out.

"But he should be here." I scan the new arrivals, the sense of unease twisting my stomach. "I don't see Robbie either. Or Minka." I look down at Charlotte and her expression of confusion. "I don't think this is it."

"What are you talking about?"

"He's got something else planned. Not here." I notice Ham trading punches with Carl, and then it hits me like a slap in the face. "It's the head office. No one is there."

"He doesn't know where it is."

"Minka does."

"He can't get in. No one can."

"Maybe he can."

Charlotte looks at me with horror. Is she remembering my words in the car the other day? *"I think I could give it a good try. I got out, didn't I?"*

I'm at the kitchen door before she can say another word. There's a door in the kitchen that leads to the alley, and if they don't have it blocked, Declan and I—

I don't see Mikhail waiting for me until it's too late.

He grabs my arm as I'm about to slip through the swinging door, slamming me back into the wall. "I told him you were mine," he says in his growly accent, with a backhand that sends my head crashing against a framed print on the wall.

"I'm not anyone's," I retort with a sharp jab to his nose.

Mikhail may not be a big man, but he's as strong as those rugger buggers who lug their boyos around on their shoulders after a win. He grabs me by the shoulder and the waist, his sweaty hands wrinkling the fabric of my dress beyond repair. He grabs me, lifts me into the air with a mighty grunt, and throws me through the window into the kitchen.

It takes only a second for me to fly into the kitchen, but it feels like forever. I notice everything in that flash of time: Tenley and Alessia standing back-to-back with minions circling them, Seamus trading blows with Benjy, and Charlotte perched on top of the bar, ready to leap onto the back of Carl, who has Ham pressed into the wall with a heavy arm across his throat.

And then I hit the counter, skidding across, sending a tray of delicate pastries flying to the floor with a clatter of broken crockery and slamming into the stove. I land in a heap of organza on the floor.

"Bloody hell," I wheeze.

"Pippa!"

I trip over my skirt, trying to get to my feet. The floor is slick with grease, sending me careening into the counter.

There's enough time to see Declan at the other end of the kitchen, trading punches with another minion before Mikhail gets hold of me and yanks me upright. The blow sends me staggering, but he's got a hold of the lace of the bodice of my beautiful dress and hits me again.

The breath's been knocked out of me, and things hurt more than they should, but I'm not out yet.

I find a handle sticking out from the stove and swing it like a cricket bat, right onto Mikhail's head.

He crumples to the floor.

"Keep your bloody hands off my dress," I snarl, kicking him in the stomach for good measure.

With my lovely cast-iron frying pan, still warm from whatever was cooking in it and heavy in my hand, I plow through the rest of the minions in the kitchen. "We've got to go." I grab hold of Declan's wrist, pulling him after me.

"We can't just leave them," Declan argues. I think for a second he means his brothers and Charlotte, but realize he's referring to the dishwasher and sous chef cowering behind him.

"No one's going to hurt *them!* Lysander's not here. He's going to hit head office."

"I don't have my car. Seamus drove me here."

"I'll find something." I hit the door with my shoulder, falling out into the alley between Thrice and a Korean place, smelling of spiced garbage and urine. The growl of a motorcycle slows as it enters the alley, with a bag strapped on the back. UberEats. "That'll do."

I head for the bike, big and billowy and beautiful in my wedding dress. The driver, young, skinny and tattooed, cringes and without a word, hops off.

"Don't hurt me!" he cries in a high-pitched voice, holding the still-running bike upright. "Take it! Take everything."

"If you say so." Trying to look threatening, I hop on the bike, tucking in the yards of fabric as best I can. "Let's go."

"I'm not getting on that thing with you," Declan declares.

"If you want to come with me, you are. I can drive." I can tell from Declan's expression he wants to argue. "We don't have time for this. Get on!"

Without another word, Declan climbs on behind me. Revving the motor, I spin in a tight three sixty and take off, leaving the delivery man still shaking behind us.

Thirty-Six

I PULL OUT INTO the evening traffic with a squeal of tires. Declan's arms tighten around my waist. My skirt billows around us like a deflated parachute, and Declan helps me tuck more of it under our bums.

"I hate this dress," I cry, swerving in front of a minivan. Horns blare and I flap my hand in apology. "It's in the way."

"I think you look beautiful," Declan says, leaning close enough for his lips to tickle my ear.

A foolish grin spreads over my face, like the warmth his words produce. "Thank you."

"Very sexy. But it is in the way. All I've been able to think about is getting you out of it." I gasp as Declan slides his hand along my ribcage. "Maybe I like you driving."

"Concentrating here!"

"You're doing a great job. Watch that car!" The tiny compact pulls out in front of me, but Declan's warning is just in time.

"Was that our first fight?" Declan asks, raising his voice over the wind.

"You not wanting me to drive? That wasn't a fight, that was you being a man."

"I thought you liked me being a man. You liked it enough earlier."

Declan has to shout for me to hear, loud enough for people on the street to hear. We're racing through traffic like a bat out of hell, and he's making me blush?

I already love being married.

"Now's not the time, Declan!"

"We'll have time later, though, right?"

I laugh out loud. Taking a hand off the handlebars, I quickly squeeze Declan's hand, the hand that is dangerously close to my breast. "Let me concentrate, willya?"

Declan chuckles, his chest rubbing against my back.

All too soon, I make a screeching turn into the parking garage of Mutual Liberty, slowing as I head down the ramp. "Do you really think he's here?" Declan asks.

I don't have to answer.

Lysander stands before the private elevator leading down to the head office. My heart sinks to see Minka and Robbie beside him.

I don't take my eyes off him as I swing my leg off the bike. I should have known Lysander would have a big-picture plan. I should have known I was small potatoes for him, that the Agency was what he really wanted.

My plan to draw him out gave him the perfect opportunity.

Robbie has a bag of tools on the ground beside him—my tools. Handy little things I've been collecting for years, allowing me to break into just about everything. It looks like he's been working on the controls to the elevator.

I hope Ida and Perry are as good with security as they claim to be.

"You look beautiful." Lysander steps forward. "A touch overdone, but nice. Let me offer my congratulations."

"We got your present," I say. "And cake blowing up? A little overdone, but at least everyone got to have a taste. It's my favourite flavour."

"I pictured you as a chocolate lover," Declan muses, standing strong beside me. I want him to run, to get away from here. Fear clutches me, making me feel like my moves are thick and gluey, but I keep my eyes on Lysander.

"There's a lot you don't know about Pippa," Lysander says. "Like her plan to get my father released."

Declan shakes his head. "That's not her plan."

"No? How about my plan for her to let us in?" Lysander draws his gun.

I don't wait to see which one of us he's going to use it on; I throw myself into a flip and then another. The fabric of my skirt billows around me, creating a curtain of white silk between Lysander and Declan. I hear the gunshot and feel the heat as it passes close to my upside-down leg.

The next one hits my arm. I waver but manage to stay steady on my feet as I finish the flips, landing on my feet in front of Lysander.

"You bloody tosser," I cry, not even glancing at my arm. "I'll never be able to get the blood out.

And then I punch him in the face, hearing the satisfying crack as I break his nose.

Ham and Charlotte and the rest of the cavalry show up moments later. Declan has already taken out Robbie as Minka stands with a bemused look on her face, not doing a thing to help either one of them.

"Good job, Declan," Seamus says, noticing Robbie's prone body on the floor of the parking garage.

"What about me?" I demand, resting my toe-crunching shoe on Lysander's shoulder.

Seamus gives me a flash of a grin as he heaves Lysander to his feet. "You'll do."

Ham brushes by me as he marches Robbie to the elevator. "We'll lock them up until Interpol comes." He glances back at Minka. "Care to join me for a chat?"

She follows him with a hint of a smile on her face.

Caleb and Seamus flank Lysander, whose murderous expression has dimmed to a sullen scowl.

I thought I'd feel guilty. I thought I'd feel bad, that this is my fault. But the only thing I feel is relief that Lysander will be out of my life forever.

And Declan is safe.

I stop them before they enter the elevator. "I never meant for any of this to happen," I tell Lysander. "I would have been loyal to you forever."

And I would have. Had I not met Declan, Lysander would have been my future. I would have trailed along behind him, taking the crumbs he threw me, grateful for the security of the pseudo-family.

I have a real one now.

"Get out of my way," Lysander sneers. How did I ever think he was good-looking? He looks like an angry boyo having a tantrum. Not attractive at all.

"I'm the only one standing in the way of you going into a very small cage, so talk to me first. Why did you kill Henry?"

Lysander doesn't even flinch. "Finally figured it out, did you? He was in the way."

"I may have loved him, but I would have stayed true to you," I say. "You should have trusted me. You should have believed in me like your father did."

"Look where it got him—locked up like a common criminal."

"No, it's going to get him released with a slap on the wrist. He'll lose all his control, and the idea of Mielson is finished, but I'm the only one with enough information to put him away for life. And I'm going to save all that for you. Everything that's been going wrong these past years is because of you, Lysander, because you're trying to take over. Eugene can keep IIP and work with us, and MI-6, rather than against us."

His expression is ugly and hateful but it doesn't scare me. "You don't have anything on me."

"Try me." I nod to Caleb and he frog-marches Lysander into the elevator. I hear the howl of frustration as the door closes.

"You said us."

I turn to see Charlotte standing beside me, her dress ripped and dirty.

"Well—*you*. I meant Eugene can work with you."

She nods her blond head. "You did good today. You kept him safe."

I find Declan in the group of agents, laughing and shaking his hand. "I'll always keep him safe."

"He'll want to do the same for you." Charlotte winks. "But he's not as good at it as you are."

Thirty-Seven

Epilogue

S IX WEEKS LATER, I finally finish the dance with my husband.

Once again, the agents of NIIA have taken over Thrice restaurant, but this time it's Charlotte wearing the white dress.

Her wedding gown is fitted, off the shoulder and covered in lace. It also has a slit that comes to mid-thigh.

"Just in case I have to make a run for it like you did," she tells me.

Ham waited for Charlotte's memories to be returned to her before getting down on one knee and proposing. He also did it during a staff meeting, to Charlotte's mortification.

Two days later, Tenley met me in the cafe with a shiny new rock on her finger, too. She was right—this wedding thing is catching.

"She looks good." Declan catches me watching Charlotte laughing with Ham. "Not as good as you, but pretty good for my little sister."

"She looks beautiful."

"You have to say that because she made you one of her brides-maids."

"I really didn't expect that." I smooth out the navy sheath, the match to Tenley and Ida's. "Are you sure you didn't put her up to it?"

"Haven't you learned anything? No one can make Lottie do anything she doesn't want to."

"I guess that goes for me too." I tighten my arms around Declan's shoulders and run my fingers into his thick hair. I never get tired of touching my husband.

"Is there anything you particularly want to do tonight?" I've come to recognize the tone of his voice and the way he looks at me.

"It'll be pretty late by the time we get home after this," I say with feigned sadness.

"I guess so. And you're helping Tenley in the morning again?"

"I'll have to be up bright and early." Declan clucks with disappointment and I lean closer. "Maybe you should let me drive home. We'd get there faster."

Declan pulls away with an eyebrow raised. "You think you're a better driver than I am?"

"I know I am. You, Declan Dodd, may think you're a hot-shit driver, but I'm here to tell you..." I pause to punctuate my words with a lingering kiss on his lips. "I'm better."

Declan kisses me, a kiss that goes on and on, and sends tingles racing through me. Enough with the trash talk. I need to shut up and see what he's got to offer.

I feel the curve of his lips against mine. "And now I've got all the time in the world to find out how good you really are."

Pippa and Declan. Tenley and Seamus. Charlotte and Ham...? They all got their happily ever afters—But there's time for one more adventure.

Charlotte saved the world, trained the next generation of spies, and married her sexy former boss. Now? She's facing her most terrifying mission yet: Christmas dinner.

With a ghost from her past, pressure to start a family, and a kitchen full of chaos, Charlotte has one last chance to decide what she really wants—before dessert is served.

Next up: The Last Stand of Charlotte Dodd.

One final mission. One unforgettable holiday. One badass woman saving the day—again.

But first...

Subscribe to my newsletter to get your exclusive copy of Cupcake Connections!!

T HANK YOU!

The Hidden Past of Pippa McGovern might just be my favorite book I've written.(Possibly because I read every line of Pippa's dialogue back to myself in an Irish accent.)

From the moment she stepped onto the page, fully formed and fearless, I knew she was something special. And pairing her with Declan—my favorite Dodd brother—was pure joy.

But Charlotte's not done yet...

Next up: The Last Stand of Charlotte Dodd

One final mission. One chaotic Christmas. One last chance at happily ever after. Don't miss the grand finale!

Love the spy girls? Want more stories, sneak peeks, and behind-the-scenes fun? Join my mailing list and I'll send you a bonus short story: Cupcake Connections—a sweet treat featuring familiar faces and a brand-new romance.

At Pain au Chocolate patisserie, cupcakes are stealing the spotlight—and so is Reuben.

A big, burly Scotsman with a soft spot for sugar, Reuben knows everything about sweets... except how to find love. When he starts falling for a charming customer, his friend Adam jumps in with a plan: makeover, matchmaking, and maybe a happily ever after.

But as Adam digs into Reuben's past, he discovers Reuben might not need help at all—just someone who sees him for who he really is.

Cupcake Connections is a heartwarming, feel-good story about finding love in unexpected places—featuring fan-favorite cameos from Beautifully Baked, Unexpectingly Happily Ever After, and The Hidden Past of Pippa McGovern.

Exclusive for newsletter subscribers so sign up now!

Thanks so much for spending time with me and my characters. I'm so glad you're here.

Holly

ACKNOWLEDGMENTS

THE HIDDEN PAST OF Pippa McGovern is the third in my Charlotte Dodd action chick lit series. Fourth, really, if you count the prequel and I guess I should.

I've loved writing Pippa.

I love all my spy girls, and my Dodd brothers, and Ham, and especially Benjy.

There's one more adventure for Charlotte, and you can bet Pippa will be along for the ride.

I read other acknowledgments pages for authors and they always have so many people to thank, with such heartfelt sentiments. I have people to thank, so here goes.

Nita and Lisa, and Glyn—thank you for being such awesome critique partners. You really help make me a better writer. You got in Pippa's head as much as I did and continually steered me the right direction. I feel like I should say something in Gaelic here, for all you did to help a Canadian girl craft an Irish badass. *Ta. Ta very much!*

Thanks to Paula for editing and proofing and being a great set of eyes.

Thanks to Pat, my editor extraordinaire, who we lost the year Pippa came out. You didn't read this one, and I would have wanted you to. I liked it when you told me you were proud of me. We miss you.

Thanks to my kids who still think it's cool that I'm a writer and their friends who ask me about my books. Thanks to Jeff who allows me to live my dream.

I also need to thank all the readers. Whether you buy a book, read an advance copy, or even just asked me what I'm working on—thank you from the bottom of my heart. I am so fortunate to be able to do what I love but writing is a solo gig and your interest makes me feel less alone. Thanks for being there!

Thanks for reading.

LOTS OF LAUGHS.
LOTS OF LOVE.

READING LIST

Love in Laandia

Royal Rumble
Royal Retelling
Royal Rising
Royal Reluctance
Royal Rebel

Suitor Science

Hating the Chemistry Teacher
Falling for The Suitor
Fraternizing with the Ex
Marrying the Billionaire Best Friend
Loving the Wrong Guy
Finding the One

Don't

Don't Tell Me You Love Me
Don't Want to Be Friends
Don't Stop Me Now
Don't They Know It's Christmas

Love & Alliteration

Perfectly Played
Beautifully Baked
Pleasantly Popped

Charlotte Dodd

The Secret Life of Charlotte Dodd
The Missing Files of Charlotte Dodd
The Best Worst First Date Ever
The Hidden Past of Pippa McGovern
The Last Stand of Charlotte Dodd

Sisters in a Small Town

Coming Home
Hanging On
Stepping Up

Unexpecting
Unexpectingly Happily Ever After

STANDALONES

Cinnamon Rolls and Pumpkin Spice - Coffee
Break with the Billionaire

Oceanic Dreams - I Saw Him Standing There

Absinthe Doesn't Make the Heart Grow Fonder

www.ingramcontent.com/pod-product-compliance
Lightning Source LLC
Chambersburg PA
CBHW072346020726
47506CB00004B/1019